"You haven't bee
Cam shot back a
you were facing
know what the hell is going on. I don't even know who you're running from!"

Tala hadn't withheld information to deceive him. She'd done it to protect him, and herself.

"You're not as innocent as you pretend to be," he said.

She sputtered with outrage. "I'm not pretending to be anything."

He stepped forward, crowding her space. "I'm not a fool, Tala."

"Why did I come here, then?"

"To torture me."

She shoved his chest. He didn't budge. "You think you're the only one who gets stir-crazy? I've been trapped inside a truck for two days, just like you. I need to move around, just like you. I feel restless, too."

"What I feel is sexual frustration, not restlessness."

"I'm aware of that."

"So you wandered over here to make it worse?"

"No. I wandered over here to make it better."

She didn't touch him. She just waited for him to touch her, and he didn't disappoint. Thrusting his hands into her hair, he crushed his mouth over hers.

* * *

If you're on Twitter, tell us what you think of Harlequin Romantic Suspense! #harlequinromsuspense

Dear Reader,

I'm delighted to take you on another exciting adventure in my latest romantic suspense novel! If you've read my previous books, you know this story is a bit of a detour for me. Cameron Hughes isn't a navy SEAL. He's not a member of Team Twelve. He's a truck driver.

I've always had a soft spot for unlikely heroes, especially the bearded-recluse type. Cam is a former police officer turned guarded widower. He embraces the solitude and remoteness of Alaska's dark highways. He doesn't want to get involved with anyone, but fate has other plans. Enter Tala Walker, the witness on the run, and an unlikely heroine in her own right. She's a waitress with a troubled past and in desperate need of a ride. Cam gives her shelter and becomes her reluctant protector. Together, they embark on a daring journey across the icy tundra.

I hope you enjoy spending time with these characters as much as I did. The setting is unusual, but the core of the story is pure romance. It's about two people who fall in love against all odds and find the happiness they deserve.

If you prefer the road less traveled, come with me.

Susan Cliff

WITNESS ON THE RUN

Susan Cliff

HARLEQUIN® ROMANTIC SUSPENSE

ISBN-13: 978-1-335-45668-7

Witness on the Run

This edition published by arrangement with Harlequin Books S.A.

For questions and comments about the quality of this book, please contact us at CustomerService@Harlequin.com.

Printed in U.S.A.

Susan Cliff is a longtime romance reader, part-time writer and full-time California girl. She loves to daydream about exciting adventures in exotic locales. Her books feature heartfelt romance, gripping suspense and true-to-life characters. Get swept away with Susan Cliff!

Books by Susan Cliff

Harlequin Romantic Suspense

Witness on the Run

Team Twelve

Navy SEAL Rescue
Stranded with the Navy SEAL

Chapter 1

December 11
62N
14 degrees

Tala Walker was a woman on the run.

She'd fled Canada six months ago and never looked back. Now she was living under an alias in Willow, Alaska. She'd rented a room at a quiet boarding house. Every day she got up early and walked to the diner where she worked.

It wasn't much, but she felt safe here.

This morning, the diner was in disarray. There were beer cans all over the countertops and broken glass on the floor. It reeked of booze and cigarettes. She sighed, shaking her head. Walt must have really tied one on last night.

A quick detour to the office down the hall revealed the man responsible for the mess. He was dead to the world, snoring away on a dilapidated love seat. His barreled chest rose and fell with every breath.

Tala didn't bother to wake him up. Walt was her boss, the designated cook and the owner of the diner. If he wanted to sleep on the job, that was his prerogative. She'd opened on her own before. She could handle the early-morning customers herself. They were heading into the dark days of winter, and business was sparse.

She cleared away the trash and cleaned the floor. She thought of Duane, the husband she'd run away from, who'd also indulged in drunken antics. Only his hadn't been as harmless as Walt's. She pushed aside those memories and focused on her morning tasks. Alaskan truckers liked their coffee. She prided herself on brewing a good cup.

At 6:00 a.m. she turned on all the lights, flipped the Closed sign to Open and unlocked the front door. Soon after, a black-and-white squad car pulled into the parking lot. An officer in a navy blue uniform emerged from the vehicle. The sight reminded her of Duane also, and she had other reasons to be nervous about lawmen, but she knew he wasn't here for her. Cops liked coffee, too. They drank it at Walt's for free.

"Morning," he said, hunkering down on a bar stool.

She put a mug in front of him and filled it up. The cream and sugar was within reach. "Can I get you anything else?"

"Just this."

Tala nodded and inched away. She felt the familiar urge to flee, so she grabbed a clean rag and started wiping down the counter. She didn't strike up a conversation with him. She didn't strike up conversations with anyone. She wasn't the friendliest waitress. Walt always told her she'd get better tips if she smiled once in a while.

A few minutes later, three roughnecks strolled in. Truckers were their regular clientele, but the diner took all kinds. These men had the weathered look of loggers or oil riggers. Tough guys weren't unusual in these parts, or where she was from. She'd been born on a land reserve in the Northwest Territories. She was no stranger to hardworking men.

She brought them three mugs and three menus, glad for the distraction. As she poured their coffee, she noticed one of the men exchanging a glance with the police officer. She got the odd feeling they knew each other.

"You need another minute to decide?" she asked.

The man closest to her had dirty blond hair and bloodshot eyes. His friends were dark-haired. One had a long, skinny face and a goatee. The other was stocky, with boyish freckles. "Three breakfast specials."

She collected the menus. "Coming right up."

The police officer watched her walk away from their table.

"Ready for a refill?" she asked him.

He checked his mug. "I'm good."

She retreated to the kitchen and turned on the griddle. She considered waking up Walt. Something felt wrong to her, like a bad spirit. Men made her nervous, especially when she was working alone. She told herself it was just her imagination. Not her past, catching up to her.

Not Duane, coming to get her.

She took a deep breath and scrambled eggs. By the time she was finished with the sausages and toast, she'd regained her composure. She brought them their plates.

They acted like normal men. The blond one looked her up and down as he bit into his toast. She'd been leered at before, so it didn't faze her.

"More coffee?"

The boyish one nodded, shoveling food into his mouth. She refilled his mug, noting that he had a better appetite than his companions. He also seemed more relaxed.

"Anything else?" she asked.

The blond one smirked, as if he'd thought of a funny joke. She waited a beat before she walked away, aware of his gaze on her backside. Her waitress uniform was a basic blue dress with white tights and a white apron. She wore sensible shoes and scraped her hair into a bun at the nape of her neck. Some customers were disrespectful, but lewd behavior was rare. Most of the truckers who frequented the diner were old married men, not young bucks on the prowl. They didn't bother her.

There was only one customer so far who'd caught *her* eye. He was quiet. Strong, but not a roughneck. He was young and fit, for a trucker. He tipped well and didn't leer. He smiled even less than she did.

Tala got busy rearranging some pies in the refrigerated case. The police officer left, tossing a few coins by his empty mug. The three men finished their breakfasts soon after. They paid in cash and walked out. She frowned as she cleared their table. Only one of the plates was clean, which was odd. Roughnecks usually ate every bite. Shrugging, she dumped the contents in the trash. It was full, thanks to Walt's late-night party.

She put on her jacket and picked up the trash, grabbing the keys on the way out. The dumpster was in the back corner of the parking lot. It had to be kept behind a wooden fence, because of bears. She hurried forward and unlocked the gate. Male voices carried on the wind, which whipped around her stocking-covered legs. It was still pitch-black outside, and the air smelled like snow. She hefted the trash into the receptacle. Then she heard a loud pop.

Gunfire.

Close-range, small-arms gunfire. She knew guns. Her dad had taught her how to shoot. Duane had been an enthusiast himself. The sound was unmistakable, and chilling. Hunching down, she peered around the fence to locate the source.

Light from the diner windows illuminated three figures in the parking lot, less than twenty feet away. The blond man who'd leered at her was holding a pistol. One of his breakfast companions was slumped on the ground. The policeman stood right next to the killer. His badge glinted like an evening star.

She ducked lower, smothering a sound of panic. She wanted to run, but she was afraid she'd be spotted.

Two men loaded the body into a car while the officer stood guard. He was watching the street with his back to her. He clearly had no idea she was there. She clapped a hand over her mouth, horrified. Someone slammed the trunk, and the officer turned around to speak. His face was angry.

"Take care of this mess," he said, pointing at the diner. "All of it."

The blond man's reply was lost on the wind.

Tala stayed hidden, trembling with terror. The officer strode to his squad car and got in. After a short hesitation, the two men headed toward the diner's front entrance. She glanced at the back door, which was still ajar. They'd come out and find her any moment.

She couldn't breathe properly. She couldn't blink. She felt like her eyeballs might freeze inside the sockets. The mental picture of her frozen corpse got her moving. The instinct to flee was impossible to ignore. She had to run, now. She leapt out from her hiding place and bolted across the parking lot. She tripped over the first cement parking block she encountered and went down hard. Gravel bit into her hands and knees. It hurt like hell, but she didn't dwell on the pain. She got up and kept moving.

There was a truck stop on the other side of a wide-open space. She ran toward it, because there was nowhere else to go. Dogs barked in the distance. She couldn't hear anyone following her, but she couldn't hear anything except her pounding heart.

She enjoyed running, under normal circumstances. She'd been on the cross-country team in high school and college. She could run for miles without tiring.

She reached a group of big rigs—huge trucks with trailers. There were four or five in a row, sitting idle while the truckers rested inside the sleeper cab or somewhere else. She didn't know what truckers did when they weren't driving. Maybe they didn't sleep. They were magical, mythical creatures.

She hid behind one of the trailers and tried to catch her breath. Her blood was half adrenaline. Her veins might burst from the overload. She was having trouble with her eyes again. Everything in her peripheral vision was fuzzy. It was as if fate had decided she only needed to see what was directly in front of her.

Ice Storm.

That was all she could see. A gray semi with decorative lettering on the door of the passenger side. Its engine purred like a tiger. Between the cab and the trailer, there was enough space for her body.

She swallowed hard. The diesel fumes made her lightheaded. She had no idea where the killers were, or if they'd followed her. She could run to the nearest building and scream for help. Or she could stow away on Ice Storm.

She bit the edge of her thumbnail. If she ran away from the row of trucks, she'd be out in the open again. She didn't know if she'd make it to safety. What if she got shot, or fell into the hands of that police officer?

She chose the Ice Storm.

Her knees shook as she squeezed into the narrow slot and crouched down behind the cab. There was a metal bar to cling to, and electrical wires to avoid. Beneath her feet, a thin metal plate. It was a dangerous place to ride, but she was desperate. She hoped the driver couldn't see her back here. The last thing she needed was an interrogation. He might call the police or leave her stranded.

She'd stowed away in a semitruck before. The day she'd left Duane, she'd climbed inside a trailer at a gas station on the outskirts of Carcross. She'd expected to go south to British Columbia. Instead, the truck had traveled north. And that was how she'd ended up in Alaska, with no money and no documentation. She'd used a stolen ID to find work and rent a room. Her biggest fear up to this point had been Duane hunting her down and dragging her back home. Now she had a whole new set of problems. The men she was running from made her ex look like a choir boy.

She tightened her grip on the metal bar as the semi

moved forward. The gravel lot turned into a gray blur. Then it was smooth asphalt. Soon they were heading north on the highway. With the increased speed came a chill that penetrated her thin stockings.

Her jacket was no joke, made for arctic weather. She zipped it up to the neck and pulled the fur-lined hood over her head. But her exposed hands started to tingle and her feet felt like blocks of ice. She told herself to endure the discomfort, even though it was acute. She had to stay hidden for as long as possible. She also had to stay conscious. If she drifted into a hypothermic state and fell into the road…

Well. That would be a fatal mistake.

She closed her eyes and summoned the strength of her ancestors. She had the blood of Yellowknife warriors flowing through her veins. Her people had thrived in polar climates, with no modern conveniences, for centuries. She could handle a little freezing wind.

She held on tight, determined to ride out the cold.

Chapter 2

Cameron Hughes deliberated for at least ten minutes before he started the engine.

He hadn't planned on going to Walt's Diner. He'd been avoiding Walt's Diner. To be specific, he'd been avoiding one particular waitress at Walt's Diner. Which was ridiculous, because she'd never acted interested in him. She poured his coffee and took his order with brisk efficiency. She didn't flirt. She didn't even smile at him. There was no reason for him to keep his distance from her.

Although she'd done nothing to encourage him, he felt uncomfortable in her presence. Her cool manner and pretty face unsettled him. The last time he'd visited the diner, he'd found himself staring at her. He'd realized, with a surge of guilt, that he was attracted to her. And he'd decided not to go to Walt's again.

This morning, he'd glanced across the parking lot and studied the neon sign in the diner's front window. He'd imagined strolling in for breakfast. He knew what would happen. He'd avert his eyes when she approached, and let them linger as she retreated. He'd think of her at night, instead of Jenny. Cam studied the picture of his wife that was affixed to the dashboard. Jenny smiled back at him, not judging.

Shaking his head, he fired up the engine and prepared to leave. Maybe Jenny wanted him to move on, but he wasn't ready.

He left the truck stop and headed north on the highway. He had a radio app with more music than he could ever listen to and several audiobooks on queue. He enjoyed mysteries and true crime. He liked stories about bad guys getting caught, and hard evidence that led to convictions. If only real life mimicked fiction.

He'd forgotten to select listening material for this leg of the trip, so he drove in silence. Some days he surfed through the CB channels to hear the latest trucker chatter. This morning he didn't bother. There was light traffic and good weather. He concentrated on the lonely lanes before him, feeling restless. He needed a workout. He'd stop at the twenty-four-hour gym in Fairbanks. Hit the weights, jog a few miles.

Stretching his neck, he continued down the road. He'd gone about thirty miles when he heard a strange thump. He checked his mirrors and didn't see anything. Maybe one of his tires had kicked up a chunk of asphalt. His gauges looked fine. He kept going. A few minutes later he heard another thump, along with a rattle.

What the hell?

It sounded like something was banging against the

metal plate behind the cab. His mirrors didn't give him a full view of the space. A loose piece of wiring wouldn't make that noise. The rattling started again, and then stopped. When he reached a long straightaway, he pulled over, shifted into Neutral and engaged the brake. It was still dark, so he grabbed his flashlight before he climbed out.

First he checked the back of the trailer, which looked secure. It was locked up tight. He dropped down to his belly to shine his beam underneath the rig. The wheels were intact. He didn't see anything amiss.

He got up and inspected the space behind the cab. To his surprise, he caught a glimpse of gray fur.

Wolf?

He blinked and his eyes adjusted, making sense of the shape.

Not a wolf. A woman.

Holy hell. There was a woman in his hitch space. A stowaway. He'd never had a stowaway before, and he'd never expected to see one here. Any hobo with a lick of sense would climb into the cab or the trailer. He kept his trailer locked, of course, and there was no way to get inside his cab unnoticed.

"Come out of there," he said. "It's not safe."

The woman didn't move. She was crouched down like a cornered animal, shivering violently.

He attempted a softer tone. "Come on out. I won't hurt you."

She didn't respond. Maybe she didn't speak English. It was difficult to judge her ethnicity because most of her face was hidden behind a fur-lined hood. She appeared to have dark eyes.

Cam turned off the flashlight and pocketed it. She'd

been here since he left the truck stop, or earlier. She might be hypothermic, unable to move. He reached into the space with both hands. She leaned sideways in a feeble attempt to escape his touch. He captured her arm and pulled her toward him. She didn't fight, but she didn't cooperate, either. He had to drag her out of the narrow space. As soon as she was free, she crumpled to the ground. Her legs were ghost-white. Other than the gray parka, she wasn't dressed for the weather.

With a muttered curse, he scooped her into his arms. She was tall and slender, but heavy. He carried her toward his open door and climbed the kick-step, grunting from exertion. He skirted around the driver's chair and deposited her in the passenger seat.

Now what?

He grabbed a wool blanket from his supplies to cover her trembling body. She had on white stockings, ripped at both knees. The sight triggered his memory. He knew those legs. Startled, he lifted his gaze to her face.

It was *her.* The waitress from Walt's Diner. The one he had a crush on, and had vowed to steer clear of.

He spread the blanket over her legs and retreated, rubbing his jaw. In any other circumstances, he'd call the police and let them handle the matter. He was reluctant to take that step with this woman. She wasn't a stranger. He knew her. She clutched the edges of the blanket in a tight grip, still shivering. His first instinct was to help her, not report her.

He closed his door and cranked up the heat. Then he removed his jacket, placing it over her lap to add another layer of warmth. He didn't think her condition was life-threatening, but it concerned him. "Do you need to go to a hospital?"

She shook her head, vehement.

After a short hesitation, he put the truck in gear and pulled forward. He couldn't leave her on the side of the road, so he might as well drive. He monitored her progress as he continued north. She shivered less and less. Some of the color returned to her cheeks. Her grip on the blanket relaxed and her expression softened. No smile, but that wasn't unusual or unexpected, given the circumstances. The only drink he had was lukewarm tea. When he offered it to her, she accepted the cup and took an experimental sip.

"You work at Walt's."

She seemed surprised that he recognized her. But every trucker who'd been to Walt's would have recognized her. There was chatter about her on the radio. Pretty young things were rare in the frigid interior.

"Why did you stow away in my truck?"

"I needed a ride," she said, passing back his mug. She inspected the palms of her hands, which were scraped raw.

"You're hurt."

She hid her hands under the blanket. "I'm fine. I just tripped and fell."

Cam knew she wasn't telling him the whole story. She wouldn't climb aboard his rig and risk serious injury for no reason. She was either lying, or crazy, or scared to death. He guessed it was the latter, and his protective instincts went into overdrive. "Are you running from someone?"

She glanced into the side mirror, as if searching for a bogeyman.

He checked the highway. It was dark and deserted. "Maybe I should call the police."

"No," she said in a choked voice. "Please."

"Why not?"

"If you don't want to give me a ride, let me out. I'll walk."

He gave her an incredulous look. She'd rather freeze than contact the authorities? "The nearest town is thirty miles away."

"I can hitchhike."

"Are you in trouble?"

She stared out the window again. Her eyes welled up with tears, but she blinked them away quickly. She had a stubborn chin, bold brows and a soft mouth that reminded him of tulips. Her upper lip had a distinctive bow formation, like two little triangles.

With a frown, he returned his attention to the road. He needed to concentrate on driving, not her mouth. He didn't care if she'd robbed a bank, or vandalized Walt's Diner. He wasn't going to leave her out in the cold.

"Are you a cop?" she asked finally.

He drummed his fingertips against the wheel. "Do I look like a cop?"

"You don't look like a truck driver."

"I'm not a cop," he said, raking a hand through his hair. Not anymore. He'd abandoned his career in law enforcement a few months after Jenny died. He'd stopped believing in justice. He'd lost faith in himself.

An uncomfortable silence stretched between them. Her defensiveness could be an indication of guilt, or another manifestation of fear. He didn't ask any more questions. He knew from experience that aggressive interrogations made victims clam up. But it didn't matter, because he wasn't getting involved. Her problems were none of his business.

"I've seen you at the diner," she said.

He cleared his throat. "Yeah?"

"You order the veggie omelet and wheat toast. Black coffee."

He was surprised she remembered him. He'd only been in the diner a handful of times. The idea that he'd made an impression on her appealed to him. She tugged off her parka, revealing some other things that appealed to him.

Cam pulled his gaze away from her. She was an enticing package, with her slender figure and lovely face. Her presence in his cab felt like an electric charge. He couldn't prevent the rush of warmth that suffused him every time their eyes met.

He'd been alone on the road too long.

"Where are you headed?" she asked.

"North," he said shortly.

"Fairbanks?"

"For starters."

"Can I come with you?"

The temperature inside the cab had gone from toasty to sweltering. Cam turned down the heat, contemplative. He'd never picked up a hitchhiker before. He'd seen his share of "lot lizards" in the lower 48. They were hard-looking women, desperate for hard-up men. Nothing like this fresh beauty beside him.

She waited for his answer in silence.

"I'll take you to Fairbanks," he said, against his better judgment. He knew it was the wrong choice. She needed help, beyond a simple ride north, and he couldn't give it to her. He had nothing left to give. "From there you're on your own."

"Thank you," she said stiffly. "I appreciate it."

He made a noncommittal sound and fell silent. It was a long drive to Fairbanks, and he didn't intend on passing the time with idle chitchat. He couldn't remember how to engage a woman in conversation. The less she spoke, the easier it would be to ignore her. He could keep his mind—and his eyes—on the road.

A part of him wanted to look at her. A part of him wanted to do more than look. He'd been living like a monk for three years. He'd isolated himself in Alaska for a reason. He'd abandoned every comfort, including female company. He couldn't imagine dating again. He almost couldn't imagine a single night of pleasure.

Almost.

He knew she wasn't offering. She wasn't a lot lizard, and he didn't prey on vulnerable women, regardless. The man he used to be, the man who'd been a good husband and conscientious police officer, would never have considered taking advantage of her desperation. The man he'd become was numb. He had no moral high ground. He was a shadow of his former self, frozen in grief. He suddenly longed for some release from the monotony of his existence. He longed for human touch.

He glanced at Jenny's smiling picture on his dashboard. Her guileless expression never changed. She wouldn't have approved of his reclusive lifestyle or his current predicament. But she was dead, and had no say in the matter. He moved his gaze to the windswept lanes ahead. His heart felt like a stone inside his chest. He didn't say anything to put his passenger at ease. He just kept driving, into darkness.

Chapter 3

Tala regretted asking him if he was a cop.

She should have just shut up and let him drive. He'd threatened to call the police, but he hadn't picked up his phone or CB. He hadn't pulled over and told her to get out. He'd questioned her safety, like any conscientious person would, and she'd panicked.

She couldn't tell him what happened at the diner. He'd take her to the nearest police station and insist that she report the crime. She had no intentions of falling into that trap. No, she was going to run until she felt secure.

Running was what she did. It was what she knew.

She slunk lower in the passenger seat, feeling nauseated. She wished she'd never come to Alaska. She wished she hadn't fled Canada like a thief in the night. Now she was in a bind, and she had no idea how to get out.

She snuck another glimpse at the man behind the wheel. She hadn't lied when she'd said he didn't look like a trucker. There was something different about him, beyond his handsome face. She couldn't put her finger on what. He was rugged and outdoorsy enough to fit in with the locals. He wore flannel shirts and steel-toed boots. He had dark brown hair that curled around his collar and a well-trimmed beard that suited his features. She got the impression that he didn't smile or laugh much. He had thickly lashed, soulful brown eyes.

He was built more like a logger than a trucker. His broad shoulders and lean physique added to his appeal. He looked stronger than most homesteaders. He could even pass for one of those elite mountain climbers who came to summit Denali. He was a man in his prime. He was also married. He wore a plain gold wedding band on his left hand. She hadn't noticed it when he'd visited the diner.

The diner. A fresh wave of memories assaulted her. She could never go back there. Thoughts of Walt trickled in, making her heart clench. She hadn't stopped to consider the danger to him. He'd been asleep inside the office. What if those men had shot him? Guilt and shame and fear struck all at once, overwhelming her.

"What's your name?" the driver asked.

"Tala."

"Tala? Is that Native American?"

In her distress, she'd forgotten to lie about her name. She'd been Abigail Burgess for the past six months. She massaged her forehead, wincing. "We don't say Native American in Canada."

"What do you say?"

"First Nations."

"First Nations," he repeated, glancing at her. "You're from Canada?"

She nodded. Now that she'd screwed up, she might as well be honest. "I was born in Yellowknife."

"They have ice roads in Yellowknife."

"Yes."

"Have you been on them?"

"No. Have you?"

"I've always wanted to. I've been on the Dalton, which has an ice road section near Prudhoe Bay."

She hadn't realized he was an ice-road trucker. Maybe that was why he reminded her of a mountain climber. Both endeavors required nerves of steel. Only the most daring truckers would drive over a layer of ice with arctic waters flowing underneath.

"I'm Cam, by the way. Cameron Hughes."

"Nice to meet you," she said automatically. It felt odd to have a normal conversation after what she'd been through. "Where are you from?"

"Tacoma, Washington."

"When did you come to Alaska?"

"Three years ago. I needed to…get away."

She could relate. Unless he meant he needed to get away from his responsibilities. Maybe he'd left a wife and children behind. He didn't seem like the deadbeat-dad type, but she didn't know him. She couldn't judge his personality on polite manners and generous tips. His nice-guy vibe could be deceiving. After Duane, she didn't trust easily.

The short exchange ended, revealing the extent of his curiosity about her. She was relieved by his disinterest. She didn't want to talk.

The sun rose over the horizon as they continued north on the highway. Warm rays penetrated her window. A few hours ago, she'd been convinced she was going to freeze to death. It had been unbearably cold in that dark space. She'd pounded her fist on the cab for help. If he hadn't pulled over to investigate, she might have died.

She moved her gaze to the side mirror. She didn't think they were being followed. The road behind them was clear. The killers must not have seen her flee. She was safe—for now. Thanks to Cam, she was warm and dry.

She folded his jacket and set it aside. Then she removed the blanket. Her stockings were ruined, her knees scraped. She had bits of gravel embedded in her skin. Her palms were raw, too. She needed to wash up.

"I have a first aid kit in the glove compartment. There's a toilet in the back. Make yourself at home."

She glanced over her shoulder. There was a narrow bunk and a mini-fridge in the berth. "Do you sleep here?"

"When I have to."

With his long legs and rangy build, he didn't look like he'd fit. She rose to her feet and ventured into the space. A sliding door led to a closet-sized bathroom. It was cramped, but clean. She washed her hands at the sink before inspecting herself in the mirror. Her hair had come loose from the bun. She combed her fingers through the tangled strands to smooth the disarray. Then she returned to the front of the cab. Taking a deep breath, she helped herself to the contents of the first aid kit. After she cleaned the minor wounds with alcohol, she applied antibiotic ointment and stuck on some bandages.

"There are drinks in the fridge," he said. "And sandwiches."

She grabbed a bottled water. "Do you want something?"

"I'm good."

He drove for several hours without speaking. It felt odd to sit next to a stranger in complete silence, but she made no attempt at small talk. Sharing personal information with him seemed unwise.

She felt self-conscious in his presence. She wished he wasn't so handsome. She couldn't pretend she hadn't noticed his rugged good looks, and the last thing she wanted to do was get caught staring. Many truckers, even the married ones, wouldn't hesitate to proposition a female hitchhiker. Cam hadn't given any indication that he expected sexual favors from her. He didn't have a creepy-predator vibe. She sat very still and tried not to imagine the worst.

He gestured to the radio. "You can change the station if you like. Or I have audiobooks."

"Audiobooks?"

"Books on tape."

She nodded her understanding. There was a device plugged into his port. She picked it up and browsed the files. A Stieg Larsson book was at the top of the queue. The other options were horror, murder mysteries and true crime. Disturbing stories of violence and mayhem.

"Is this what serial killers listen to?"

He frowned at the question.

"Sorry," she said awkwardly. "That was a joke."

He changed gears, glancing her direction. "I guess my selections are pretty stark."

"They're fine."

"I choose books that will help me stay awake. It's a trucker trick."

She set aside the device. "I've never listened to an

audiobook. I don't think they make them for the books I like."

"Why not?"

"I read graphic novels. They have pictures." She flushed at the admission, as if it was something to be ashamed of. Duane always said her "comics" weren't real books. But Duane never read anything, so what did he know?

"Where do you get graphic novels?"

"I've bought a few at a used bookstore, but they're hard to find. In Canada, I checked them out from the library. I don't have a card here."

"How long have you been in Alaska?"

"Six months."

He didn't ask her why she'd come. She wouldn't have told him.

"What's Canada like?"

"Cold."

He smiled at her answer. "Were you a waitress there, too?"

"I was before I got married."

"You're married?"

She searched his face for judgment and found none. "It didn't work out."

"Is he the one you're running from?"

"None of your business."

A muscle in his jaw ticked with displeasure, but he dropped the subject. She crossed her arms over her chest to hide her trembling hands. Although she wasn't naturally meek or shy, she'd learned to avoid conflict with men. She'd managed to escape Duane and his hair-trigger temper. This morning, she'd stumbled into more danger. Witnessing a murder hadn't improved her opinion of strangers. She half expected Cam to lash out at her.

When he didn't, she released a slow breath. Her first instinct was to apologize again, but she squelched it. They had to establish some boundaries. Certain topics were off-limits. She couldn't tell him why she was running.

To his credit, Cam took her prickly attitude in stride. He didn't interrogate her further. He continued driving, steady as a rock. He didn't exceed the speed limit or take unnecessary risks. They entered Denali State Park, which offered spectacular views. She looked out the window and watched the rugged landscape pass by.

They stopped for lunch around noon. Cam gave her a sandwich and a drink from the mini-fridge. Then he put on his jacket and went outside to check his load. She was surprised by how hungry she was. She bit into the sandwich with relish.

He came in from the cold, his cheeks ruddy, and they hit the road again. He ate his sandwich on a long straightaway.

Tala thought about the last man who'd given her a sandwich: Walt. He'd always been kind to her. The day she'd walked into his diner, he'd hired her on the spot. He'd fed her and offered her some pocket money at the end of the shift. His generosity reminded her that there were good men in the world. Men like her father, who'd raised her to be strong, to fight back, to take care of herself. She wondered if he'd have been disappointed in her, had he lived.

Cam seemed like a good man. Maybe a little too good, with his healthy eating habits and unflappable demeanor. It occurred to her that he might call the police after they parted ways. If something had happened to Walt, Cam would hear about it. He'd want to help. He would tell them everything. Her name, birthplace, nationality. It was more than enough information to identify her. She'd fled the scene of a crime. She could be arrested just for that.

Trying not to panic, she nibbled the edge of her thumbnail. Maybe he wouldn't go to the authorities. He was a trucker, not a Boy Scout. She sensed a certain amount of detachment in him, which made sense for a married man who wanted to stay true to his wife. He was giving Tala a ride to Fairbanks, nothing more. When they got there, she was on her own. She had no idea what she'd do.

She didn't know anyone in Alaska, other than Walt, her landlady and her coworkers. She had no family here. She hadn't seen her mother in years. She'd been closer to her father, who'd died almost a decade ago. She still missed him.

Blinking away fresh tears, she pushed her anxieties aside and focused on the present. There were majestic mountains in the distance. She hadn't seen much of the state in her short time here. She'd passed by Denali once on her way toward Anchorage. It was a sight to behold, immense and breathtaking.

Her father had been an avid outdoorsman. He'd shared his love of the land with her. Traveling through this beautiful country reminded her of him. *Live simply*, he'd always said. *Take only what you need.*

She closed her eyes and held those thoughts for as long as she could. When she opened them, she was strong again.

Chapter 4

Fairbanks, AK
65N
2 degrees

It wasn't a pleasant drive from Denali.

Another rig had jackknifed on the icy road before McKinley Peak, causing a major pileup. Traffic was stopped for miles in both directions. There was no way around the wreck, no alternative route. Cam had to sit and wait for several hours. Tala didn't complain about the delay. She didn't say a word. The sun set early and daylight faded. They reached the outskirts of Fairbanks in the evening hours.

"Where should I drop you off?" he asked.

"Anywhere is fine."

He didn't feel right about abandoning her on a street

corner. It was getting late. "You have family around here?"

"No."

"Friends?"

"I can get by on my own."

He wanted to ask how, even though it was none of his business. She appeared to have no belongings, other than a serviceable parka and a cheap waitress uniform. She wasn't carrying a purse or backpack. If she stood out in the cold, she'd get another ride. That much was certain. Someone would pick her up. Someone with ill intentions, most likely.

"I'll find work."

"What kind of work?"

Her eyes narrowed at the question. "Not the kind you think."

"You need a change of clothes before you go job-hunting."

She fingered the torn fabric at her knees, sighing.

"I don't want to leave you on the side of the road."

"I'll be fine. Don't worry about it."

That was the problem: he was worried about it. He'd assumed a certain amount of responsibility for her when he'd agreed to give her a ride. He'd decided not to call the police, against his better judgment. Now he couldn't just walk away. He was standing between her and danger, whether he liked it or not. He felt obligated to see her off safely. If he didn't, he'd think about her all night. He'd obsess over worst-case scenarios. He'd imagine her climbing into a stranger's car. Or freezing to death.

He hadn't been able to save Jenny, and he'd never recovered from the loss. The helplessness. The soul-crushing futility.

He didn't have to *save* Tala, per se, but he could at least offer her shelter for the night. He could give her a few bucks for clothes in the morning. She could find a job tomorrow. She was young and resourceful. She'd survive. It was no hardship for him to dig into his pockets, and it might make all the difference in the world for her. A minimal cost and effort on his part could keep her from doing something desperate.

"Are you hungry?" he asked.

She moistened her lips, not answering.

"I have to deliver this load first. Then we can grab some dinner."

"You don't have to buy me dinner."

"I know."

Her eyes narrowed with suspicion. "Why are you being so nice to me?"

"Not the reason you think."

"No?"

"No."

She crossed her arms over her chest, still wary. "What would your wife say about this?"

He gave her a puzzled look. "My wife?"

"Aren't you married?"

"No."

"You're wearing a wedding ring."

He rubbed the band on his left hand absently. He'd forgotten it was there. "I'm not married anymore."

"What happened?"

"She died."

Her lips parted in surprise. Then her features softened with sympathy. "I'm sorry."

"It's okay," he said, clearing his throat. Saying the words out loud wasn't easy, even after three years, but he'd learned to swallow the pain. Then the numbness returned to his chest and he could breathe again.

Maybe Tala felt sorry for him, because she didn't reject his dinner offer. He continued to the stockyard to deliver the trailer. He'd get a new load tomorrow morning before he traveled north on the Dalton. The Dalton Highway was both his savior and his nemesis. The route wasn't for the faint of heart. It was a death-defying stretch of snowpack, black ice and whiteouts, with avalanche-prone areas and roller-coaster turns. He relished every mile.

He'd come to Alaska to be an ice-road trucker. Nothing else got his blood pumping like the Dalton. There was nothing more exciting, more addictive, or more life-affirming. Except maybe sex. It had been so long since he'd had any, he couldn't quite remember. He'd stayed true to Jenny's memory. He still wasn't ready to move on.

He hadn't lied to Tala about his intentions. He wasn't being nice to her in hopes of getting laid. She was incredibly attractive, but he couldn't imagine hooking up with her. Even if he was in the market for female company, she wasn't an appropriate choice for a one-night stand. She'd had a close call this morning. She was on the run from someone. She needed protection, not seduction.

He unloaded the trailer and returned to the cab, invigorated by the chill in the air. It was perfect ice-road weather, with temperatures dropping below zero. He climbed into the driver's seat and pulled out of the yard.

There was a good burger joint off the main drag, so Cam headed in that direction. It was crowded with customers, despite the late hour. Tala kept her hood on as they entered the building. She chose a back booth in the corner, glancing around warily. Cam knew they hadn't been followed from Willow. He'd checked his rearview mirror at regular intervals. He figured her skittishness was a side effect of past trauma, not an indication of current danger, but he made a point to stay alert.

The waitress arrived quickly. He ordered a salmon burger, iced tea and french fries. Tala asked for chicken strips and a strawberry soda. After the food was delivered, he offered her some of his fries, because he had a mountain of them.

"You like to eat healthy," she said, grabbing a fry.

"I do."

"That seems unusual, for a trucker."

"I grew up on a farm in upstate Washington. My parents made me learn about sustainable agriculture and organic produce. We ate food we grew ourselves." He shrugged, picking up his salmon burger. "It stayed with me."

She nodded her understanding. "We ate food my dad caught."

"Was he a fisherman?"

"He did a little bit of everything. Fishing, trapping, hunting. It was hard in the winter, but we got by."

Cam swallowed the bite he'd taken. "You lived off the land exclusively?"

"Yes."

He couldn't hide his surprise. He thought his childhood had been atypical. Eating fresh farm produce instead of junk food was nothing compared to eking out a meager existence in the Northwest Territories.

"He died when I was sixteen. He was only forty at the time."

"Jesus," Cam said.

"He had a good life," she said. "Short, but not wasted."

"Is that what you want?"

She shook her head. "I'd rather take after my grandmother. She lived to be eighty. She used to say my dad used up all of his spirit in half the time because he never sat still. He never stopped working."

"How old are you?"

"Twenty-five. You?"

"Thirty-four," he said gruffly.

"That's a good age," she said, grabbing another fry.

Cam tried not to be captivated by her, and failed. She had a slight accent that sounded woodsy and pleasant to his ears. She was interesting, as well as beautiful. A wave of sexual awareness washed over him, heating his blood and kicking up his pulse. He felt mildly alarmed by his response to her. He needed to pump the brakes, and stop asking so many personal questions. This wasn't a date.

She stuck a straw in her soda bottle and took a sip, drawing his attention to her mouth. Tulips in spring.

"What about you?" she asked.

"What about me?"

"Would you rather have a short life or a long one?"

He made a noncommittal sound and kept eating.

"You're an ice-road trucker, so I'm guessing short. Then again, you eat healthy and take care of your body." Her gaze traveled over him. "You work out, right?"

He flushed at her perusal. "I don't work out to live longer."

"No?"

"I sit in a truck all day. I'd get stir-crazy if I didn't exercise."

"It's not natural to spend so much time inside a vehicle."

Cam couldn't argue there. The lack of activity didn't bother some truckers. They each had their own vices. Chain-smoking and snacking were common ways to stay awake. The long hours of limited movement were difficult, but it was part of the job. He embraced the restrictions as much as the freedoms. He relished the danger and the solitude. He hadn't become a trucker to take it easy. He'd done it to disconnect with the rest of the world, and from himself.

He also didn't exercise just to combat inactivity. He did it to assuage his grief, to punish himself for living, and to sleep at night. The more grueling the workout, the better. He'd become obsessive. He'd made an effort to cut down last year, after pulling a muscle in his thigh. Overdoing it wasn't healthy, either.

They were almost finished eating when a pair of uniformed officers walked in. Cam watched them dispassionately, reminded of his former self. Tala rose from the table after the officers paused at the front counter.

"I have to go to the bathroom," she said.

Cam paid the check while she was gone. The waitress came and went. So did the police officers, who ordered their coffee to go. Cam drummed his fingertips against the table. It dawned on him that Tala had taken her parka with her, which was odd.

He wondered if she'd ditched him. It wouldn't be a big shock. She'd wanted a ride to Fairbanks, and here they were.

Curious, he went looking for her. The women's restroom was at the end of the hall. An emergency exit on the opposite side of the restaurant offered the only escape. He paused outside the door, listening for a moment. Then he pushed it open. There were two stalls and two sinks under a big mirror. "Tala?"

No answer. Just a sharp intake of breath.

He waited another beat. "The officers are gone, if that's what you're worried about."

"I'll be right out."

Frowning to himself, he shut the door. What had he gotten himself into? It was one thing to risk death on the ice roads, quite another to risk arrest by harboring a female fugitive.

She emerged from the bathroom a second later, feigning innocence. They walked into the night together and approached his rig. He glanced in her direction, noting she was tight-mouthed and ghost-pale. He didn't ask her why she'd been hiding from the police. She probably wouldn't tell him, and he wasn't sure he wanted to know. He couldn't afford to get wrapped up in whatever trouble she was in. He had to leave tomorrow.

She paused in the parking lot, her breaths visible in the frozen air. "Thank you."

"I haven't done anything."

"You've done a lot. I won't forget it."

He realized she was trying to say goodbye. He shook his head in protest. "Come with me. I know where we can stay for free."

"Where?"

"Ann's Cabins."

"Why is it free?"

"I split wood for her every time I'm in Fairbanks. We trade services."

She searched his face for hints of deception. He was stretching the truth a little. Ann gave him a discount, but he hardly ever stayed at the cabins. He split wood because he liked doing it, not because he cared about saving money.

"Are we trading services, too?" she asked.

He laughed, rubbing a hand over his mouth. Then he realized it was a serious question. She wanted to know what he expected of her, and she was smart to be cautious. Very few men would offer her a bed without intending to share it.

He held her gaze. "No. We're not."

She stared at him with undisguised curiosity. "Why are you helping me?"

An icy fist of grief squeezed around his heart. He couldn't answer her question honestly. He couldn't bear to talk about Jenny and his inability to save her. He opened his passenger door. "I didn't bring you in from the cold just to let you freeze somewhere else."

She didn't appear satisfied with the response, but she climbed inside his truck. She must have trusted him more than another stranger. The next trucker she met might not be a gentleman. He might demand sexual favors in exchange for a ride. If she said no, he could leave her stranded on the side of the road. Or worse.

Cam got behind the wheel and started the engine. Ann's was within walking distance of a major shopping center. Tala could rest tonight and look for work tomorrow.

The cabins were quaint and secluded. Romantic, even. Although it wasn't a trucker hangout, it was known to truckers because the owner was a trucker's widow. Her husband had died on the Dalton a few years ago, in an avalanche. Cam had heard chatter about it on the CB last winter. The truckers pitched in to help Ann with odd jobs. One of them said she needed someone to chop firewood for her. Cam had jumped at the task.

Turning off the main drag, he drove toward the cabins. He parked in the back of the lot and went inside the office while Tala waited in the truck.

The front desk was empty, so he rang the bell. Ann came out to greet him. She reminded him of Mrs. Claus, with her round-framed glasses and curly white hair. "If it isn't my woodcutter," she said with a smile. "How's the season going?"

"It's good. I'm keeping busy."

"Have you been on the haul road?"

"I'm heading that way tomorrow."

"You be careful out there."

"I will."

She toggled the mouse on her computer to check him in. "The only cabin left is a double. My singles are under remodel, so they're all closed."

He took out his wallet, considering. Would Tala stay with him in one room?

"I'll give you a double for the single price, if it's just you."

His neck heated with embarrassment. "I have a guest, actually."

Ann gave him his discount and handed him the key. If she was curious about his companion, she was discreet enough to pretend otherwise. "Ring me if you need anything," she said, winking.

He left the office and approached cabin 4, which was at the end of the first row. He opened the door and turned on the lights. It was a cozy room with two beds, a fireplace and a bathroom. Tala got out of his truck and walked across the parking lot, her parka hood obscuring most of her face. She didn't object to the sleeping arrangements. Maybe she hadn't anticipated having her own space. He followed her inside, his heart racing.

She sat down on the far bed. She bounced on the mattress to test its firmness. "This is nice."

Cam glanced around for something else to look at. His gaze settled on the fireplace. There was a bin full of logs he'd split. The evidence of his last good deed unsettled him. He crouched down to build a fire with shaking hands. He didn't know what he was so nervous about. They were here to sleep, nothing more. He wasn't going to touch her. Even if he was capable of a clumsy seduction attempt, which he doubted, he wouldn't try anything. He might be numb and emotionless, but he wasn't a liar. He'd given her his word.

She stood, shrugging out of her parka. "I'm going to take a shower."

He watched her disappear into the bathroom. She locked the door behind her with a click. He turned his attention back to the fire. When he had it blazing, he got up and dusted off his hands. Then he moved to the far corner of the room, by the window. There were logs stacked up near the chopping block. He considered going outside to split wood. Tala might appreciate the privacy. He turned his attention to the bathroom door, picturing her naked. Wet, dark hair. Warm, soap-slick skin.

His blood thickened with arousal. He could feel that, if nothing else. He was still capable of desire. He scrubbed a hand over his eyes, but the images didn't cease. He was ten steps away from a nude woman. He could hear the water running, streaming over her body. Erotic thoughts filled his head, fantasies and memories combined. He remembered how it felt to join a lady in the shower. To lift her up against the tiles and take her. To drink water droplets from her skin.

His hands curled into fists and his groin tightened to a painful degree. He didn't know what to do, or where to look. Staring out the window didn't help. It was as if his brain had short-circuited from the sensory overload. He was afraid she'd emerge from the bathroom and see him standing there with an erection.

He sat down on the edge of the mattress, his heart pounding. He tried to think unsexy thoughts, but it was no use. He was too wound up. He took deep breaths, fists clenching and unclenching. Unfortunately, his arousal didn't ebb. He'd denied himself pleasure too long. His body was staging a full-on revolt. He needed to get out of here.

Springing to his feet, he walked outside, into the frigid air. He gulped it into his lungs, staring at the clear night sky. It was bracingly cold. He felt better. He wanted to stretch his legs, so he started jogging. He did a few laps around the neighborhood, his breaths puffing out in the black night.

After he regained control of his body, his thoughts cleared. He returned to the chopping block outside their cabin. There was a stack of heavy logs beneath a covered awning. The ax was in the shed. He placed a log on the stump and brought the ax down, splitting it in one strike. He repeated the process over and over, until his mind was numb.

Chapter 5

Tala ducked into the bathroom and locked the door.

Even though Cam had made it clear that he didn't expect her to sleep with him, she couldn't stop her heart from racing. She shouldn't have come here. Now she felt trapped. She was at his mercy.

What if he made a pass at her? He might think she was fair game for a one-night stand, despite his reassurances. The poor guy's wife had died. He was lonely. He was young and strong and healthy. It was only natural for him to seek out female company, and he liked her. She could see it in his eyes. When his gaze settled on her, awareness sizzled done her spine. Because she liked him, too.

She studied her anxious expression in the mirror, feeling conflicted. She wished she'd asked him to take her to the airport. She could have spent the night on the benches. It wouldn't have been comfortable, but she'd endured worse. At the airport, there were multiple exits. If she needed to, she could run.

Cam wasn't holding her against her will, of course. She'd agreed to stay with him. She didn't think he was a physical threat. It wasn't so much that she was afraid of him. She was afraid of men, period. She was afraid of letting down her guard, and of getting attached. She hadn't escaped Duane to become reliant on another man. She couldn't make that mistake again. She had to take care of herself before she could feel safe with anyone else.

She turned away from the mirror and stripped off her clothes. As she stepped into the shower, memories from this morning crept up on her. She started shivering again, even though the water was piping hot. When she closed her eyes, she imagined the scene in the parking lot. Blood spraying from the gunshot wound, spreading from the body in a dark circle. She scrubbed at her skin, as if the trauma had sullied her.

After she rinsed off, she felt lightheaded and slightly nauseated. She stepped out of the stall, wrapping a towel around her body. She didn't have anything to wear besides her uniform, which wouldn't double as pajamas. Her tights were ruined, so she tossed them in the trash. Then she washed her underwear in the sink. They were nylon, so they'd dry by morning. She hung them on the hook behind the door.

She was reluctant to leave the bathroom without clothes on, but whatever. She'd have to climb into bed in her towel. Maybe Cam wouldn't notice. Maybe he wasn't that interested. She'd been told she was pretty often enough, but she'd also been told otherwise. Duane had yelled at her to shut her ugly mouth, or move her skinny ass. She didn't think she was ugly, and she definitely wasn't skinny, but his criticism had eroded her self-confidence.

Tension welled up inside her. A part of her wanted Cam to find her attractive. She just didn't want him to do anything about it. She hoped he wouldn't consider her near nudity a sign of encouragement.

Taking a deep breath, she opened the door and ventured out. She tried not to worry about Cam's reaction, or overestimate her appeal. With her tangled hair and skinned knees, she wasn't some irresistible femme fatale. He might not look twice at her.

As it turned out, Cam didn't look once. Because he wasn't there.

She clutched the towel to her chest, bewildered. He must have gone outside. There was no reason to run for cover now, so she stood in front of the fireplace. It was crackling with new flames, bright and warm. If Cam didn't return, she'd spend the night in the cabin and figure out her next step in the morning. She'd have to look for work at another café or diner. While she finger-combed her hair, letting it dry, she became aware of a familiar sound. Someone was splitting wood. She approached the window and peeked through the curtains.

It was Cam. He swung the ax in powerful strokes, bringing it down hard. When he had a nice stack of split pieces, he carried them to the shed. Then he started over. He set a punishing pace, his brow furrowed. She didn't know what demons were inside him, or why he worked so hard for physical release, but she enjoyed watching him. His strength was impressive and his tortured-soul expression captivated her imagination. She assumed he was still grieving. He was still in love with his late wife.

That was why he didn't want to "trade services" with Tala. That was why he seemed so detached and alone.

She left the window, her heart heavy, and sat down to fix her hair. She made two braids and secured the tails. She hadn't worn her hair like this since she'd left Canada. She hadn't wanted to look Indian while she was hiding out in Alaska, but she was proud of her heritage. The blood of her ancestors flowed strong and true inside her. Unlike her self-esteem, it could never be weakened or changed. It could never be beaten.

Cam came in from the cold, breathing hard. His face was flushed from exertion. He had a duffel bag in his hands. He did a quick scan of her towel-clad form. Then he unzipped the bag and took out a red-checked flannel. He thrust it at her, averting his gaze. "You can wear this to sleep in."

She accepted the shirt with gratitude.

"I'm going to shower," he muttered, and ducked into the bathroom.

After the door closed, she brought the flannel to her nose and inhaled. It smelled nice, like cozy man and laundry detergent. She put on the shirt, securing the buttons. Then she climbed into bed and stared up at the log-beam ceiling. Her thoughts whirled around and around before settling on the obvious. She pictured Cam naked in a soapy lather. She wondered if he was hard-muscled all over, or if he carried most of his strength in his arms. Was he hairy, with a thick pelt on his chest to match his beard? Maybe he had ugly feet. She smiled at the thought. Surely he had flaws. He was just a man like any other.

When he emerged from the bathroom, she had to revise her opinion. He was shirtless, in a pair of gray sweatpants. She couldn't find a single imperfection. Splitting wood had brought his muscles into sharp definition. His shoulders were broad, his stomach tight. His biceps looked as hard and crisp as McIntosh apples. The smattering of hair across his chest didn't qualify as a pelt, but it added to his rugged masculinity.

He turned off the lights and headed toward the other bed, ignoring her. She watched him get settled under the blankets. They were quiet for several moments. She listened to the wood crackle and pop in the fireplace.

It became clear that he wasn't going to try to climb into bed with her. She didn't have to worry about him demanding sexual favors in exchange for the ride to Fairbanks. Maybe she'd mistaken simple kindness for desire on his part.

Maybe he didn't want her.

She should have been relieved by his decency. She could relax now that she knew where she stood with him. For some reason, she felt sad and restless. Although she was exhausted, sleep wouldn't come.

She turned toward him in the dark. The light from the fire didn't reach his face. Although she couldn't see his features, she sensed his tension. The reason for it eluded her. He hadn't seemed anxious before they entered the cabin. Something had triggered him. While she showered, he'd gone outside to chop wood in a frenzy. "Are you awake?"

"No," he said in a clipped tone.

She smiled at his curt response.

"Do you need something?" he asked.

"I don't want to bother you."

"I don't mind."

"What happened to your wife?"

He paused for so long she thought he wasn't going to answer. Then he said, "She was in an accident. Hit-and-run. They rushed her to the hospital and tried to save her. She was in a coma for a few months."

"She never woke up?"

"No. She didn't."

Her heart constricted with sadness. "I'm sorry."

He didn't say anything.

"Is that why you came to Alaska?"

"Yes."

"You needed to get away from the bad memories."

He shifted on the mattress, seeming uncomfortable. "I thought if I kept moving, I could...move on."

"Did it work?"

"What do you think?"

"I think you're too hard on yourself."

He fell silent again.

"It's okay to grieve, even for a long time."

"Let's talk about you," he said.

"Me?"

"You're on the run for a reason."

It was her turn to be quiet.

"You won't tell me about it?"

"No."

"You don't trust me?"

That wasn't it. Right now, in the dark of the cabin, with flames crackling in the fireplace, she trusted him. She didn't think he would hurt her or take advantage of her. But she also couldn't expect him to rescue her from this mess. She had to rescue herself.

"I don't want to involve you," she said finally.

"Why not?"

"It's not your problem."

"Maybe I can help."

She shook her head in denial. "I just have to lay low for a while. I've done it before."

He grunted at this admission, as if it didn't surprise him.

"I'll be okay. I can find a job."

"Where?"

"At a diner."

"A diner with no cops or truckers? Good luck with that."

"I'm not worried about truckers."

"You should be, because they'll recognize you."

"So?"

"They'll talk about you on the radio."

"They will not."

"Sure they will. They already do. I've heard them."

She moistened her lips, incredulous. "What do they say?"

"Complimentary things. Some of it's a little crude."

Those bastards. She curled her hands into fists. If truckers talked about her on the radio, she'd be in trouble. Anyone could listen to those stations, including the cops—and the killers. But maybe Walt was okay, and no one would come looking for her. Maybe no one would worry about a missing waitress.

"I'm sure you'll be able to find work on your back, if nothing else."

She sat up in bed, her eyes narrow. He wasn't insulting her to be mean. He thought he was helping her. "You're trying to scare me into going to the police."

"You should go to the police."

"Why do you care?"

He tucked his hands behind his head. "I don't know."

She settled back down and hugged a pillow to her chest. Cam meant well, but she didn't trust the police. She could take care of herself. Cam felt responsible for her because he'd given her a ride, and now she was like… his cargo. He wanted to deliver her safely. But she knew better than to expect him to stick around.

He was a trucker. He'd move on in the morning.

She closed her eyes and tried to rest. Visions of murder and violence plagued her. She burrowed deeper in the blankets. When she finally drifted off, the nightmares closed in. She was back at the diner. There was a bloody pile of innards sizzling on the griddle. She plated the mess and took it out to her customers. The killers were sitting at a table in the parking lot. She dropped the tray and started running, but her legs didn't work. She couldn't escape, so she climbed inside the dumpster to hide.

Walt was at the bottom. He'd been disemboweled.

She let out a terrified shriek, covering her mouth. A figure emerged from the shadows. It was Duane.

"I knew I'd find you in the trash with another man."

He struck her across the cheek, and everything went black.

Tala woke up screaming. Her skin crawled with creepy sensations, and blankets were tangled around her ankles. She kicked them aside to free herself, flinging out her hands. She connected with someone, but it wasn't Duane. It was Cam.

He put his arms around her. "Shh. You're okay now. I've got you."

She stopped struggling and went quiet. It was dark in the room. She could see the pleasant glow of the fire in the hearth. The only sound was her ragged breathing.

A sob rose up to her throat. The breakdown she'd been fighting all day caught up to her with a vengeance. She couldn't prevent the tears from coming, and they were long overdue. She hadn't cried since she'd left Duane.

Cam stroked her hair and made soothing noises.

She finally calmed down enough to speak. "Walt was in the dumpster. He was dead."

"It was just a dream."

"Duane was there, too. He hit me."

"Did he?"

She heard the edge in his voice and eased away from him. There were tissues on the nightstand, next to a bottle of cold water. She used a tissue and took a soothing drink. Little by little, her tears abated.

"Better now?"

"Yes."

"Duane is your husband?"

"He was."

"Are you divorced?"

"Not legally, but I left him."

"Because he hit you?"

Her stomach clenched with unease. It was a deeply personal question, but they weren't strangers anymore. They'd passed that point and entered another territory. He'd opened up to her about his wife. She'd wept in his arms.

She'd never told anyone about the abuse she'd suffered in her short marriage. She'd been too ashamed. Her father had raised her to be strong and proud. She wasn't the victim type. She was a survivor, and a fighter. Somehow Duane had taken that away from her.

Maybe talking about him would help her get it back.

He didn't deserve to be protected. She couldn't excuse his actions, and she was done keeping his secrets.

"He was abusive," she said, letting out a slow breath. "Mentally and physically."

"Do you want to talk about it?"

A cold calm passed over her, and she nodded. "He got more violent and controlling as time went on. It was so gradual, I almost didn't notice it. Or I didn't want to acknowledge it. Then he snapped, and I couldn't pretend it wasn't happening anymore."

"What do you mean, he snapped?"

"Well, he changed after we got married. It wasn't a huge transformation, because he'd always had a temper. He'd yell at me and act jealous and get drunk and stupid. I thought it was regular boyfriend stuff. Then we got married, and we moved to a very rural area. He started treating me like his property, instead of his wife. He'd have these dark moods that scared me. He didn't want me to leave the house without permission. One day, I snuck out to go to the library. When I got back, he hit me."

"What did you do?"

"Nothing. I was too stunned to move. He cried and begged me to forgive him. He said he'd never do it again."

"But he did."

"Yes."

"Is he a cop?"

She was startled by the question. "How did you know?"

"Just a hunch. Go on."

"We stayed together for a few more months. He flew into another jealous rage and hid my purse so I couldn't go anywhere. I realized things weren't going to get better. The next time he hit me, I hit him back."

"What happened?"

She touched her face, remembering. "I bloodied his nose. I don't think he expected that, and he got really mad. He knocked me out. As soon as I could move, I packed a bag. I left in the middle of the night while he was sleeping."

"How did you get to Alaska?"

"I stowed away in a trailer."

"You're kidding."

"No. I wasn't planning on leaving Canada. I thought the trucker was going south. Instead he went west, and here I am."

"Are you here illegally?"

She shook her head. "Have you ever heard of the Jay Treaty?"

"No."

"It allows First Nations people the right to come to the US from Canada and vice versa. There's really no such thing as an undocumented Indian, but I don't have my tribal card or any ID to prove my status. I left everything in Canada.'

"I'm glad you escaped."

"So am I."

She looked away, contemplative. Cam didn't seem to think less of her for having an abusive husband. She knew it wasn't her fault, but a part of her felt responsible for what had happened. She should have been smarter, and more aware of Duane's true nature. She shouldn't have rushed into marriage. She should have identified the threat sooner.

Tala closed her eyes to clear the bad memories. Her

relationship with Duane was over. She'd left him, and she'd never have to suffer his abuse again.

Unfortunately, she'd traded up as far as personal problems went. Now she had to worry about the other men she was running from.

Goose bumps broke out across her flesh. She'd kicked off the blankets in the throes of her nightmare. Her legs were bare and cold. So was Cam's chest, she realized with a start. She'd been too distressed to notice that before. The faint glow of the fire revealed an intimate scene. They were in bed together, close enough to touch. He was shirtless, his torso outlined against the pale sheets. She was wearing his flannel without a stitch underneath. She tugged the comforter back into place, flushing.

"I should let you sleep," Cam said.

"Don't go," she whispered. "Please."

He glanced in her direction, brow furrowed. He seemed uncomfortable with her proximity, and was possibly confused about what she wanted from him. Tala struggled to pinpoint it herself. She knew he was hung up on his wife, and not interested in sex. Or not interested in her. Whatever his reasons, she felt safe with him.

She wouldn't drag him into her problems, but she could ask him for one small thing. "Will you…hold me?"

He drew in a ragged breath, as if tortured by the thought.

"Just until I fall asleep," she said, to make her wishes clear. "Nothing more."

"I don't think that's a good idea."

She searched his features in the dark, uncertain what he meant. His eyes glinted with something she'd seen before. Something he'd been trying to hide. The desire she'd sensed earlier flared between them, like a new spark.

He wasn't so disinterested.

She altered her request. "Can I hold you?"

After a short hesitation, he rolled onto his side, facing away from her. She hugged his back, spoon-style. It was the best of both worlds. She could cuddle him and enjoy the simple pleasure of human touch without worrying about him getting aroused. He could lay there and be her teddy bear, no strings attached.

She slipped her arm around him and closed her eyes. He was warm and hard-muscled. Solidly built, like a protective shield. She could feel his heartbeat under her palm, strong and sure. He covered her hand with his and linked their fingers together. Her throat tightened with emotion. She hadn't felt peace or contentment in such a long time. His presence filled an empty place inside her she hadn't known was there.

She savored him for as long as she could before she fell asleep.

Chapter 6

December 12
65N
-5 degrees

Cam got dressed in the dark.

He pulled on his jeans over thermal underwear and shoved his feet into steel-toed boots. His long-sleeved T-shirt provided minimal warmth against the morning chill, but he didn't grab his jacket. He wanted to feel the cold bite of winter, and he did. It had snowed overnight. Powder crunched beneath his soles as he crossed the dark, deserted parking lot. Frosty air filled his lungs and penetrated his clothing.

He made his way toward the front office, which was open but unmanned. The smell of fresh-brewed coffee awaited him. He helped himself to two cups. He didn't know if Tala liked cream and sugar, so he grabbed packets of both.

"There's oatmeal," Ann said, emerging from another room.

He glanced at the cooking pot next to the carafe. His stomach growled with interest, but his hands were already full. "I'll come back for it."

"I can deliver two bowls to your cabin."

A flush crept up his neck at the thought of Ann coming to his door and catching a glimpse of Tala in his bed. He felt like a teenager who didn't want his mom to find out his girlfriend had slept over. "No need."

Ann smiled at his quick response. "Thanks for splitting logs."

"I enjoy the work."

She nodded, and he escaped the cozy space in a hurry. He had no reason to be embarrassed. He hadn't done anything wrong. He'd slept next to Tala without crossing the line. Even if their night hadn't been innocent, so what? Surely Ann had seen worse in her days as innkeeper. Drunken hookups, seedy affairs, hard partying. She wouldn't blink an eye at Cam's pretty young guest. Unless she assumed he was married, which might be the case. He was still wearing his wedding ring.

He winced at the oversight. He'd put it on again a few weeks ago, after a disastrous Thanksgiving at his parents' house. His mother had invited one of Jenny's friends—one of her *single* friends—in a clear attempt at matchmaking. He'd left as soon as possible, claiming he had an important delivery.

Women had flirted with him before, and he'd felt nothing. No whisper of temptation. No need to armor himself with proof of his lack of availability. This time was different. He hadn't been interested in Jenny's friend. He'd thought of the waitress at Walt's Diner, someone he hardly knew, and he'd been struck by a wave of intense longing, mixed with sorrow. It hit him like an avalanche, knocking him off-balance. He'd found his ring and slipped it on. He'd needed a protective shield, because his attraction to the waitress had triggered new pain. His grief had felt staggering, insurmountable.

That was the problem with moving on. It hurt more than standing still.

He took the coffee to the cabin and set the cups down on the mantel by the fire. He poked the ashes and added some wood. Tala stirred at the sound. She sat up in bed with an abruptness that suggested she'd forgotten where she was. Her gaze connected with his, and recognition dawned. She returned to a reclining position, her trepidation fading.

She trusted him not to try anything sexual. Which made sense, he supposed, because he'd kept his hands to himself all night. But if she could've read his thoughts in the wee hours of the morning—or right now, for that matter—she wouldn't look so relaxed. Because he wanted to climb into bed with her. He wanted to kiss away the hurt her husband had caused and show her how a real man treated a woman.

Heat crept up his neck at the thought. Of course he wasn't going to make a move on her. He wasn't ready for that kind of intimacy. He was still wearing his wedding ring. The only way to stay numb was to keep his distance.

"I brought you a coffee," he said. "Do you want oatmeal?"

She nodded, rising to her feet. She looked rumpled

and sexy in his flannel shirt. Her eyes were sleepy, her legs a mile long. When she tugged on the fabric to make sure she was covered, he averted his gaze. He knew she was bare beneath it. He'd seen her pale blue panties hanging in the bathroom. He'd touched them this morning—to see if they were dry. To feel the silky material and imagine it against her skin.

After she went into the bathroom, he released a slow breath. He needed to get a grip before he embarrassed himself. He cleared his throat and left the cabin, sucking in the cold air. There were two servings of oatmeal in disposable cups with lids at the front desk. He carried them back to the room, plastic spoons in hand. Tala was sitting by the fire, sipping coffee. They shared a simple hot breakfast in silence.

He wasn't eager to get on the road again, despite his discomfort in her presence. He wanted to make sure she was safe before he left town. He hadn't expected to be so concerned about her welfare, but they were in an unusual situation. They'd spent the past twenty-four hours together. They'd shared personal stories. They'd even *held hands*.

Cam might be numb, but he wasn't dead. His protective instincts were working overtime. So was his libido, if he was being honest.

"Do you have another load to deliver?" she asked.

He nodded. "I'm supposed to pick it up this morning."

"What direction are you headed?"

"North, on the Dalton."

It wasn't a trip she could take with him. The Dalton Highway was the deadliest stretch of road in Alaska. There were almost no facilities, and constant obstacles. Whiteouts, avalanches, ice patches, snowdrifts.

"You could stay here," he said, on impulse.

"In Fairbanks?"

"In this cabin."

Her lips parted with surprise. She hadn't expected him to make this offer. That made two of them.

"I know the owner of this place, like I said. She might hire you."

"To split logs?"

"Or for lighter work."

"I can handle heavy work."

He believed her.

"The owner is a woman?"

"Yes."

"How well do you know her?"

Cam rubbed a hand over his jaw. "Her husband was a trucker. He died on the Dalton. Since then, I've been coming around to do chores for her."

"Do you really trade services?"

"She gives me a discount. Also, I like it."

"You like helping women?"

"I like splitting logs."

She studied his face with skepticism. "Is there anything else you enjoy doing for her?"

He smiled at her question. "Like what?"

"You know what."

"She's pushing seventy. My generosity doesn't extend quite that far."

Tala set her coffee mug aside. "These cabins aren't cheap. Even if she hired me, I couldn't afford to stay here."

"I can afford it."

She shook her head in refusal. She wouldn't allow herself to depend on him, or anyone else, and it pissed him off. She had no belongings, no money, no job, no resources. She didn't even have a change of clothes. But she'd rather strike out on her own than kick back in this cozy cabin on his dime.

What was wrong with her? What was wrong with *him*, for that matter?

He should never have given her a ride in the first place. His contract prohibited picking up hitchhikers. She was clearly in trouble with the law. He should be cutting her loose, not trying to keep her around. He didn't understand what he was doing. He'd made a series of bad decisions upon meeting her. Emotional decisions that threatened his current, stark existence. He'd brought her inside his rig to get warm, and warmed himself in the process.

If he wasn't careful, the protective layer of ice he'd been hibernating under would thaw. Then the real pain would come.

"At least let me buy you a change of clothes," he said. She had nothing to wear. He wasn't leaving her on a street corner without any *pants*. "I have to go to Walmart and get some supplies anyway."

She nodded her agreement and ducked into the bathroom to get ready. She had to borrow his sweatpants. Even with the drawstring tightened, they rode low on her hips. Her black waitress shoes were for indoor use only. She needed warm clothes and winter boots no matter what her future plans were. She couldn't job-hunt in her old uniform, or his pajamas.

The big-box store was about five miles away. He parked on the outskirts of the lot and accompanied Tala inside. He grabbed a cart, swamped by memories of

Jenny. Their Sunday shopping trips. Rainy mornings in Seattle. They'd been good together. They'd been content.

He headed toward the women's clothing department, where Tala browsed the racks. She selected black leggings and an oversize sweatshirt. When he gestured for her to continue, she added a pair of jeans to the cart. They strolled through another section with packages of socks and underwear. She chose basic white cotton, seeming embarrassed.

"That's all you want?" he asked.

"You don't have to buy the whole store."

"This is Walmart. Everything's cheap."

"I'm going to owe you."

"Consider it a gift."

"No," she said, her face solemn. "I'll pay you back."

Warmth suffused his chest at her assertion. He admired her pride, even though he cursed her stubbornness. The thought of reuniting with her after he returned from the Dalton appealed to him—and not because he wanted to collect on a debt. He'd like to see her again, despite his wariness toward women, and his general misgivings about the trouble she was in.

"You should let me introduce you to Ann," he said.

She continued walking alongside him, not answering. It was a good sign, he supposed. She hadn't refused outright. They found the shoe racks. He left his cart at the end of the aisle and accompanied her on the search for practical footwear.

"You know what you said about moving on?" she asked.

"Yeah."

"I have to do that, too. I have to keep moving."

"You're running away from your problems."

"And you aren't?"

He didn't answer. Of course he was. They both were.

"If you stay in the same place, your past catches up with you." She turned to study the opposite side of the aisle. "When I first came to Alaska, I went from town to town. I hitchhiked here and there. I didn't feel safe unless I was on the go. It took me almost a month to settle down in Willow."

It was on the tip of his tongue to tell her that she didn't have to run anymore. He could help her. He used to be a cop. His brother was still a cop. Cam could make some inquiries about her husband. He could probably have the guy arrested, with or without Tala's cooperation. Cam didn't extend the offer, because he sensed it wouldn't go over well. She didn't trust the police, obviously. She wouldn't trust him if she knew he'd been a patrol officer.

He also had his own issues with faith and justice. And family, for that matter. Calling his brother would open him up to uncomfortable questions. He'd disconnected from everyone in Washington. He hadn't spoken to Mason since Thanksgiving.

He massaged the nape of his neck, feeling guilty. It was better to keep his secrets and protect his privacy. Stay distant. Stay numb.

She reached into a large box on a lower shelf and fished out a pair of sturdy black boots. They looked warm and practical, with faux fur trim. She sat down on the floor to try them on. "They fit."

He grunted his approval. "What else do you need?"

She walked back and forth to test the comfort of the boots. Then she removed them. "This is more than enough, Cam."

"You don't have to pay me back."

"I want to. How long will you be on the Dalton?"

"Three days, maybe."

"Do you have a cell phone?"

"Of course, but there's no service. You can leave a message."

"Give me the number."

He handed her a business card with his information. She tucked it into the front pocket of his flannel.

"You can go to the cabin anytime. I'll tell Ann to run a tab."

She nodded, avoiding his gaze. He didn't press, because he was afraid to scare her off. Maybe she'd call him in a few days. Maybe she'd rethink his offer to stay at the cabins. She had nowhere else to go, after all.

They headed toward the front of the store together. She added a couple of travel-size toiletries to the cart, along with a simple canvas backpack. He didn't really need any supplies, but he grabbed a few boxes of snacks. The store was busier now, at the start of the morning rush. He paid for the items in cash.

"I'll change here," she said, gesturing to the restrooms.

He went to wait for her near the entrance. There was an in-store restaurant with a café. He sat down at an empty booth. A mounted TV in the upper corner displayed local news. He listened to the weather report with interest. There was snow in the forecast, as usual. Then a photograph of Tala flashed across the screen.

Cam's blood froze at the sight. Newscasters launched into a story of a missing waitress from Walt's in Willow. The photo of Tala appeared again. It had been taken at the diner, probably by a patron. Tala was standing at the counter next to Walt.

The caption under her face read "Abigail Burgess." Viewers were asked to call a number for the Willow Police Department if they had any information. The segment lasted sixty seconds at the most. He blinked and it was gone, like a figment of his imagination.

Abigail. *Abigail?*

He tried to remember hearing her name in the diner, or over the radio. The other truckers used terms like "honey" or "cutie" for an attractive waitress. Tala was a distinctive name, and he wouldn't have forgotten it. She must have lied to him. He was disappointed, but not particularly surprised, by the realization.

Cam pondered this latest development. There was no mention of a crime committed, by her or anyone else. She didn't have any family in the area to report her disappearance, and she'd only been gone twenty-four hours.

And yet, her story had made the morning news.

What the hell had happened at Walt's? He got the feeling it was something more serious than a brief sighting of her ex. She'd woken up screaming last night. She'd mentioned a dream about Walt in the dumpster. Dead.

He glanced toward the restrooms, uneasy. She was taking too long to change clothes. Either she'd ditched him to avoid saying goodbye, or she'd run into some more trouble. The first option was far more likely, and it filled him with dark emotions. He hadn't been able to say goodbye to Jenny because she'd never woken up. He couldn't bear to relive the moment his wife had slipped away.

He had issues with saying goodbye. Major issues.

Stomach roiling, he rose to his feet. Women who weren't Tala breezed in and out of the restrooms. Had she walked by him while his eyes were glued to the television screen? No. She couldn't have left the store, unless there was another way out. He spotted a garden section in the opposite corner.

Damn it.

Cam strode past the potted plants and fertilizer. Sure enough, there was an alternate exit at this end. He moved forward and shoved through the doors, searching the dark for a wolf-quick girl in a fur-lined parka.

There.

She was in the parking lot—and she wasn't alone. A man had his hand locked around her upper arm. He appeared to be leading her away by force. She looked over her shoulder at Cam. Their eyes met for a split second. Then the man, who must be her abusive ex, jerked her forward. She stumbled and almost fell.

Cam's vision went red. He was already on edge, filled with angry tension. The sight of her being manhandled made him completely snap.

He rushed toward them, intent on introducing himself with his fists.

Chapter 7

Tala had checked her reflection before she went out to meet Cam.

The form-fitting jeans flattered her figure and the oversize sweatshirt was cozy. Her dark eyes glittered with a mixture of emotions. Fear, excitement, hope. She liked Cam, but she couldn't accept his offer to stay in the cabin. It wasn't the right place to lay low. She needed a cheap, anonymous hotel where no one asked questions. Also, her instincts told her to keep moving. She had to run until she felt safe.

She wanted to be cautious with her heart, as well. She didn't know Cam well enough to trust him, and what she did know gave her pause. He was still in mourning. He was quiet and reserved. He wanted her physically, but he might change his mind about that. She wouldn't be surprised if he started to have second thoughts about her as soon as they parted ways. He wasn't ready to let go of his wife's memory.

There was also the small matter of Tala being on the run from the law. Cam wasn't the kind of man who would disregard her suspicious behavior. He'd continue to ask questions. He'd insist on helping.

She tugged on her parka, her spirits low. She didn't want to say goodbye to Cam yet. He made her feel sexy and tingly and warm inside. More importantly, he made her feel safe. Tearing her gaze away from the mirror, she picked up her backpack and left the bathroom. She searched the crowd for Cam and found someone else.

The police officer from Willow.

He was in plainclothes, but she recognized his face. He was standing less than twenty feet away, blocking her path to the exit. His mouth stretched into a menacing smile. Pulse racing, she whirled around and headed the opposite direction. She rushed through the garden section, trying not to panic. It was filled with indoor plants and herbs. Alaskans liked to grow stuff, even in the dead of winter.

She spotted another exit sign in the corner. She started running toward it. She knocked over a garden gnome and kept going. Then she was outside in the cold, dark morning. The parking lot lights beckoned. She didn't see Cam's truck, but it didn't matter. She needed to escape without involving him. She sprinted away from the danger, picking up speed with every stride. Running had always come naturally to her. She'd won several medals for her college cross-country team.

Unfortunately, she got tripped up before she could reach the road. A man jumped out from behind a parked car and pushed a shopping cart directly into her path.

She couldn't hurtle it, and she was going too fast to stop. She avoided the cart, but collided with the man. They both went sprawling.

When she tried to scramble away, he grabbed her by the arm. He was skinny, but strong. He rose to his feet and dragged her upright. She recognized him as one of the killers from the diner. With his free hand, he brandished a wicked-looking knife. When he twisted his wrist, the blade glinted in the dark.

She stopped struggling.

"Walk," he ordered.

She moved forward, swallowing hard. A glance over her shoulder revealed Cam emerging from the garden section. He bolted toward them. She didn't want him to get hurt, but she needed his help. Her captor pulled her along, wrenching her arm painfully.

Five.

She counted down the seconds until Cam struck.

Four.

The man at her side continued walking, staring straight ahead.

Three.

Cam was almost on them.

Two.

She jerked her elbow from the man's grasp and dove to the ground like a bomb was about to go off. And it kind of did. Cam was the bomb. He exploded with brutal force, punching her captor in the back of the neck. The skinny man staggered forward and dropped his knife, which clattered to the asphalt. He looked stunned, but he didn't fall down. He turned to fight, raising his fists protectively.

Cam punched him again, in the jaw, and that was all it

took. The man spun around and crumpled to the ground like a leaf. Cam kicked the knife away. He said a few choice words, his mouth twisted with fury.

Tala stayed down, afraid to move. She thought Cam might continue his attack. He stood over his opponent, as if evaluating his condition. Then he left the guy alone and came to Tala. When he offered her a hand, she took it.

"Are you all right?"

She stood, testing the strength of her knees. "Yes."

The parking lot wasn't deserted. There were cars driving past, people coming and going. She glanced around for the police officer, her legs shaky. He wasn't there, but someone else emerged from the shadows. It was the man who'd leered at her at the diner. His jacket was open. He had a revolver tucked into his waistband.

Cam used one arm to move Tala into the space behind him.

"What's the trouble?" the man asked.

Tala gripped Cam's elbow, terrified. Cam didn't answer. A car passed by in the next lane, its headlights illuminating the scene. The man closed his jacket. He squinted at the curious onlooker in annoyance. Then he nudged his friend with the edge of his boot.

"Get up."

The skinny man rose to his feet slowly. The man with the gun helped him stagger away. He shot Cam a threatening look over his shoulder. Then they both disappeared into the dark recesses of the parking lot. An older-model SUV, maybe a Ford Bronco, took off in the opposite direction. There were other vehicles in motion. It was difficult to tell which one held the men who'd attacked her.

Cam picked up her backpack. "We have to go back inside to call the police."

Fear spiked through her. "No. We can't."

"Why not?"

"There was another man in the store. He's with them."

His eyes narrowed with suspicion. He glanced toward the front entrance. "Okay, we'll call from my truck."

She didn't argue, because she wanted to get out of sight. They crossed the parking lot in long strides. Cam unlocked the door for her. She climbed in, taking the backpack from his hands. He walked to the driver's side and got behind the wheel.

"Please," she said. "Let's just go."

A muscle in his jaw flexed. He fired up the engine and left the parking lot. A delayed reaction to the close call struck her. She started shaking uncontrollably. Tears flooded her eyes. She drew her knees to her chest, making a tight ball with her body. She thought about Duane, the last man who'd been violent toward her. He'd said he was going to kill her once. She didn't know if he meant it, or if he was capable of murder. He seemed pretty tame compared to the men she was currently running from.

When she lifted her head, they were parked on the side of the street, in front of an auto repair garage. There was a café and a bookstore across the street. Cam turned off the engine and gave her a measured look.

"I have to call the police," he said again.

Fresh tears filled her eyes. She blinked them away. "I won't talk to them."

"That guy pulled a knife on you."

"He'll deny it."

"Was that your husband?"

"No."

"Which one was?"

"None of them."

"None of them?"

"Cam, you shouldn't get involved. The police won't help me. If anything, they'll arrest you for assault."

"That's bullshit."

"You struck first."

"I had cause!"

She flinched at his vehemence. She hadn't meant to put him in danger, but she had. Now he was on the killers' radar. They knew his truck. They'd seen his face. She shouldn't have gone shopping with him. She shouldn't have let him get so close, or shared so much personal information. She grasped the door handle, ready to bolt.

His gaze searched hers, missing nothing. He didn't reach for his CB. She didn't move. It was a standoff. After a long moment, he broke eye contact with her and squinted into the distance. He wasn't the type of man who casually disregarded the law. She was asking him to go against his natural instincts.

"I want to help you," he said. "But you need to tell me the truth."

"I wouldn't lie to you."

"Wouldn't you, *Abigail*?"

She drew in a sharp breath. "Where did you hear that?"

"It was on the news when you were in the bathroom. Missing waitress from Walt's Diner, Abigail Burgess."

"Was there any news about Walt?"

"No."

She twisted her hands in her lap. She hoped Walt was okay. She had to tell Cam her story, or at least part of it. He was already involved, and he needed to know what they were up against. But if she said too much, he'd call the police for sure. "When I first came to Alaska, I didn't have any ID, and I couldn't get a job. So I stole one from a lady's wallet. She was about my age, with dark hair. She was Abigail Burgess. My real name is Tala."

"Who were those men?"

"I don't know," she said. "They came into the diner yesterday."

"Do they work for your husband?"

She stared out the window, across the dark stockyard. Snow flurries had begun to fall. Cam had unwittingly given her the perfect lie. Of course he thought Duane was behind this. A girl could only have so much unrelated bad luck.

"How did they find you?"

"They must have followed us from Willow."

"No one followed us from Willow."

She moistened her lips, nervous. The killers would have looked for her outside the diner. She'd left the trash gate open and the keys dangling. They knew what she'd seen, and could guess where she'd gone. The truck stop was the only option. Since then she'd been in several public places with Cam. "Maybe someone talked about us on the radio."

"You don't have a cell phone they can track?"

"I had a cheap one, but I left it in the diner. I left my purse, keys, everything."

He fell silent, his expression skeptical.

"You don't believe me."

"I believe that you have an abusive ex, and that you're in trouble. I don't understand why you haven't gone to the police."

"I told you. He *is* the police."

"In Canada. Not here."

"I have a criminal record," she said, with reluctance.

"For what?"

"Civil disobedience."

He arched a brow. "Civil disobedience? That's it?"

She stayed quiet.

"Do you have priors?"

"No, but I missed my court date. Now there's probably a warrant for my arrest."

"So you think you'll be extradited to Canada if you file a police report? You think you'll go to jail instead of him?"

"Yes, I do," she said, frowning at his incredulous tone.

"That's crazy."

"It's not crazy, Cam. He's a white man who works in law enforcement. They'll believe him over me."

He deliberated for a moment, giving her point the weight it deserved. "They won't believe him over *me*. I'll give a statement about what happened in the parking lot. I'll make sure you're protected."

Tala was touched by the offer, but she couldn't accept. She didn't trust the police in Alaska or anywhere else. Even before she met Duane, she'd been wary of law enforcement. Her people had a history of being targeted unfairly in Yellowknife. She'd learned to avoid men in uniform at a young age. She didn't know why she'd ever trusted Duane. She'd been lost and alone, after the deaths of her father and grandmother. She'd been flattered by the attention. She'd made a mistake.

She hoped she wasn't making another one with Cam. He seemed like an honorable man. He'd been kind to her, and he'd come to her rescue without hesitation. She shivered at the memory of his brutal use of force in the parking lot. He could certainly handle himself in a fight. But did he have a dark side, like Duane?

"I'm sorry," she said, shaking her head. "I have to take care of this on my own."

He massaged his right hand, contemplative. His knuckles were scraped and swollen.

"You need ice."

"I'm fine. I'll put some snow on it in a minute."

She felt guilty for dragging him into this mess. He'd gotten hurt because of her. He could have been shot. Those men were clearly willing to kill again. They'd come all the way to Fairbanks to eliminate her as a witness.

"You can't stay here," Cam said.

She murmured an agreement.

"Where will you go?"

"I've thought about heading to Montana. I have family there."

"You'll be safe with them?"

"I think so," she said. Her mother and two half-brothers lived on reserve land, with her stepfather. The tribal police would protect her. She doubted the killers would be able to track her that far. They didn't even know her real name.

"How will you get there?"

"I'll hitchhike."

His jaw clenched with displeasure. "That's a stupid idea."

"Do you have a better one?"

"Yeah, but you shot it down."

"I could go with you."

"On the Dalton?"

"Why not?"

"It's too dangerous."

"And staying here isn't?"

"The weather is extreme. The roads are treacherous. There are constant storms, avalanches and snow drifts. It's white-knuckle all the way. If you break down or crash, you can freeze before help arrives."

"I'm from the Northwest Territories, Cam. Cold doesn't scare me."

"Cold is an understatement."

"I understand that, and I can handle it. My people have been thriving in polar climates for thousands of years."

"Not in eighteen-wheelers, they haven't."

"They lived in sod houses with no heat. Your truck is a four-star hotel compared to those lodgings."

"Did you live in a sod house?"

"No, I grew up in a two-bedroom trailer. But I've camped in the snow before. My dad was an outdoor expert. He taught me all sorts of winter survival skills. I can handle rough weather."

He raked a hand through his hair, sighing. She could sense his capitulation. He didn't want to leave her behind, alone and unprotected. And maybe he wanted someone in his bed, to help him forget about his wife. His eyes traveled down the length of her body. "I can't afford to get distracted on the road."

"I won't be a distraction."

"Right," he scoffed, his gaze searing.

"I'll ride in the back. I won't make a sound."

"And when we return? Then what?"

"I don't know."

"I can't take you to Montana."

"I didn't ask you to."

"I'm contracted to work exclusively on the Dalton for the next few months. I'll be hauling loads to Deadhorse and back."

"I'll figure something out," she said, more confident now.

He tightened his grip on the wheel. "Okay," he said, letting out a huff of breath. "You can come with me on one trip. You'll have to stay out of sight as much as possible. We'll spend the night at the basecamp in Coldfoot. It's rustic."

"I like rustic."

"There are separate bunks for men and women. We won't be together."

She nodded her understanding.

He turned on the ignition, his jaw clenched. He seemed irritated about the arrangement. He was bringing her along and not getting anything he wanted out of the bargain. She didn't promise to make it up to him. The tension between them was already high. There was no reason to fan the flames of their attraction.

"I have to get my truck worked on," he said, digging into his pocket for a few dollars. "Buy yourself a cup of coffee while you're waiting. I'll keep an eye out for trouble."

She smiled in relief. Leaning toward him, she kissed his bearded cheek. "Thanks, Cam. You're a good man."

He grunted his response, his neck ruddy. She climbed out and shut the door, zipping up her parka to ward off the chill. The temperature would climb after sunrise, but only a little. Winter days were cold and short. She inhaled the brisk, snow-laden air. She didn't see any other vehicles on the road.

Cam pulled forward, gravel spitting from his tires.

He drove the short distance to the entrance of the auto repair shop. Tala headed the opposite direction, toward the café. Coffee was huge in Alaska, and she liked it as much as the next girl, but the lights in the bookstore beckoned. She bypassed the café and headed inside. An elderly man in glasses muttered a greeting as she walked in. He was immersed in a taxidermy project. There were stuffed puffins and other frozen birds scattered around.

She strolled up and down the aisles, her hands in her pockets. After a few minutes of browsing, she found a small stack of graphic novels on a bottom shelf in the back of the store. She spotted a book that Duane had ordered for her last Christmas. She plucked it off the shelf, her throat tight. Fresh tears flooded her eyes and her knees went weak. She sank to a sitting position on the floor.

Her marriage to Duane had devolved into a prison of intimidation and abuse, but it hadn't started that way. She wouldn't have fallen in love with him if he'd been cruel every moment. They'd had good times, especially in the beginning. The man who'd abused her seemed like a different person than the man she'd married.

She felt guilty about her attraction to Cam, which was ridiculous. Duane didn't deserve her loyalty. She was angry with him for hurting her, and angry with herself for choosing him. She should have run at the first sign of trouble. She should have seen the darkness inside him before it closed in on her.

Her father had warned her that some people weren't what they seemed. Some men were wolves in sheep's clothing. She hadn't remembered his advice until it was too late. She wouldn't forget it again.

Her fingertips skimmed the novel's dusty cover. It

was one of her favorites. The artwork depicted a man with horns and a woman with a baby at her breast. Duane had torn her copy to shreds in a jealous rage one day.

Blinking the tears from her eyes, she set the book aside and chose another.

Chapter 8

Cam pulled into an empty space in the garage, letting the engine idle.

His rig needed a few modifications before he could drive it on the ice road. The adjustments would take almost an hour, and Cam didn't need to watch the process. He could have joined Tala in the bookstore. He could have brought her into the shop, for that matter. The company mechanic wouldn't report him for having a female companion in Fairbanks. On the Dalton, it was another story. He wasn't allowed to transport a passenger without permission and a liability waiver. If a safety supervisor spotted Tala with him, he'd be screwed.

He didn't know why he'd agreed to bring her along.

Okay...he *knew* why, but he couldn't believe he was doing it. He'd become infatuated with her, against his better judgment. He was letting his emotions take over.

He hadn't been himself since he'd found Tala in his hitch space. Every decision he'd made after that moment had been questionable. He wasn't usually a rule-breaker, but he'd been numb for so long. She made him feel alive, and he wanted to hang on to that feeling. He wasn't ready to let her go.

If he left her behind, he'd lose her. He felt it in his bones. She'd run away from Fairbanks and he'd never see her again. He'd never get the chance to save her. He'd never know what might have been.

He studied the smiling photograph of Jenny. He was forgetting her, little by little. Her face wasn't as clear in his mind as it used to be. Her voice didn't pop into his head as often anymore. He didn't hear echoes of her bright laughter.

After a long moment, he removed the photo from the dash and put it in the pocket next to his seat. Then he worked the ring off his finger, tucking it away with the picture. Before he could rethink his actions, he grabbed his cell phone and climbed out of his rig. He nodded at the mechanic as he left the garage. Snowflakes drifted down in soft flurries, adding to the fresh powder on the ground. The knuckles on his right hand throbbed.

He hadn't brought Tala to the garage because he needed space. He wanted to cool down and clear his head. He also wanted to have a conversation without her listening in. His older brother, Mason, was a detective with the Seattle Police Department. Cam scrolled through his short list of contacts. Then he bit the bullet and called him.

Mason answered on the second ring. He didn't sound happy, which wasn't a surprise. "Cam," he said simply.

"Mason."

"Where are you?"

"Fairbanks," he said, looking up at the bleak sky. "Do you have time to talk?"

"You want to talk now? Really?"

Guilt speared through him. He fell silent, because he deserved Mason's vitriol. He also figured that letting his brother vent was better than trying to forge ahead as if he'd done nothing wrong.

"You didn't want to talk in Tacoma."

"I felt ambushed."

"Give me a break," Mason scoffed. "Nobody ambushed you. Mom invited a friend of Jenny's and you freaked out."

"It was a setup," Cam said.

"So what? You didn't have to leave early, or treat the girl like the goddamned plague. You made Mom cry."

Cam swore under his breath. "I'll send her some flowers."

"Who, Jenny's friend?"

"No, *Mom*. I'm not interested in Jenny's friend, or anyone else Mom tries to throw at me. I know she means well, but she needs to back off."

"Stop living like a recluse and she will."

"I didn't call for a lecture."

"You think you're the only person in the world who's ever lost someone?" Mason continued, undeterred. "You're the only one grieving? The only one whose life didn't work out the way you expected?"

Cam tried to tamp down his anger, and failed. "Don't compare yourself to me, brother. Your wife is still alive. She just doesn't want you anymore."

It was a low blow, and Cam regretted the words as soon as he spoke them. Mason's silence indicated that the barb had hit its mark. Their conversations tended to be contentious, which was why Cam avoided calling. He wished there wasn't so much animosity between them. They used to lift each other up, not tear each other down.

"I'm sorry," Cam said gruffly. "That wasn't fair."

"You're an asshole, you know that?"

"I need your help."

Mason made a heavy sound into the receiver. But he didn't hang up. "With what?"

"I met a woman."

"You met a woman," Mason repeated in a flat tone.

"She was stowed away behind my cab, so I gave her a ride to Fairbanks."

"You're high, aren't you? You're on trucker drugs."

"I'm not high," Cam said, rolling his eyes. He told an abbreviated version of his adventures with Tala, omitting the overnight stay in the cabin. That was too personal to share. "I think she's in trouble, and I want you to look into it."

"What's her name?"

"Tala."

"T-A-L-A?"

"I guess."

"I need more info than that, Cam."

He gave as many details as he could remember, including the Abigail Burgess alias. "She's from Yellowknife, in Canada. She has family in Montana. Her husband is some kind of cop named Duane."

"What's her description?"

"She's about five-nine, maybe one hundred and forty pounds, long black hair, brown eyes. Unusually pretty."

"How old?"

"Twenty-five."

Mason grunted with derision.

Cam rattled off short descriptions of the two men in the parking lot.

"Why are you asking me to do this?" Mason asked. "You can call the local cops anytime."

"She doesn't want me to call them."

"That's a red flag, Cam. A big red flag."

"Maybe the local PD is in on it."

"Maybe she's a liar."

"I don't think so."

"Want to know what I think?" Mason didn't wait for a response. "I think you've gone off the deep end. You've been teetering on the edge for three years, and now you've tipped right over."

"I've been doing the best I can."

"Have you?"

Cam didn't answer.

"This girl could be a criminal, or a teen runaway—"

"She's not a teen runaway. I haven't gone that far off the deep end."

"Why are you ordering a background check, if you trust her?"

"I want to help her," Cam said, raking a hand through his hair. "I like her."

"She's unusually pretty, with a hot body?"

"I didn't say that."

"I'm glad you're not dead below the waist, Cameron. I'm just concerned about your mental state."

Cam scowled at the phone. "Are you going to run her or not?"

"I'll do it on one condition."

"What?"

"Come home for Christmas."

Cam smothered a groan at the request. Christmas was in the middle of the ice-road season, and the holidays were the most difficult time of year for him. Going home always reminded him of Jenny. She'd died the last week of December.

"Well?" Mason prompted.

"You're killing me," Cam said.

"You're killing Mom."

Cam told Mason to screw himself, and Mason said it right back. It was just like old times. "Okay, you rotten bastard. I'll come home."

"Lay off the crystal meth, too."

"It's hard to be the ugly brother, isn't it?"

"I wouldn't know. How's sitting on your ass all day working out for your metabolism?"

"You tell me, desk jockey."

Mason laughed, taking no offense. For most of their lives, they'd been close, with good-natured teasing between them instead of deep rancor. "I'll meet you on the basketball court and we'll see who's getting slow."

Cam smirked at the challenge. "I won the last round."

"Only because you cheated."

He shook his head in disbelief. Mason was such a sore loser. They'd been battling on and off the court since they were kids. "Text me the details as soon as you can. I'll be on the Dalton, so I might not be able to reply right away."

"Whatever," Mason said. "Stay safe."

"I will," Cam said, and hung up. He pocketed the phone, his spirits lighter. He'd expected Mason to be surly and judgmental, and he had been, but he'd also agreed to help. Their conversation had ended on a positive note. His brother had sounded almost jovial. They'd laughed together, like they used to. Maybe Mason was getting over his divorce. Maybe, in time, Cam could get over Jenny.

He scooped up a handful of snow and covered his knuckles, hissing at the sting. Then he walked inside the lobby to wait. He could see the bookstore and the coffee shop from the front window. The stockyard was less than a mile down the road. Although the trucking company had several mechanics on site, they were always swamped with repairs. Cam preferred this place. Whenever he could avoid a crowd, he did.

As he iced his hand, he mulled over his brother's criticism. Mason exaggerated a little, but he didn't lie. Cam *had* overreacted at Thanksgiving. Their mom was a classic meddler, unable to accept Cam's withdrawal from society. She wanted him to come back to Tacoma, settle down with a nice woman and live happily ever after.

She wanted the same for Mason, who'd disappointed her as much as Cam, if not more. Last year his brother had been the target of her matchmaking efforts. She'd invited Lisa to her Thanksgiving celebration in an obvious attempt to reunite the estranged couple. It hadn't worked. Shortly after their separation, Lisa had started dating a firefighter. Mason had feigned indifference, but Cam knew better. His brother hated losing, and the dissolution of his marriage had devastated him.

Cam still didn't know why Lisa had left. Mason wouldn't talk about it, and Cam was basically a ghost at family functions. He'd been a shadow of himself since Jenny died, buried in his own grief. Disconnected from everyone who cared about him.

He felt guilty about abandoning his brother in a time

of need, but his guilt hadn't spurred him into action. It was another weight to carry, another feeling to escape.

He turned his thoughts to Tala, whose troubles offered a refreshing diversion. He didn't have to face his problems when he could focus on hers. She was pleasant company, beautiful to look at and interesting to listen to.

Cam understood his brother's concerns. Her story didn't add up. She was hiding something, refusing to answer certain questions. Her husband had sent a couple of thugs after her instead of coming himself. That seemed odd. Cam wondered if the guy was a dirty cop with sinister connections, not just a run-of-the-mill abuser.

Cam didn't really care how dangerous her ex was. Cam didn't need anyone's approval. He liked Tala, and he wanted to help her.

The snow melted on his knuckles and dripped from his fingertips. The physical discomfort added to a growing sense of unease. Mason had always been critical of Cam's decision to come to Alaska. Cam's family hadn't understood his need to withdraw. They didn't approve of his chosen profession. Maybe he wasn't doing his *best* here, but he'd been working steadily. He'd been surviving, one day at a time.

If he wasn't moving forward…at least he was moving.

No one could convince him to come home, because home offered no comfort. Tala did. One night with her had changed something inside him. He couldn't deny that he wanted her. He wouldn't pursue a relationship with her, however. Whatever happened between them, he couldn't afford to get attached. It would only lead to another heartbreak. Falling for her could send him over the edge Mason claimed he'd been teetering on. But maybe that was what Cam was seeking. Total ruin, instead of cold apathy.

They couldn't bunk together in Coldfoot, so he didn't have to worry about curbing his baser instincts tonight. Beyond Deadhorse was Prudhoe Bay, an industrial wasteland filled with scientists and oil riggers. There were several hotels. They could share a private room at the end of the ice road, on the outermost edge of civilization.

When his truck was ready, he drove back to the spot where he'd left her. She was sitting in the café with a cup of tea and a stack of books. She turned toward the door when he came in. She seemed relieved to see him.

"I spent some of your money on books," she said, tugging on her parka.

"Find anything good?"

"Yes."

She held the books protectively, as if she thought he might try to take them away. Her eyes looked red and swollen. "Are you okay?" he asked as they walked outside. She'd taken a spill in the parking lot earlier.

"I'm fine."

"You still want to come with me?"

"Of course."

He didn't try to talk her out of it again. If they were heading toward disaster, so be it. "I'm going to the stockyard now to pick up the load."

"What are you delivering?"

"I don't know. I'll find out when I get there." He opened the passenger door to let her in. She crawled into the berth with her stack of books. She'd have to stay back there until they left Fairbanks.

A trailer filled with building supplies was waiting

for him at the yard. He signed the paperwork and secured the load, pleased with the assignment. He'd hauled worse. Oversize loads, hazardous chemicals and cargo that exceeded recommended weight limits weren't uncommon. All of it had to be delivered to the drop-off zone as fast as possible, in order to facilitate the lucrative work on the pipelines.

Oil was big business in Alaska, and black gold flowed in any weather. The coldest months of the year were among the busiest, because the ice roads made it possible to drive the short distance from Deadhorse to Prudhoe Bay. When the ice melted, the route was closed. Goods for the pipeline and its employees had to be delivered by air or sea. It was that remote and inaccessible.

Cam filled up his gas tank before he headed out of town, toward the Dalton. It was about a hundred miles west of Fairbanks. The entire length of the highway could be traversed in one long day, if you started early enough and the weather cooperated. Cam was getting a late start, by trucker standards, and the snow flurries reduced visibility. He'd be lucky to hit Coldfoot, the halfway point, by early evening.

Tala stayed in the berth, reading one of her graphic novels. She closed the book after about thirty minutes. "Can I come up front?"

"Sure," Cam said, shrugging. No one would be able to see her in the snowy dark. Most drivers kept their eyes on the road and minded their own business, regardless. Cam wasn't that worried about getting reported by another trucker.

She settled into the passenger seat. "Should I duck if we pass someone?"

"Nah."

"What about after the sun comes up?"

"I'll let you know. If it keeps snowing, we're okay."

She gave him a tremulous smile. "Good. I'd rather sit beside you."

He searched her face, which looked a bit pale. He hoped she didn't get carsick, because the Dalton was twisty as hell. He focused on the drive, saying nothing. Her eyes darted to the side mirror to check the highway behind them. It was the same thing she'd done on the ride from Willow to Fairbanks.

"You think they'll follow us?" he asked.

She seemed startled by the question. "Can they?"

"They could try. There's no checkpoint or regulations."

"So anyone can drive on the Dalton?"

"They can, but they don't. It's too dangerous. You need special modifications so your engine parts don't freeze. We might see a tourist bus, or some smaller vehicles that belong to safety officials. Otherwise, it's just ice rigs."

She nodded her understanding. "How far is it to the entrance?"

"Sixty miles."

They fell into an uneasy silence as dawn broke over the horizon. It was almost ten o'clock, but they only had about six hours of daylight here. In Deadhorse, at the end of the road, there would be less than two.

Cam was on a long straightaway when a black SUV appeared behind them, moving fast. He straightened in his seat, squinting into the rearview mirror. He had a handgun in a locked box in the berth, out of reach. It was a memento from his cop days, packed away carefully with his photos of Jenny.

He considered asking Tala to grab it for him as the SUV veered into the passing lane. Then he dismissed the idea, because trading gunfire on a snowy highway at this speed would be stupid, even in self-defense. If they got shot at, he'd have to run the SUV off the road.

Tala followed his gaze, her expression wary. The driver moved into the space beside him. Cam got a glimpse of two young faces as the SUV surged ahead and crossed over the broken yellow line. Snowboarding stickers covered the back bumper. They were teenaged boys, not the men from the parking lot. Not a threat.

Cam glanced at Tala, who was visibly shaken. "You okay?"

She moistened her lips. "I'm fine."

"I can pull over."

"No. Just drive."

He didn't argue. She sounded defensive, as well as rattled. Maybe she was worried that he'd change his mind about bringing her along if she showed any weakness.

"I didn't use to be like this," she said in a low voice.

"Like what?"

"Afraid of everything. Jumping at shadows."

His chest tightened with empathy. "It takes a strong person to admit fear."

"I don't feel strong right now."

"You were just attacked. Give yourself a break."

She nodded, taking a deep breath. "What are you afraid of?"

"Nothing," he joked.

She laughed, which broke the ice a little. He'd forgotten how much he enjoyed hearing female laughter, and she had a great smile. She was stunning. He pulled his gaze away from her, clearing his throat.

"I'm serious," she said.

"I'm afraid of getting attached."

"To another woman?"

He shrugged, though she'd nailed it. He was afraid of women, dating…feelings.

"You're afraid to let go of her."

It was an uncomfortable insight, impossible to deny. Of course Jenny was at the crux of the matter. If he found someone else, he'd have to move forward. He'd have to get over the loss, instead of wallowing in it. "You're right."

"Do you want to talk about her?"

"No."

She gave him a chiding look. "That's no way to move on."

He didn't want to move on, especially if it meant baring his soul. He was more interested in physical release than an emotional overhaul.

"Tell me something easy."

"Easy?"

"A nice memory, you know. Not sad."

He mulled it over. "Okay, I have one."

She clasped her hands together in anticipation. Most women wouldn't be so eager to hear about an ex. It occurred to Cam that Tala saw him as a friend, nothing more. She hadn't cuddled him last night because she wanted his body. She'd needed comfort.

Cam felt reassured by the thought. It would be easier to resist temptation if she didn't give him any encouragement. He wouldn't try to cross the line with a woman who wasn't attracted to him. She could keep her secrets, and he could hold on to his grief, like a shield to hide behind.

"She was a teacher," he said.

"Primary or secondary?"

"Fourth grade, so nine- and ten-year-olds."

She waited for him to continue, her lips pursed.

"During her first year of teaching, one of her students got sick. He was admitted to the Seattle Children's Hospital, and his family needed financial help, so she decided to do this fund-raiser. It was a mud run."

"What's a mud run?"

"It's 5K run with a challenge course. She talked me into going with her. We had to wade through mud and climb over walls, stuff like that."

Her expression grew wistful. "Sounds fun."

"It was. We had a good time. Jenny promised to jump in the mud pit if she raised a certain amount. She met her goal and then some, because she was the kind of person who could get everyone involved. She had that infectious enthusiasm thing." He paused, glancing at Tala. "You know what I mean?"

"Yes."

"Anyway, at the end of the course, she really went for it, like completely submerged herself in the pit. When she came out, she was unrecognizable. Just blue eyes and white teeth. I took a photo so she could show her class."

"Did they love it?"

"They did," he said, his throat tight. The happy memory morphed into another one, steeped in sadness. "They came to her funeral."

"Her students?"

"The boy she'd raised money for came with his family. He'd recovered by then. All of the students from her current class came. They brought handwritten sympathy cards." Cam remembered standing there like a statue while weeping kids presented him with their heartfelt letters, colored in crayon.

"That must have been difficult," she murmured.

His chest ached with the same agony he'd felt three years ago. He gripped the steering wheel until his knuckles went white. After a few deep breaths, he could speak again. "This is why I don't talk about her."

"Because it hurts?"

"Yes."

"If you keep your feelings bottled up, they cause more pain."

He made a noncommittal sound. Bottling up his feelings was a defense mechanism, necessary for survival. He couldn't just open up and release his emotions like a jar of butterflies. They were a nest of hornets, ready to sting.

"I have another idea," she said. "Tell me about her bad side."

"She didn't have a bad side."

"Surely she had flaws. Did she leave her towels on the floor, or drink milk out of the container?"

"That was me."

"She was perfect? You never argued?"

"We argued."

"About what?"

He sighed, shaking his head. "Stupid things. I wanted her to spend more time at home. She was too busy with her students and colleagues. She had a lot of friends. Everyone liked her. *Men* liked her."

"That bothered you?"

"Yeah, it did. She was…flirtatious."

Tala's eyes widened with interest. "Really?"

"She was always touching some guy's arm, or laughing at his jokes. She flirted with my brother a lot."

"What did he do?"

"Nothing. He enjoyed it, that bastard."

She laughed at his disgruntled expression. Cam didn't laugh with her, but he felt the heavy weight of sadness slip away. He hadn't thought about Jenny's flirty nature in ages. It had been a minor issue between them, easily forgotten.

They'd argued about more important things, too. Private things, like when to start a family. Cam hadn't been ready. He'd wanted to *travel*, which was ironic. Now all he did was travel, without getting anywhere.

The entrance to the Dalton loomed in the distance. Once they started down that road, there was no turning back.

"This is it?" she asked.

"This is it."

She grasped the armrests at her sides, as if bracing herself for a roller-coaster ride. She seemed committed to the journey, if only because she thought coming with him would be safer than staying in Fairbanks on her own.

For both their sakes, he hoped it would be.

Chapter 9

The first fifty miles on the Dalton were uneventful.

Tala shifted in her seat, watching the tree-lined snowbanks pass by. It wasn't picturesque, like Denali National Park. She checked the side mirror every few minutes. Even though Cam had expressed doubt over anyone following them, she wanted to stay alert. The killers were intent on hunting her down. They'd already tracked her from Willow to Fairbanks. They wouldn't be easily deterred.

She turned her gaze to Cam, her gallant rescuer. He drove with his right arm extended and the heel of his hand resting on top of the steering wheel. His knuckles didn't appear to be bothering him, so he must not have broken any bones. He was wearing a gray thermal undershirt with a navy blue flannel. His beard was the kind that real men grew, thick and dark and dense, without any patches.

"What did you do before you came to Alaska?" she asked, studying him.

He kept his eyes on the road. "I did a lot of different things."

"Such as?"

"I had a job in public service."

"Doing what?"

"Road safety, traffic control, stuff like that."

"Like a construction worker?"

"Sort of. Before I graduated from college, I worked on the farm."

"You went to college?"

He scratched his jaw. "Yeah."

"What did you study?"

"Sociology."

She gaped at his answer. "Sociology?"

"Why is that so hard to believe?"

"Because you're a truck driver. I can't think of a more antisocial job."

"You've got the wrong idea about truckers."

"Do I?"

"We aren't antisocial. We interact on the radio all the time. We have our own lingo, our own network. It's a tight-knit community."

His radio was on, at a low volume. She'd heard some chatter, but she hadn't paid much attention to it, and he hadn't picked up the receiver once since she'd been with him. "Do you talk to the other truckers?"

"Sure."

"What about? Cute waitresses?"

He shook his head. "I try to keep it professional. There are female truckers who listen in. Some guys don't care, but I do."

"Would you speak freely if it was just men?"

"Probably not."

"Who do you talk to about personal stuff?"

He fiddled with the controls on his dashboard, seeming reluctant to answer. He didn't want to speak about his ex-wife, or his former profession. She got the impression that he'd be quite happy to drive all day in silence.

"You're not close to anyone?" she pressed.

"My brother."

"Older or younger?"

"He's two years older."

"Is he your only sibling?"

"Yes."

"Where does he live?"

"Seattle."

"I have three brothers," she said. "Two half-brothers and a stepbrother. They're in Montana with my mom. I haven't seen them in years."

"Why not?"

"It's a long story."

"It's a long drive."

She tucked her legs under her body, getting comfortable. Maybe it would be easier to have a conversation with him if she did all the talking. "My parents got divorced when I was ten. They weren't happy together. My dad was Yellowknife Dene, and my mom is Plains Cree, so they were kind of a mismatch from the start."

"How do you mean?"

"Well, my mom is from Stony Plain, near Edmonton."

He gave her a blank look. "Is that in Canada?"

"Yes. Edmonton is a big city in Alberta. It's nothing like the Northwest Territories." She tried to think of an analogy he would understand. "Imagine a New York City girl marrying an Alaskan from the bush."

"Oh," he said, nodding. "Got it."

"They met at college. My dad only went for one semester, but it was long enough for him to fall in love with my mom. They got married and he brought her to Yellowknife. I guess she expected to have a different kind of life. My grandma said she was the prettiest girl in Stony Plain. She had a lot of admirers."

"Does she look like you?"

"People say that."

He grunted an acknowledgment.

"We went to see her family about once a year. At some point she reconnected with an old boyfriend, and she decided to leave my dad for him. He told her she could go, but she couldn't take me with her."

"Did you want to go?"

"No. I loved Yellowknife, and I loved my dad. I loved hunting and trapping and living off the land."

"So you stayed."

"I stayed. My mom moved to Montana and started a new family. I spent a month with them every summer."

"How was it?"

"It was hard," she said honestly. "I felt abandoned and forgotten, and I didn't get along with my stepdad. I hated him for taking my mom away, and I resented my little brothers for having a mother when I didn't. The only one I liked was Bear."

"Bear?"

"My stepbrother," she said, her cheeks heating. "I had a crush on him."

Cam arched a brow. "Did he encourage you?"

"Not at all," she admitted. "He ignored me. One day

my mom caught me spying on him, and we both got in trouble. My stepdad yelled at Bear, even though he hadn't done anything. My dad wasn't happy about it, either. The next summer, he let me stay home. Then he died, and I went to live with my grandma. She passed away three years ago. My mom and brothers came to her funeral. I haven't seen them since."

"Are you still in touch?"

"I send my mom messages on Facebook, but we don't talk much. I haven't told her I left Duane."

"Why not?"

"I don't know," she said, tugging on one of her braids. "I was so angry with her for leaving me and my dad. I pushed her away for years. It seems hypocritical of me to reach out to her for help now."

"It's not hypocritical," he said, his gaze steady.

"I judged her pretty harshly."

"You were just a kid. How were you supposed to feel?"

She tried to put her thoughts into words. "What I went through with Duane changed my perspective. I realized it wasn't fair to lay all the blame on my mom for their divorce."

"Sometimes it *is* fair to lay all the blame on one person."

She looked out the window, pensive.

"Your ex, for example. He hit you. That's not a mutual failing. It's totally on him."

"I could have done some things differently."

"Like what? Ducked?"

She frowned at his sarcastic tone. "I'm not making excuses for Duane. I'm just saying that I'm more sympathetic toward my mom than I used to be. I know what it's like to marry the wrong person and feel trapped."

Cam focused on the highway, his mouth tight. She got the impression that he wouldn't mind meeting Duane in a dark alley, but he didn't say it out loud, and she was glad. She'd had her fill of violence.

Tala wasn't sure she could mend the relationship with her mother. She wished she hadn't been so rebellious and resistant. Her little brothers were teenagers now. Bear worked in law enforcement. Her stepdad was a large, intimidating man. She might not feel like part of their family, but she'd be safe with them.

They passed a sign that said Coldfoot 289 miles.

"How long will it take to get there?" she asked.

"About eight hours, depending on the weather and road conditions. It's possible to drive all the way through in sixteen hours, but we're not supposed to."

"Why not?"

"Anything over fourteen consecutive hours is a code violation."

"So you're required to stop in Coldfoot?"

"We're required to take breaks, and Coldfoot is the only place with services."

"Where is the final stop?"

"The end of the gravel road is in Deadhorse. From there to Prudhoe Bay, it's pure ice."

"Will we go on the ice?"

"Probably. They have to test the thickness every week. If it's safe, you can drive on it."

"What if it's not safe?"

"Then they restrict access."

"And you have to take the load back to Fairbanks?"

"Not this early in the season. You can leave it at the

yard in Deadhorse and someone else will deliver it after the conditions improve. Supplies pile up there. Last year I spent a couple of weeks going back and forth on the ice road. When it turns to slush in spring, they shut the whole thing down."

She went quiet for a few minutes, staring out the window. They passed by a sparse forest of spruce trees. A slow climb, followed by a series of hairpin turns, caused her pulse to kick up a notch. She gripped the armrests, trying not to show fear. They entered a straight section that was incredibly narrow. Trucks going the opposite direction flew by at a breakneck pace, as if they were on a roomy highway instead of a thin ribbon in the snow.

"How are you doing?" Cam asked.

"Fine," she said, releasing a pent-up breath.

"This is the easy part."

"Where's the hard part?"

"Atigun Pass is coming up. It's a steep incline along a sheer cliff."

"Sounds great."

He smiled at her sarcasm. "We have an hour before it starts, so you can relax."

She peeled her hands off the armrests. As they gained elevation, the landscape changed into a winter wonderland with snow-speckled trees. Rugged mountains loomed in the distance, promising sharp turns and dizzying plummets. The road followed the same path as the pipeline, which bisected the entire state of Alaska. The Trans-Alaska Pipeline had caused a boom to the economy and contributed to several unnatural disasters.

"I've heard of Prudhoe Bay," she said. "It's on the list of places with frequent oil spills."

He didn't seem surprised by this news. "Are you an activist?"

"I used to be. I started getting into it after my dad died."

"What happened to him?"

She glanced at the snowy tire tracks in the road. There were no markers, fences or telephone lines to guide their way. At least they had the bleak light of day. She didn't know how Cam would drive after sunset. "He got in a sled accident. He was cutting across a frozen river on a section of land that had been closed off due to arsenic contamination from the gold mine. It was discovered in the drinking water. They've been trying to clean it up for decades. They were testing some geothermal equipment, which taps heat from deep in the ground and brings it up to the surface. The process was melting the ice at the mouth of the river, but they didn't post a warning, because no one was supposed to be there."

"He broke through?"

She nodded. "The mining company gave me a small settlement. I used it to pay for college in Edmonton."

"What did you study?"

"Earth science. I was in my third year when my grandma got sick. She'd lived in Yellowknife for most of her life. The doctors said that stomach cancer is a side effect of low-level arsenic poisoning."

He made a sympathetic sound. "I'm sorry."

"I didn't get angry after my dad's accident," she said, thinking back. "Maybe I was too young, or too numb. But my grandma's death hit me hard."

Cam downshifted as they reached another sharp curve. She tensed in anticipation of a sideways slide into the embankment. He navigated the space with confidence, clearing a turn that appeared impossibly tight, before continuing uphill.

She released a shaky breath.

"Go on," he said, glancing her way.

"I'd been researching the impact of pollution on native communities, and I started getting involved with local protests. I actually met Duane at a rally. He was there because he hated the government, not because he cared about First Nations people or the environment, but I didn't realize that until later."

Cam flipped a switch overhead. His dashboard looked like the controls for an airplane. There were lights and dials and toggles everywhere.

"What's wrong?" she asked.

"Nothing. I turned off my jakes."

"What are jakes?"

"Compression brakes. I don't need them on an ascent."

She catalogued that into her mental files and checked the side mirror, which revealed an empty road behind them. So far, so good. Cam hadn't lied about the difficult driving conditions. It was unlikely they were being followed. "Where was I?"

"You'd just met Duane."

"Right," she said, moistening her lips. "Are you sure you want to hear this?"

"Why wouldn't I?"

"It's kind of a heavy topic."

"So?"

"We don't know each other that well."

"We're getting there."

She gave him an assessing look. If he wanted to avoid getting attached, they shouldn't be sharing so much personal information. Maybe he wasn't as afraid of intimacy as he claimed. Or maybe his only goal was to bed her, and he wouldn't have any trouble moving on after the deed was done. Either way, she felt obligated to tell him about herself. He'd risked his life to help her. The least she could do was make conversation, and part of her longed for a deeper connection. Her attraction to Cam went beyond physical needs. The emotional comfort and closeness he could offer was incredibly tempting.

She didn't just want to be touched. She wanted to be *held*.

"Duane was angry and rebellious," she said. "I liked that. I was mad at the world, and so was he. We both wanted to burn everything down. But he also had a sweet side, if you can believe it."

"I can."

"He gave me gifts and constant attention. He was obsessive. At the time I thought it was romantic."

"How old were you?"

"Twenty. We'd only been dating six months when he got stationed in Carcross, in Yukon. He asked me to come and live with him. I said no, because we weren't married. He bought a ring the next day."

Cam arched a brow, but didn't say anything.

"We moved too fast."

"I'm not judging."

"Did you and Jenny wait a long time before you got married?"

"We dated for a couple of years, but I knew she was the one right away. I could have asked her sooner."

She cleared her throat and continued. "With me and Duane, it was rocky from the beginning. He was unhappy with his assignment in Carcross. We didn't know anyone in town. He drank too much and didn't sleep enough. I wanted to hike and ride sleds and raise animals. Instead I ended up hiding in the bedroom whenever he was home."

"How long were you married?"

"A little over three years. I found a job as a waitress, just to get out of the house. There weren't a lot of women in the area, and Duane treated every man we encountered like a rival. Sometimes he accused me of encouraging them. He'd come to the café and sit in the parking lot, watching me. I finally had to quit."

"He knew you were out of his league."

She crossed her arms over her chest, considering. Duane hadn't been ugly. Not on the outside, anyway. But he'd been insecure and accusatory, even paranoid. "Maybe that's what he thought, but he didn't say it. He said mean things."

"About your looks?"

"Yes."

Cam studied her for a moment before turning his attention to the road. "You're beautiful. If he said otherwise, he's a liar."

Her cheeks warmed at the compliment. She believed he meant it. Admiration flashed in his eyes when he glanced at her, along with a sincere interest in her as a person. He cared about what she was saying. Men had complimented her before, Duane included, but she couldn't remember the last time one had made her feel special.

Waitresses didn't get a lot of respect. Some customers stared at her body as if she was on the menu, or demanded smiles for a tip she'd already earned. She wouldn't do it. Smiling for no reason didn't come naturally to her.

Cam didn't smile much, either. He seemed intent on holding on to his grief, as if letting go would insult his wife's memory. He'd resigned himself to a life of solitude on the road. Never staying in one place, but never truly moving on. Her gaze fell to his right hand, knuckles scraped from defending her.

"You took off your ring," she said, startled.

He flexed his fingers absently, as if they were sore. She'd remind him to ice his knuckles the next time they stopped.

An hour later he pulled over at the base of a steep incline. Snow flurries reduced visibility, which was probably a good thing. She didn't want to see too much. "I have to put on my chains," he said.

"Do you need help?" she asked, hopeful of a chance to stretch her legs.

"You're supposed to stay out of sight."

"Right," she said, shifting in her seat. She'd love to get out. Sitting still had never been her strong suit. "No problem."

He smiled at her answer, as if he knew she was getting antsy. He shared her need for physical activity. If he didn't, he wouldn't be so eager to chop wood for lonely widows. "Put your parka on."

"Really?"

"You can walk around on the passenger side. That's it."

She made a little squeal of excitement, reaching for her parka. She didn't bother to zip up, because she wanted to feel the invigorating chill. He didn't wear a parka at all, just gloves. He kept the engine running while he worked. She walked up and down along the snowy roadside. She hopped and jumped and twirled in circles. Then she watched him tug the heavy chains into place. She enjoyed the sight of his strong shoulders and hard-muscled arms. He winced as he placed the last set.

She scooped up some snow, striding toward him. "How's your hand?"

"Fine," he said gruffly.

"Let's see."

He removed his glove to show her. His knuckles were slightly swollen. She covered them with snow and lifted her gaze to his face. Although it was cold, he looked hot. His cheeks were ruddy, his eyes bright. The strenuous task had warmed his blood.

She held the snow in place for as long as she could. After it melted off, she brought his knuckles to her lips for a soothing kiss. His gaze flared with heat, and her pulse throbbed with awareness. Maybe he'd taken off his ring because he was ready to move on—with her.

"What are you doing?" he asked sharply.

She released his hand, flushing. "Nothing."

Or…maybe not.

Another truck came barreling down the hill, emerging from a snowy fog. Despite the speed of travel and thick air, she could see the faint outline of the driver. Which meant the driver could see them.

Cam stepped forward and grasped her waist, cursing. He crushed her against the passenger side and held her there. Her breaths puffed out in the chill air above his shoulder. Her parka was open, allowing him entry. His torso pressed tight to hers. When the tension drained from his body, she knew the danger had passed. She glanced up at him, moistening her lips. A muscle in his jaw flexed, but he didn't ease away from her. Her heart thumped with excitement, from the close call, and his close proximity.

Ready or not, his desire was clear. It glimmered in his dark eyes and radiated between them. He needed this, and so did she. He seemed uncertain about how to proceed with her, however. She wondered if he knew the attraction was mutual, or if he was waiting for her to give him an overt signal. Something even more obvious than kissing his knuckles.

She twined her arms around his neck. His gaze dipped to her lips. Then his mouth descended.

Yes.

She threaded her fingers through his hair as he kissed her. He started with a soft touch, his lips warm. The snowflakes in his beard melted on impact. She opened her mouth for his tongue, tentative. He groaned and deepened the kiss. It was an explosion of heat, tongues tangling. His hands gripped her hips and her back met the metal door. She made an encouraging sound, wanting more. He gave it to her. More tongue, exploring her hungry mouth. More hands, roving lower. He cupped her denim-covered bottom with a low growl. His erection swelled against the juncture of her thighs.

He broke the kiss and stepped away. Cold air filled the space between them. His eyes still smoldered, his breaths puffing hot.

"Get in," he said, opening the passenger door.

She climbed the metal steps, disconcerted. She engaged in a brief fantasy in which Cam followed her inside and pushed her down on the bed in the berth. There was hardly room for him, let alone the two of them, but they could make it work.

He slammed her door and walked around to the driver's

side. When he got behind the wheel, his jaw was clenched. She shrugged out of her parka, her cheeks warm. Everything was warm. Her breasts felt full, her mouth swollen. She slumped in her seat, embarrassed by her runaway desire. The seam of her jeans tugged at her tingling sex. She wanted to rub herself there to ease the ache.

His eyes traveled down the length of her legs and lingered between them, as if he could sense her arousal. She squirmed at his perusal, her pulse throbbing.

"Get in the back," he said in a low voice.

"Why?"

"I need to focus on driving."

"I won't bother you."

He gave her a look that said she was already bothering him, after she'd promised not to. She'd wanted to leave the cramped confines of the truck. She'd wanted him to kiss her. It was his fault as much as hers, but this issue wouldn't have arisen if she'd stayed in Fairbanks, so she didn't argue. She climbed out of the passenger seat and entered the berth.

Lying down, she found it even more difficult to ignore her physical needs. She hadn't been touched in a long time. She hadn't touched *herself*, either. Her body had gone into hibernation after she'd escaped her abusive marriage. Cam had brought her back to life. She'd forgotten how it felt to enjoy a man's attention.

She reached for one of her graphic novels as they ascended the steep cliff. She didn't like not being able to see the road, but maybe ignorance was bliss. The incline felt alarming, the engine shuddering from exertion.

It occurred to her that Cam had been angry with her for tempting him, and angry with himself for surrendering to temptation. Maybe he was angry about not being able to finish what they'd started, too. Either way, he hadn't yelled at her or done anything violent. He hadn't blamed or belittled her. He'd accepted the situation as it was, and found a solution that allowed him to continue driving.

He was calm and in control. That was comforting.

The book in her hands offered another level of comfort. She concentrated on the story, the illustrations, the characters. Despite the precarious road conditions, she felt safe and cozy, as well as highly desired.

Cam wanted her. He wanted her so much that he had to remove her from his sight in order to do his job.

Smiling, she turned the page.

Chapter 10

December 12
67N
-1 degree

Atigun Pass was as nerve-racking as usual.

Cam had to increase his speed steadily in order to make the climb. Slowing down meant risking a dangerous backwards slide. If his rig stalled or malfunctioned, he couldn't pull over. The weight of his load would cause the wheels to slip. It was a recipe for a jackknife—or worse. One wrong move could send them hurtling over the edge. Other truckers had taken that icy path before. They'd plummeted down the snowy cliff. There were no survivors in these accidents.

He was glad Tala had agreed to ride in the back, because this stretch of road demanded his total concentration. Through no fault of her own, she was a distraction. He couldn't afford to sneak glances at her luscious mouth or fantasize about their kissing session. He had to keep his mind calm and his thoughts clear.

She wouldn't have enjoyed the view, anyway. She'd seemed nervous on easier sections of the Dalton. It was better for her to sit tight in the berth. Reading her comics, or whatever she was doing.

When he reached the summit, he breathed a sigh of relief and flexed his fingers, which had been clenched around the wheel. A glance into the back revealed Tala, lying on her stomach on his bed. He couldn't see all of her, just the midsection.

She had a body made for blue jeans. Long, lean legs. Her curves were lovingly cupped by snug denim. The twin pockets seemed designed to lift her pert bottom in invitation. They had silver studs and gold thread. He imagined climbing on top of her, gripping her hips and pressing himself against her.

Swallowing hard, he returned his attention to the road. He'd drifted slightly off-course. He corrected in a calm, practiced motion.

Jesus.

This woman was dangerous in more ways than one. He'd risked his life to rescue her from two assailants this morning. Now he was lust-struck after a single glance. If he wasn't careful, he was going to veer into a snowbank.

For the next few hours, he concentrated on driving. The technical difficulty of navigating a loaded rig in inclement weather kept his thoughts occupied. He could hear subtle movements in the berth. The whisper of turning pages or shifting limbs. She switched positions often. He wondered if she was struggling to stay focused on her book. If she was distracted by memories of their kiss, and imagining other, sexy scenarios.

His neck flushed with heat. Now that he knew she felt the same desire he did, it would be harder to resist her. He'd assumed she wasn't attracted to him. He'd been wrong. Over the course of the day, he'd started to notice some signs of interest. She looked out the window a lot, but she also looked at him. She studied his body as if she wanted to touch him. She studied his hands as if she wanted *him* to touch *her*.

He hadn't been absolutely sure until he'd kissed her. The way she'd responded had removed all doubt. She'd moaned and clutched at his hair and devoured his mouth.

He tried not to think about her physical reactions, or possible sexual frustration. He tried not to wonder what kind of panties she was wearing, or if they were damp. Gritting his teeth, he cracked his window to let in a cold blast of air. It worked to clear his head. As the sunlight faded into another early evening, she set her book aside.

"You can turn on the lamp," he said.

"I'm okay."

"Are you hungry?"

"I can wait."

He didn't tell her that they were still hours from Coldfoot. Like most truckers, he preferred to drive as long as he could without stopping, and there weren't many places to pull over on this section of the Dalton.

She curled up with his wool blanket. It obstructed his view of her body, which was probably for the best. Darkness enveloped the cab. Her slow, even breaths told him she'd drifted to sleep. A warm feeling settled in the center of his chest. It was part satisfaction, part tenderness. She didn't trust easily, but she trusted him enough to take a nap in the back of his truck. She trusted him to protect her.

He wasn't sure if he deserved the honor, or if he could keep her safe in the long term. He balked at the responsibility. There were too many emotions, too many entanglements involved. He couldn't afford to get attached to a woman in jeopardy. He didn't want to control her fate, or make any life-or-death decisions.

He'd done that with Jenny, and it had almost killed him. Everyone had agreed that the breathing machine was prolonging the inevitable. Everyone had been ready to say goodbye—except him. He'd preferred limbo and false hopes to that soul-crushing end.

Tala slept peacefully for more than hour. He made good time in some tricky sections, charging over bone-white roads with nothing but vague tracks to guide his way. Snow flurries danced in his headlights. He expected storms and delays on the Dalton, but the weather was supposed to hold steady tonight. He hoped it wouldn't take a turn for the worse. All he needed was a blow, or a full-on blizzard, to trap them in Coldfoot. When visibility was nil, truckers had to pull over and wait for the conditions to improve. Sometimes they closed the road altogether until the storm passed.

It would be difficult to stay a single night at Coldfoot Camp with Tala. He'd have to keep his distance and pretend they weren't traveling together. If they got stuck there by bad weather, the ruse would fall apart. She wasn't a woman who could go unnoticed for long.

While he considered ways to address this problem, she stirred in her sleep. She mumbled something unintelligible and kicked her legs, as if running away from a threat. Then she sat upright with a start. Her eyes were wide, lips parted in distress.

"You were dreaming," he said helpfully.

She drew in several ragged breaths. "Yes."

"Everything's fine. You're safe."

"Is anyone following us?"

"No."

Wrapping the blanket around her shoulders, she held it clutched tight over her chest. "How far to Coldfoot?"

"Another hour. You can come up front."

She brought the blanket with her to the passenger seat. After she buckled up, she shot him a curious look.

"We need to discuss your story."

"My story?"

"You can't tell people you're a stowaway or a hitchhiker."

"Why do I have to tell them anything?"

He smiled at the question, which he understood on a visceral level. He'd spent the past three years avoiding social interactions whenever possible. "It's better to have a story ready. Someone might ask if you're a trucker."

"I don't look like a trucker."

"No, you don't. More importantly, you don't talk like one. You don't know the lingo."

"What else can I be?"

He mulled it over. Tourists visited the Dalton on occasion. Mostly the road was populated with truckers, oil rig workers and engineers. "Keeping it close to the truth is easier. You can say you're a waitress, and you've got a job lined up at a hotel in Prudhoe Bay. They're always desperate for help."

"Okay."

"We'll see how busy it is when we get there. If it's

crowded, we might be able to come in without causing a stir."

"Why would we cause a stir?"

He arched a brow.

"Because I'm a woman."

"You're a young, beautiful woman, in a place where there are only men."

She fell silent, watching the snow-packed road. Then she turned her gaze on him. "You're a beautiful man."

He tensed at the compliment. He'd been called handsome before, but never beautiful. The term didn't fit him.

She studied his face with interest. "Do they hit on you?"

"Who?"

"The other men."

"No," he said, flushing. "Hell, no."

Her lips curved into a smile. "Maybe you cause a stir all by yourself."

"I don't think so."

"Are you sure? Some of those truckers could be pining away for you."

"If they are, I don't want to know."

She laughed at his reaction, seeming pleased with herself. He realized he didn't have any idea how it felt to be the object of unwanted desire. As a waitress, she'd probably dealt with lewd behavior and grabby hands, not just crude comments on the radio. After escaping her abusive husband, she must have been wary of strange men. Even so, she'd served them with calm efficiency. He admired her grit. It took a lot of courage to stare down truckers and pour their coffee with a steady hand.

"What if it's not crowded?" she asked.

"Then I can't pretend we didn't arrive together."

"Will you get in trouble?"

"I doubt it."

"But you'd rather not attract attention."

"Exactly."

"I get it."

He shifted into a lower gear as they climbed another steep slope. As soon as he was clear of the danger, he glanced in her direction. "I didn't mean to offend you by saying you'd cause a stir."

"I wasn't offended. I'm used to it."

"Used to what, being stared at?"

"But not really seen."

He nodded his understanding. He knew what other men saw when they looked at her—long legs and long hair and pretty lips. Obviously, he noticed her surface beauty, but he saw other things in her. Strength, determination, vulnerability. A fighting spirit.

"I see you," he said, after a pause.

She smiled at his simple statement. "I know."

Before they reached Coldfoot, the snow flurries turned into a swirling whiteout. Visibility was reduced to almost nothing. He crept along at a snail's pace for the last stretch, grateful it was a straight shot to their destination. By the time he pulled over in the camp parking lot, it was late evening, and he was dead tired.

Luckily, the lot was full. Several other trucks had just arrived. The rustic restaurant was packed with hungry men. Cam's stomach growled for a hot meal. He grabbed his parka and removed a few bills from his wallet.

"Here's the plan," he said, giving her some cash. "You pay for a bunk and get settled while I buy dinner. I'll bring you a plate."

"How will you know which room I'm in?"

"There's a separate hall for women. I think it's just one room with a few bunks. I'll knock on the door."

"Where will you eat?"

"At the counter."

Although she didn't appear pleased with the arrangement, she said nothing. She understood the need for discretion. She put the cash in her pocket and pulled her hood up, obscuring her face. Then she caught sight of a tour bus pulling into the space next to his rig. "Arctic Adventures" was written across one side.

"Tourists spend the night here?" she asked sharply.

"Only on weekends," he said, stroking his jaw. He'd forgotten it was Saturday. "They travel to Coldfoot and back."

"Anyone can sign up?"

"I guess so."

Her brow furrowed with unease. They hadn't been followed by her assailants—at least, not in the usual sense. Cam hadn't seen any standard vehicles on the road, and every trucker required special paperwork. There was a lengthy permit process, drug testing and other regulations.

Tourists, however, could hop on a bus without much trouble. If there were seats available, tickets would be sold on the spot. Her pursuers could have paid for a tour this morning. He drummed his fingertips against the wheel as about a dozen people piled out of the bus. He couldn't see most of their faces. They were all bundled up in hooded jackets and appeared to be headed toward the restaurant.

"What do you want to do?" she asked.

"Stick to the plan. You pay for a bunk and get out of

sight. I'll sit down at the restaurant. If I spot your friends, I'll let you know."

"They're not my friends."

"Whoever they are."

She didn't ask what their options were. There wasn't anywhere else to go tonight. In an emergency, they could sleep in his rig. He'd have to keep the engine running all night, or they'd freeze to death. She pressed her lips to his bearded cheek, leaving a trace of heat and softness. "Be careful."

"You, too."

She grabbed her backpack and climbed out of the cab. There was a door nearby with a glowing Vacancy sign in the window. The bunkhouses were basically a series of connected trailers crammed with narrow beds. Although most of the space was designated for men, there was a private room for women behind the front office.

He waited a few minutes before shutting down his dashboard and making his exit. The restaurant was half-full, even at this late hour. Dinner service appeared to be winding down. He took a seat at the counter, studying the faces in the crowd. They looked like regular truckers and tourists to him. He didn't see the lowlifes they'd tangled with earlier. If they were here, they were blending in.

Cam snorted at the thought. Those guys were thugs. They didn't blend in. Subtlety wasn't their strong suit. They'd tried to kidnap Tala from a public parking lot.

He ordered two plates of pasta with grilled chicken and broccoli, one to go. He knew from experience that the food here was good. Truckers had hearty appetites, and when they were sidelined by a snowstorm, there wasn't much else to do. There was no cell service or

Wi-Fi. A single television mounted in the corner offered news and weather reports. Cam caught up on the forecast while he waited for his meal. It was going to be cold and clear.

He took his phone out of his pocket to check for texts from Mason. Sure enough, his brother had come through with a cryptic message.

Call me. Important info.

Cam frowned at the words on the screen. Mason knew Cam couldn't call from here. If the information was so goddamned important, why hadn't he texted it? Sighing, he rose from his seat and approached the register. There was only one phone in the joint, and access wasn't free. Cam paid for a ten-dollar card to call his brother in Seattle.

"Who's this?" Mason answered.

"It's me."

There was a scrambling sound, as if his brother had dropped his phone. Then a whisper of sheets and a feminine murmur.

"I'm returning your call," Cam said.

"Hang on."

Mason's footsteps padded across a hardwood floor. He lived in a drafty old loft in a run-down area near the red-light district. It was an unusual space, straight out of a horror movie. He called it "industrial." Everyone else called it creepy.

"Do you have company?"

"No."

"I thought I heard a voice."

"It was the TV."

"You don't have a TV."

"I have internet. Livestreaming."

"Livestreaming? Is that what they call it now?"

"I'd explain, but you've been in Alaska too long to understand technology."

Cam grunted his disbelief, shifting the phone to his other ear. "I only have five minutes. What's the info?"

"I found Tala Walker in a criminal database. She has a record."

"I know."

"Funny, you didn't mention it."

"She said it was a minor offense."

"Not quite."

Cam waited for Mason to continue, his stomach clenched with unease.

"She was arrested nine months ago at a rally in Whitehorse, Canada. A few hundred people were protesting a pipeline expansion project by a local oil company. It started out peaceful, but ended in chaos. Riot police were brought in to handle the more aggressive activists, and they clashed."

Cam didn't automatically assume the activists were to blame. He'd worked crowd control before. Some protests attracted unpredictable weirdos and violent extremists. But there were also overzealous officers who added fuel to the fire, and inexperienced rookies who didn't know how to defuse tense situations.

"According to the report, your girlfriend assaulted an officer."

"How?"

"She broke a beer bottle over his head. He had to get stitches."

Cam squeezed his eyes shut. Damn.

"There's more," Mason said.

"I'm listening."

"She spent a night in jail and was released on her own recognizance. Then she missed her court date, which was a huge mistake. If she hadn't skipped bail, she might have ended up with a slap on the wrist. Now she's basically a fugitive. She's got warrants for her arrest."

"Was her husband involved in the altercation?"

"I don't know. I haven't gotten that far in the background check. I actually have better things to do than assist you on your latest foray into self-destruction."

Cam squinted at the harsh words. "Foray into self-destruction?"

"That's what I said."

"You sound like a depressed poet."

"I'll jot that down in my black notebook."

"What better things do you have to do, besides that stranger in your bedroom?"

"She's not—"

Cam pounced on the bitten-off protest. "She's not a stranger? Or you're not doing her?"

Mason sighed into the receiver. "Are you going to ignore the information I gave you?"

"No. I'm taking it seriously."

"So you're done with this girl?"

"I didn't say that."

"Cam, I get it. I've seen her photo. She's hot. By Alaska standards, she's a supermodel. But she's a wanted criminal, not an innocent victim. She's on the run from the law."

"Did you find anything on the husband?"

"Duane Laramie, age twenty-six. He's a customs officer stationed in Carcross, near the US-Canada border. No record, but he's got an extensive gun collection. Seven registered weapons. Some hunting, some home-protection."

Cam didn't like this news any more than he liked the report on Tala. "What about the diner in Willow?"

"Oh, yeah. I talked to a sheriff's deputy about that. Said I was looking into another missing girl case. He told me there was no indication of foul play, but the waitress left her purse at the scene."

"That didn't raise any red flags?"

"It raised some red flags about her being a thief. She had a stolen ID in her wallet."

Cam dragged a hand down his face. "I have to go. My time's almost up."

"What's your plan?"

"For tonight?"

"And tomorrow."

Cam didn't answer. He had no intention of ditching Tala, no matter what his brother said. Maybe she was nothing but trouble. It didn't matter; he still wanted her. When he looked at her, he didn't see a liar or a criminal. He saw a beautiful, desirable woman. Every time they touched, his heart thawed a little more.

"Cam?"

"I haven't decided what to do," he said finally.

He needed more information from Tala. He'd ask her some questions and gauge her responses. If she wasn't honest with him, he'd have to rethink this whole arrangement.

He should probably keep his distance, regardless. She was a terrible choice for a no-strings fling. The man he used to be wouldn't have entertained the idea of sleeping with a fugitive who assaulted cops. That man wouldn't have considered an affair with a desperate stowaway, either.

The man he was now didn't even feel ashamed.

He felt alive.

"Be careful," Mason said.

"I will," Cam lied.

Chapter 11

Coldfoot, AK
67N
-9 degrees

Tala stepped inside the empty room and looked around.

There were four narrow beds, spaced a few feet apart from one another. A single nightstand with a lamp sat in the center. She locked the door behind her and set her backpack on the nearest bed. Then she inspected the bathroom. It had a toilet, sink and shower stall. She didn't see any towels, just a stack of washcloths.

The space was chilly and lacked ambience. Thin carpet, drab walls, beige bedding. She crossed her arms over her chest, shivering. It wasn't much, but she'd stayed in worse places, and she didn't mind the cold. She'd roughed it in the Yellowknife wilderness more times than she could count. Once she'd spent the night in a hole her father had dug out of snow, after they'd been forced to take shelter from a sudden blizzard.

Tears welled in her eyes at the memory. She didn't miss Duane, but she missed home. She'd left all her personal belongings in Carcross. Priceless artifacts that had been handed down from generation to generation. Tools her father had made with his own hands. Her grandmother's blankets and furs.

She spent the next ten minutes curled up on the narrow bed, feeling sorry for herself. Then she pushed aside her sadness and got up. She rummaged through her backpack for a change of clothes. She could wear her leggings and sweater as pajamas. A hot shower would be nice, if she could find a towel.

She searched the dresser, which had nothing in it except a Bible. She ducked into the bathroom anyway. Her hair didn't need washing, and there was no shampoo or conditioner. She stripped quickly and stepped into the shower stall, securing her braids at the nape of her neck. The water was pleasantly warm, which made her wish for a longer soak. Eyes closed, she let the warmth flow over her bare shoulders. Then she unwrapped a tiny soap to lather her body. Her hands swept over her breasts, lingering on the tight points of her nipples. The flesh between her legs pulsed with arousal. She bit down on her lower lip, trying to ignore the sensation. She considered stroking herself to climax, for the comfort and release.

Instead of giving in to the urge, she finished washing and turned off the water. Cam's hot kisses and smoldering looks had left her wanting. The book she'd been reading this afternoon hadn't helped. It had been surprisingly explicit, with a series of sexy scenes. One image featured a topless woman lying on her back in the hero's bed. She was a typical male-fantasy character—perfect breasts, slim waist, flowing hair. Her face was contorted in ecstasy. The hero wasn't in the frame at all. Tala had puzzled over that for a moment before she realized he was going down on her. It was a beautiful drawing, despite the subject matter. Or because of it. Tala wasn't sure. She'd never experienced that particular pleasure.

After she'd set the book aside, squirming, the image continued to haunt her. She wondered if the act itself was as enjoyable as the artist's depiction. Duane hadn't attempted that kind of foreplay, and she hadn't asked him for it. Near the end of their relationship, she'd avoided his touch as much as possible. His lack of finesse in the bedroom had been the least of their problems.

Cam struck her as a generous lover. Eager to please, willing to go slow. He probably wouldn't hesitate to kiss her wherever she wished. He might even do it without any prompting. Her cheeks flushed at the thought.

She stepped out of the stall and dried off as well as she could with two washcloths. The chilly air gave her goose bumps, but that was okay. She needed to cool down. Shivering, she tugged on fresh panties, socks and leggings. She didn't bother with a bra under her sweatshirt. She let down her hair and combed the waves with her fingers. As she finished dressing, she heard a noise outside the bathroom.

Voices.

Tala froze, listening to shuffled footsteps and low murmurs. Someone was in the room. More than one person, by the sound. She swallowed hard, gathering her belongings to her chest. There were no windows in the bathroom, no escape routes. Nothing to use as a weapon. There were only washcloths. Two damp, two dry.

She opened the door and looked out. Two female strangers stared back at her. One had dark hair with purple and blue streaks. The other was older, with short gray hair. They both wore black leather vests with patches on the front. The older woman offered Tala a tentative smile.

"Hello," she said. "I'm Fran, and this is my daughter, Lily."

"Tala," she replied, nodding hello. She walked toward the bed she'd claimed earlier and started rearranging her backpack. She felt jittery and paranoid, though the women were clearly not a threat. She was glad she hadn't charged out of the bathroom with her fists raised. Fran and Lily didn't seem to notice anything amiss. They got settled on the opposite side of the room, chatting about their dinner plans.

"Are you a truck driver?" Fran asked Tala.

"No, I'm just tagging along with one." She told the story Cam had suggested about catching a lift to a waitress job in Prudhoe Bay.

"We're with the tour group," Fran said. She pointed to the patches on her vest. "Denali Devils Motorcycle Club. We ride the Dalton together every summer. This year we decided to check it out in winter."

Tala folded her jeans and tucked them away. "Is everyone on the tour in your motorcycle club?"

"Yep. The rest of the members are all men. Lily's the youngest in the club."

Lily rolled her eyes at her mother's proud announcement, but Tala thought it was sweet. She was also relieved by the information. If everyone on the bus was a

Denali Devil, the killers weren't among them. That was one less thing to worry about tonight.

"You should have dinner with us," Fran said. "Then you don't have to eat with the truckers."

"I don't mind truckers," Tala said.

A knock at the door interrupted their conversation. Tala went to answer it, but Fran was closer. The older woman opened the door to Cam.

"Hello, there," she said, blinking up at him. She seemed startled by the sight of a tall, broad-shouldered man in the hallway.

Cam nodded a greeting and looked past Fran. "I brought your dinner," he said to Tala in a gruff voice.

Tala moved forward to accept the offering. Fran smiled at her encouragingly. Instead of introducing him, Tala stepped into the hall and closed the door behind her. She knew Cam didn't want an audience for their conversation.

"Making friends?" Cam asked.

"The entire tour group is a motorcycle club. They're all together."

"Okay," he said, shrugging.

She studied his handsome face. He looked tense, and tired. His thick brown hair was slightly disheveled, his eyes bloodshot. There was something else in his gaze, a cold wariness she hadn't seen since Willow. It was as if he'd decided, in the hour they'd been apart, that she wasn't worth the trouble.

Her heart clenched at the thought.

She wished she could wrap her arms around him and stroke his rumpled hair. She'd soothe his fears and ease his fatigue. She'd kiss away whatever ailed him, and in doing so, heal herself. But she couldn't do those things, because they weren't in a private place, and she wasn't free to touch him.

"Are you going to bed?" she asked.

"I might hit the gym first."

"There's a gym?"

"There's a weight bench and a few barbells. It's not for you."

She didn't argue. She'd love to stretch her legs and burn off some excess energy, but she understood his position. He'd taken a risk by bringing her here. It was better if she stayed out of sight, as planned.

"We leave at six, sharp."

"I'll be ready," she said. "Sleep well."

He gave her a dark look and strode down the hall. He seemed irritated with her. Maybe he regretted getting involved in her problems. Maybe he just needed space. She went back inside the room, rattled by his brusque attitude. Lily and Fran wore curious expressions.

"Was that your trucker?" Fran asked.

"I'm riding with him, yes."

"Now I see why you don't mind truckers," Lily said.

Fran winked at Lily. "I wouldn't either, if they all looked like that!"

Both women laughed merrily. Tala didn't join in. She returned to her spot on the bed, feeling glum. She avoided eye contact, and they didn't ask her any more personal questions. After they left the room, she inspected the meal Cam had brought her. It was a tasty pasta dish with chicken and vegetables. She ate every bite. Then she brushed her teeth and crawled under the blankets, wide awake.

She shouldn't have taken that nap earlier. She was going to toss and turn all night. She tried reading, but she couldn't focus on the story. She kept flipping back to the sexy bits and staring at the bare-breasted woman.

Groaning, she buried the book in her backpack.

When Fran and Lily returned, she closed her eyes and pretended to be asleep. They were nice enough, but she didn't want to talk. She wanted to curl up with Cam and make them both feel good again.

Someone turned off the lights. It was dark and quiet. Tala couldn't stop thinking about Cam. His hot kisses and bold hands. The feel of his muscles beneath her fingertips. Heat built between her legs. She pressed her thighs together, unable to ease the ache. She couldn't touch herself with two strangers in the room.

After an interminable length of time, she gave up on sleeping. She rose from the bed, grabbed her shoes and tiptoed out the door.

There was nowhere to go, of course. She couldn't take a walk outside in swirling snow and below-freezing temperatures. The lights in the restaurant were dimmed. Lily had complained about the camp being "dry." There wasn't a bar or alcohol of any kind. There wasn't even internet or Wi-Fi.

Tala knew they had a phone in the front office. She imagined calling her mother and explaining her predicament. She'd have to spill all the details about Duane and admit that she'd made a mistake in marrying him. While she was baring her soul, she might as well say she wished she'd been a better daughter.

She rejected that depressing idea. There would be no tearful confessions tonight. She wasn't going to call her mother at this late hour. She wasn't going to break down and cry in the middle of the hallway, either.

She needed some other kind of release.

Cam had been clear in his instructions. Stay in the room, stay out of sight. She couldn't go around knocking on the doors to the men's bunks. What would she say if she found him? *Excuse me, I know you're in a bad mood, but could you please do page 36 to me?*

She choked on a laugh as she crept down the hall. There was a light at the end, beckoning her to explore farther. She moved toward it with silent steps. She could hear the sounds of clinking metal and ragged breaths.

The gym!

She paused at the end of the hallway, which split into a T. The light was coming from an open door on the left side. She continued forward, her pulse racing. When she reached the threshold, she peered inside.

Cam was there. He was alone, stretched out on his back on a weight bench. He lifted a bar away from his chest, arms fully extended. Then he lowered it, releasing a breath. His biceps quivered and glistened with sweat. Up, down. Up, down. It was mesmerizing.

He was wearing a basic gray T-shirt, despite the chill. Clearly, he wasn't cold. His legs were covered in a pair of charcoal gray sweatpants. Athletic shoes took the place of his steel-toed boots. His stomach clenched with every lift, drawing her attention to the flat muscles there. And lower, where he wasn't flat. The hem of his T-shirt had ridden up, and the elastic band of his underwear was visible at his narrow waist. With his feet planted on either side of the bench, powerful thighs spread, she had an unfettered view of his crotch. The soft fabric of his sweatpants did nothing to disguise his manhood.

Her mouth went dry at the sight. She'd never understood why some people objected to women wearing leggings in public, but not men wearing sweatpants. The second was more revealing, considering the outward projection of male anatomy.

On his next rep, Cam placed the bar on the rack and sat up. He used the edge of his T-shirt to wipe the sweat from his face, treating her to a glimpse of his washboard abs. He didn't look pleased to see her, but it was too late to retreat. She'd already been caught staring. She might as well stay and brazen it out.

"What do you want?" he asked.

Oh, boy. *That* was a loaded question. "I couldn't sleep," she said, venturing into the gym. It wasn't much of a gym. There was a weight bench, some barbells and a wrestling mat. One of the walls was mirrored.

He stretched out on his back and did another ten reps. She stood there with her arms crossed over her chest, trying not to ogle him.

"Isn't it dangerous to lift weights like that?" she asked.

"Like what?"

"Without a spotter."

He returned the bar to the rack. "I don't need a spotter for light reps. I'm not going to get trapped under a hundred pounds."

She nodded her understanding. His gaze trailed over her body, as if wondering how it might feel to get trapped underneath *her*. Although she weighed quite a bit more than a hundred pounds, she imagined he could lift her up and down with ease.

He arched a brow. "Is watching me work out going to help you sleep?"

"Probably not," she said, glancing around. There was a jump rope sitting in a plastic crate in the corner. She picked it up and started her own workout.

Jumping rope without a bra on was not recommended. She stopped after about two minutes, her cheeks hot. Cam's lips twitched with amusement, but he didn't say anything. He also didn't avert his gaze. She returned the rope to the crate and switched to yoga. Although it was a low-impact exercise, it wasn't easy. Holding the poses required strength and endurance. She tried not to feel self-conscious about twisting and bending over in snug leggings. Her sweatshirt rode up several times, exposing her belly.

Cam didn't sit idly for long. Nor did he continue smiling. Jaw clenched with irritation, he grabbed the jump rope and approached the mirrored wall. He did a Rocky Balboa routine that was almost as impressive as his weightlifting. He jumped with both feet together, lightning-fast, never tiring. The man was a machine.

A beautiful machine, with broad shoulders and a tight butt.

She moved into a challenging position and held it for as long as possible, eyes closed. Breathing in and out. She didn't achieve total zen, but she felt better when she was finished. She collapsed on the mat. Cam sat down on the bench again. They were both sweating. He didn't seem more relaxed, post workout. He was still on edge.

"Where did you learn yoga?" he asked.

"At the library in Willow. They had free classes several days a week."

He grunted in response, wiping his face with his T-shirt.

She hugged her knees to her chest. "Is something wrong?"

"You told me you were arrested for civil disobedience."

"Yes."

"Was that it? Nothing else?"

Her stomach fluttered with unease. "Why do you ask?"

"Because I'm taking a risk by traveling with you, and I have the right to know who I'm getting involved with."

His request wasn't unreasonable. She liked the sound of them "getting involved." Maybe a frank conversation would make him feel better and break the tension between them. He'd listened to her talk about Duane without judging. She could tell him this. "The charges were civil disobedience and assaulting an officer," she admitted.

"Did you plead guilty?"

"I told you, I never went to court."

"Were you going to plead guilty?"

"I wasn't sure. I didn't want to lie under oath."

"What do you mean?"

She swallowed hard. "Let me start at the beginning. I went to a protest rally in Whitehorse with Duane. He wouldn't let me go alone, and I was desperate to leave the house. I thought it would be good for both of us. Like old times."

"But it wasn't."

"No. He put on a black ski mask as soon as we got there, because he didn't want to be recognized. There was a big crowd, with military police in heavy gear. He started drinking heavily and acting really aggressive."

"More aggressive than usual?"

"Yes. I wanted to leave, but he refused. We were following a group of guys with their faces covered, like him. They were kicking over trash cans and breaking stuff. The police used smoke bombs, and most of the protesters dispersed. Duane bought me a beer, which I accepted to placate him. Then something set him off. I'm not sure what. He grabbed the bottle from me and chucked it at one of the officers. It hit him in the back of the head." She touched her own head, shuddering.

"What did Duane do?"

"He ran in the opposite direction. I didn't see him go, because I was walking toward the officer. I wanted to see if he was okay. When I knelt down beside him, two other officers tackled me and handcuffed me."

"Why did they think you did it?"

"I kept saying I was sorry, and… I was afraid to say anything else."

"You were willing to take the blame?"

"I didn't make a statement one way or another. I asked my public defender to file for a postponement, and she did. Duane said he'd lose his job if I told the truth, but if I pleaded guilty, I'd get community service."

"He's full of shit. No one gets community service for assaulting a police officer. Not even in Canada."

She narrowed her eyes at his certainty. "You're familiar with the law?"

"Yeah, I am," he said in a flat voice. "I used to be a cop."

Her heart plummeted. She scrambled to her feet, thunderstruck. Panic and betrayal washed over her in cold waves. She'd told him intensely personal things. Incriminating things. She shouldn't have trusted him.

"You lied to me."

He rose to his full height. "I didn't lie."

"I asked if you were a cop, and you said no."

"I'm not a cop anymore. I quit."

She shook her head in denial. He still acted like a

cop, with his protective instincts and Boy Scout attitude. Her gut reaction had been right. "You kept it secret for a reason. You knew I wouldn't stay with you if you told the truth."

"What about your secrets?" he shot back angrily. "You haven't been honest with me, either. You never said you were facing serious charges. I don't know what the hell is going on. I don't even know who you're running from!"

She swallowed a protest, even though the criticism felt unfair. She hadn't withheld information to deceive him. She'd done it to protect him, and herself.

"You're not as innocent as you pretend to be," he said.

She sputtered with outrage. "I'm not pretending to be *anything*."

He stepped forward, crowding her space. "I'm not a fool, Tala. I know you didn't come here to work out."

Her hand itched to slap him. He was making insulting accusations. They'd both been dishonest—and they were both suffering from the same malady. He wanted her. That was his real problem. She was upsetting his grieving-widower applecart. She was getting under his skin. "Why did I come here, then?"

"To torture me."

"You're delusional."

"Am I?"

"Yes," she said, shoving his chest. He didn't budge. "You think you're the only one who gets stir-crazy? I've been trapped inside a truck for two days, just like you. I need to move around, just like you. I feel restless, too."

"What I feel is sexual frustration, not restlessness."

"I'm aware of that."

"So you wandered over here to make it worse?"

"No. I wandered over here to make it better."

His eyes flared with heat. "Don't tease me."

"I'm not teasing."

She didn't touch him. She just waited for him to touch her, and he didn't disappoint. Thrusting his hands in her hair, he crushed his mouth over hers. She parted her lips eagerly, inviting him inside. He plundered her with his tongue, groaning. She wrapped her arms around his neck and reveled in him. His taste, hot and demanding. His hard chest and strong shoulders. The smell of damp cotton and warm man.

He took her mouth, again and again. His hands moved to her bottom, cupping her firm flesh and lifting her against him. His erection swelled at her belly and her unbound breasts flattened against the wall of his chest. She moaned, digging her nails in his skin. The heat between her legs became an intense ache. She'd never been this aroused before, and she desperately needed relief.

"Please," she said, biting his lip.

He glanced at the open door. Either the threat of discovery was low, or he dismissed it as unimportant. Instead of taking his hands off her, he backed toward the weight bench and straddled it, pulling her on top of him. Her soft sex met his hard length. She gasped at the sensation. His mouth covered hers again, tongue thrusting.

She moved her hips in a slow circle. His hands groped under her sweatshirt and found her bare breasts. He grunted in pleasure as his thumbs strummed over her nipples. She rocked faster, lost in sensation. There was no penetration or direct stimulation, but it felt too good to stop. Incredibly, she was close to orgasm.

She broke the kiss, uncertain. He stared up at her with half-lidded eyes. Lifting her shirt, he placed his mouth over her breast. The combination of heat, moisture and suction almost sent her over the edge. She whimpered, trying not to grind harder. His erection throbbed against her. He was impressively built, which added to her excitement.

But he seemed to know what she needed, even if she didn't say the words. He gripped her hips and slid her along his thick length. She made a strangled sound of encouragement, her hips jerking. Her breaths came in short pants and her stomach quivered. She strained toward climax, beyond embarrassment. Waves of arousal crashed over her, drowning out everything. There was only this moment, pure and raw and physical.

When she opened her mouth to scream, he thrust his hand in her hair and brought her lips down to his. She exploded in ecstasy, shuddering against him. He swallowed her cries with a thorough kiss.

Then it was over. She stared at him in awe, her head spinning.

"Wow," she said, panting.

The corner of his mouth tipped up. He was still unsatisfied, hard as a rock against her, his forehead lined with restraint. She slid off his lap like a wet noodle and moved into a kneeling position at his feet. He inhaled sharply, but he didn't object. He wanted this. Taut desire was written all over his face.

She wanted it, too. She wanted to touch him and kiss him and blow his mind. She untied the drawstring at his waist, giddy with anticipation. He stroked her hair softly. His hot gaze seared her parted lips.

The sound of approaching footsteps interrupted the moment.

His hand tightened in her hair. She froze, eyes wide.

"Get up," he ordered.

She scrambled to her feet. There wasn't a closet or a corner to hide in. She smoothed her sweatshirt and tried to look innocent. The intruder never arrived, thankfully. A door slammed at the end of the hall.

"He's in the men's room," Cam said. "Go now, before he comes back out."

She hesitated, reluctant to end their encounter. They'd just shared the most intense sexual experience of her life, and he hadn't even removed any of her clothes! He'd given her an orgasm that made her see stars. She didn't want to leave without returning the favor. She didn't want to leave at all. But she also didn't want to get caught, or land him into trouble. They couldn't afford to attract attention.

So she snuck out the door quietly. As she rushed down the hall, it occurred to her that she still wasn't sure where she stood with Cam. They'd been interrupted before she could give him pleasure, and they hadn't really finished their conversation. She'd accused him of deceiving her. He thought she'd done the same. They'd both been angry when they started kissing. But how did he feel about her now? His willingness to get physical didn't indicate a future commitment, or any tender feelings.

He knew she was a criminal, not just a victim. He was a former cop, not just a trucker. He might reconsider traveling with her. What if he took off without her tomorrow? She'd never see him again, and she couldn't do anything about it.

Her heart plummeted with distress. He might not have any tender feelings, but she did. She reentered the women's quarters and slipped into bed. She stared into the dark for a long time, too anxious to sleep.

Chapter 12

Cam squeezed his eyes shut and attempted to regain control of himself.

He hadn't meant to take things so far. He hadn't meant to touch her at all.

When she'd appeared in the gym doorway, he'd been mulling over the information his brother had given him. Cam hadn't wanted to listen to Mason's advice in real time. But after he hung up, doubt had crept in.

The world was a terrible place, full of terrible people. Cam knew that from experience. It was the reason he'd fled to Alaska. He couldn't accept the circumstances of Jenny's death. Someone had struck her with their car, critically injuring her, and driven on. They'd gotten away with murder.

The trauma of this loss had darkened Cam's soul forever. He wasn't capable of optimism. He'd disconnected from his emotions. Emotions were pain, and he'd had enough pain. He preferred staying numb.

Tala didn't fit into the cold life he'd carved out for himself. She was too young and hot. She had too much baggage. She'd been arrested for assaulting an officer. Cops, even former cops with no faith in criminal justice, didn't take such actions lightly. The fact that she'd fled the country was a bad sign. Innocent people didn't do that.

Cam hated it when Mason was right.

He'd considered confronting her in the hallway, but the space hadn't been private enough, and he didn't want to attract attention. He also wasn't sure how to broach the subject. He'd retreated to the men's bunks, weighing his options. Maybe he shouldn't interrogate her. Why should he delve into her problems? The less he knew, the better.

They didn't have to talk at all.

After staring at the ceiling for an hour, he'd gone to the weight room to burn off steam. And wouldn't you know it, Tala had walked in.

She hadn't come for a workout. Not with her hair falling in loose waves down her back. Not braless and heavy-eyed, her lips parted in invitation. She'd watched him lift weights hungrily. He didn't mind her appreciation of his muscles or whatever, but he preferred being on the other side of the equation. Watching her.

He couldn't enjoy the show for long before he became uncomfortable. In some positions, her sweatshirt rode up, exposing her flat belly and slender rib cage. Her breasts shifted beneath the fabric, nipples taut. She raised her arms high, then bent over and dipped her head low. Her leggings clung to her curvy bottom like they'd been painted on. They also failed to disguise her natural shape in front. He could see the faint outline of her feminine cleft. It wasn't polite of him, but his eyes kept dipping to that spot. He had to jump rope for twenty minutes to get rid of his raging hard-on.

He'd believed her story about Duane. He felt himself getting sucked in again. Instead of demanding more answers, he wanted to wrap his arms around her and make everything better. The thought of losing his heart to her scared him.

So he'd dropped that bombshell about being a cop. He had to tell her who he was. He'd turned his back on the law, but he still had a lot of respect for men and women in uniform. He wasn't stupid, or naive. He was just broken.

Somehow, he'd ended up kissing her. All roads seemed to lead in that direction for him. The argument got his blood pumping. He'd said something accusatory. She'd been defensive. Then they were all over each other.

He hadn't decided what to do with her yet. He was on the fence about…everything. Traveling with her. Sleeping with her. Letting himself feel again. He was tempted to lift her against the wall and go for it.

He'd held himself in check, just barely. Three years of abstinence had wrecked his self-control. There were certain lines he couldn't cross. If he slid his hand into her panties and felt her wet heat, for example—that would be his breaking point. It would be like tasting the frosting on a cake he couldn't eat.

He wanted to eat the cake.

So he didn't touch her below the waist. He'd still managed to get her off, under the false assumption that he could walk away after she was finished. Wrong. The sight of her in the throes of orgasm had undone him. He'd almost come with her. Then she'd dropped to her knees, and he'd lost his mind.

Maybe a stronger man could have said no. He couldn't.

He stayed on the weight bench after Tala left, breathing in and out. The stranger emerged from the bathroom and went back down the hall. Cam waited for several more minutes. His arousal didn't abate.

With a strangled groan, Cam got up and hobbled to the men's room. It was empty. There were two shower stalls. He stripped down for a quick shower. His soapy hand brought some much-needed relief.

He went to his room, crawled into a bunk and slept for six hours. The sleep of the dead, dreamless and deep.

He woke at 5:30, feeling rested. He was used to long days and short nights during the ice-road season. Most of the other truckers were already up, milling around the restaurant. There was a special on ham and egg sandwiches. Cam ordered two, with coffee.

While he sat at the counter, he watched the weather report. The temperature wouldn't rise above zero, and it wasn't even snowing. Welcome to Alaska. A short newsbreak followed the weather update. A ruddy-cheeked journalist in a heavy parka stood in front of yellow police tape on the side of the road.

"A man's body was found in this snowdrift on the outskirts of Willow last night," she said, gesturing to the scene behind her. "The sheriff's office hasn't released a statement about the cause of death, but they are investigating this incident as a homicide. The victim hasn't been identified. They believe he was killed elsewhere."

A chill traveled down Cam's spine as the newscasters

discussed the details. Willow was a small, quiet town, not a hotbed for violent crime.

"First a missing woman, and now this," the newscaster said. "We certainly hope the police find the answers they're looking for."

The photo of Tala appeared on the screen, along with the number for the sheriff's station. No mention was made of the alias she'd been using. They didn't give a name at all. Cam wondered if his brother had clued them in about her true identity.

If he hadn't, he would now. Mason was a homicide detective. He wouldn't hesitate to assist an investigation.

It occurred to Cam that Tala might have fled the scene of a murder. She was in more danger than he'd realized. He glanced around the restaurant, cursing under his breath. He hoped no one had gotten a glimpse of her in the hallways. The two women she was rooming with weren't in the crowd. He needed to get her out of here before someone recognized her as the missing waitress.

There had to be a connection between Tala and the homicide victim. She was probably a person of interest in the investigation. Maybe she'd witnessed the crime—or been an active participant.

What if the dead man was Duane? What if he'd attacked her at the diner, and she'd killed him in self-defense? She'd been rattled and half-frozen when Cam had found her. She looked like she'd seen a ghost. He didn't know how the body had ended up in a secondary location, or who the other men following her were. There were a lot of things Cam didn't know, because Tala hadn't told him.

He should have tried to get more answers from her last night, but he'd lost focus the instant his lips touched hers. Instead of wringing the truth out of her, he'd wrung an orgasm. He couldn't say he regretted it, either. She had a powerful effect on him. Whenever she was near, his thoughts turned to sex.

Cam smothered a groan of self-derision. He was glad he didn't have cell service. Mason would be blowing up his phone with frantic texts.

Cam needed to talk to Tala before he decided what to do next. His first instinct was to protect her, not himself. He refused to put his own safety above hers. He didn't care about her arrest record. He didn't care about the risks involved. What he cared about was getting her out of Coldfoot, and into his bed.

It wasn't smart to be this obsessed with having her. He realized he was traveling down a slippery slope, throwing caution to the wind. But damn if it didn't feel good to make bad decisions once in a while. It felt good to pursue a desirable woman, after years of denying himself pleasure. He wasn't the same man he used to be, because her possible involvement in a homicide didn't dissuade him. If anything, it added an extra rush of excitement.

When his breakfast sandwiches were ready, he left the restaurant and went to Tala's door. She answered his quiet knock in seconds. Her hair was neatly braided, her face solemn. She already had her backpack on.

"Morning," he said.

She closed the door behind her. "I'm sorry about last night. I'll make it up to you."

He wasn't sure what she was talking about, but they didn't have time to chat. He had to get her out of here and back on the road. As they walked by the front desk, he put his body between Tala and the clerk to shield her from view. Bitter cold enveloped him in the parking lot. He grasped Tala's elbow and headed toward Ice Storm.

Her expression indicated distress, which concerned him. As much as he wanted this thing between them to be purely physical, it wasn't. He unlocked his truck and opened the door for her. Then he climbed behind the wheel, studying her face. She looked close to tears.

"What's wrong?" he asked.

"I was afraid you were going to leave without me."

He started the engine to let it warm up. Had she overheard the news report, and assumed he'd ditch her? "Why would I do that?"

"Because of my criminal record," she murmured. "Then we…you know, and we didn't finish. I mean, I did, but you didn't."

He gave her a curious glance. She didn't know about the homicide investigation. Cam decided not to bring it up. He had no idea how she'd react. "You thought I'd leave you stranded in the middle of nowhere because you came and I didn't?"

She nodded.

He didn't know whether to laugh or feel insulted. Her husband had been a real piece of work. He'd made her assume that all men were selfish and cruel. Cam hoped that Duane Laramie was the human Popsicle from the snowbank, frozen forever in hell. If he wasn't, Cam would like to send him there.

"I didn't mind. I enjoyed it."

Her brow furrowed. "You did?"

"Of course."

"Wouldn't you rather it be…mutual?"

He shrugged. "There's no crime in giving without taking. Haven't you ever done that?"

"Yes. Too often."

"Every time?"

She looked out the foggy window, not answering.

"For the record, I wouldn't leave without saying goodbye. And one orgasm is hardly worth keeping tabs on. When I make you come five or six times in a row, we can start worrying about me getting mine."

Her eyes widened in surprise. "You're kidding, right?"

He smiled, checking his gauges. He wasn't kidding. He was exaggerating a little, but he didn't doubt he could satisfy her. They had good chemistry. Rhythmic stimulation wasn't rocket science. Maybe her husband hadn't bothered to learn the basics, but Cam knew his way around the female body. Even so, he shouldn't be making any promises. He should be thinking about how they were going to get out of this mess. She couldn't run forever. He had to convince Tala to turn herself in before the law—or worse—caught up with her.

There were hundreds of miles between Coldfoot and Deadhorse, which led to Prudhoe Bay. They'd be together all day. Over the next ten or twelve hours, he'd find a way to get some answers from her. But he also had to tread carefully. She wouldn't be easy to interrogate. She had a fiercely independent streak, and she didn't trust law officers. She panicked every time he mentioned calling the police. She'd need a lot of convincing before she cooperated with an investigation. And she wouldn't be pleased to discover that he'd asked his cop-brother to do a background check on her.

He winced, massaging the nape of his neck. He couldn't change what he'd said to Mason. Cam regretted the deception, but not the actions.

They ate breakfast and drank coffee in silence. He enjoyed her company, as always. She had a quiet strength about her, even during moments of stress. He liked her voice, when she chose to speak. Her words carried weight, like her smiles. He wondered if he'd ever learn the truth about why she was running. She might refuse to talk to him. She might bolt at the first sign of trouble. His chest tightened at the thought.

"Maybe I should stay in Prudhoe Bay," she said out of the blue.

"Why would you do that?"

"If they're desperate for workers, it's not a bad idea. I could apply at one of the hotels."

"With what ID?"

She avoided his gaze. "Not every employer requires ID. Some people get paid under the table."

He knew what kind of job she could get "under the table," and he didn't approve. She'd have to make some seedy arrangement with a stranger who wouldn't have her best interests in mind. There were predatory men in Prudhoe Bay who'd take her up on any offer. Rough men who'd left civilization behind. Lonely men, like Cam.

"You're frowning," she said.

He touched his forehead to confirm her claim.

"You don't think I can find work?"

"That's not the problem."

"What is?"

"Prudhoe Bay is about 95 percent men."

"Walt's Diner catered to truckers. Mostly men."

"It's not the same."

"Why not?"

"You weren't trapped at Walt's Diner. Prudhoe Bay is incredibly isolated. If you want to leave, you'll have to buy a plane ticket or hitch a ride with a trucker during the ice-road season, which is only a few months a year."

"It's hard to get out, but it's also hard to get *in*. Maybe I'll feel safe there."

He made a noncommittal sound. They'd already talked about her beauty causing a stir with the truckers in Coldfoot. It would be the same situation in Prudhoe Bay, only worse. There were almost no other women. There were certainly no young, sexy women. She'd stick out like a sore thumb.

"What about your family in Montana?"

She looked away, not answering.

"I'm sure they'd like to hear from you."

"I'm not."

He dropped the subject. He hadn't meant to end the whole conversation, but his comment had that effect. She didn't speak for several hours. Which was fine, because he needed to concentrate on driving. The second leg of the Dalton was even hairier than the first. Avalanche Alley loomed in the distance. Cam had hit a moose on this precarious stretch last year. He was lucky he hadn't gone over the edge.

Most of the morning eked away and the sky brightened. Snow-heavy clouds draped the horizon, promising another blustery winter storm. He hoped for a swift commute and passable weather. The Northern Lights were spectacular in this area, when it was clear.

His thoughts kept returning to last night's furtive encounter. Despite the complications, he couldn't wait to touch her again. He didn't know if any romance could flourish after they tackled the following difficult topics: Did You Kill Your Husband? and Sorry, I Asked My Brother to Investigate You.

Cam raked a hand through his hair, uncomfortable. He could always take her to bed first and save the talking for later. That would be shady as hell, and he'd ruin the chance of ever sleeping with her again, but maybe that was a plus. He wasn't looking for a long-term relationship.

Cam had gone out of his way to help Tala. He'd rescued her from two attackers. If she wanted to share her body with him, why should he deny her? He'd give her pleasure. She'd be well satisfied. They didn't have to make any promises. There were too many secrets between them, too many obstacles to overcome. This was a hot affair, doomed to go down in flames. He might as well end it with a bang.

He didn't have to interrogate her, or convince her to go to the police. He was tired of doing the right thing. He wasn't a cop anymore. He wasn't the strong-but-sensitive husband who went to farmers' markets and charity fund-raisers. He was a cold, hard Alaskan now. He could engage in a one-night stand and walk away. There was nothing wrong with no-strings sex.

She glanced his direction as he shifted gears. "Can I ask you a question?"

"Go for it," he said, pulling his thoughts out of the gutter. They were on an easy stretch of road, with no obstacles in sight.

"Are you still in touch with your family?"

"Yes. They're relentless."

"What do you mean?"

"If I don't call, they badger me. If I don't visit on holidays, I never hear the end of it."

"Who do you call?"

"My mom and my brother."

"What do you talk about?"

He shrugged, evasive.

"You're not much help," she commented.

"You want tips from me on how to reconnect with your family?"

"Do you have some?"

He sighed, shaking his head. She was barking up the wrong tree. "I don't get along with them as well as I used to."

"What happened?"

"My brother and I were close, as kids. He was a typical big brother. He was good at everything. Sports, school, making friends, beating me up."

"He beat you up?"

"Sure. That's how brothers show love."

She chuckled at the assertion. "If you say so."

"I wanted to be like him. He was driven, competitive. He still is."

"Is that bad?"

"It's not bad. He's just sort of…rigid."

"He's rigid?"

"You think I am?"

"You're wound up pretty tight."

Cam considered her perspective. "I'm hard on myself. He's hard on everyone else."

"Ah."

"It's because of his divorce," Cam said. "His wife left him right after mine died. He didn't see it coming, and he doesn't like to lose. So he's been kind of an asshole for a few years, but I think he's getting better."

"Does he look like you?"

"Like me, but clean-cut."

"You're clean-cut. For an Alaskan."

"He wears suits."

She curled up in the passenger seat, tucking her knees to her chest. "What about your mom?"

"What about her?"

"Is she hard on you?"

"She has her moments."

"Give me an example."

"I went home for Thanksgiving a few weeks ago. She invited one of Jenny's friends over without asking me. It was like a blind date that I didn't agree to. She wants me to fall in love and get married again."

"What a monster."

He laughed at her dry response. "You're mocking me, but her guilt trips are legendary. I'm in the doghouse right now for not playing along with her matchmaking. Apparently, I was supposed to be charming, instead of sullen."

"Was she pretty? This friend?"

"She was okay."

"What was wrong with her?"

"Nothing. She reminded me of Jenny."

"Have you been with anyone else?"

"No."

"Not in three years?"

"I haven't even looked at other women. Until you."

"Why me?"

He glanced in her direction. She was young and beautiful, but that wasn't it. There was something else between them, a connection that went beyond physical chemistry. "You pour a great cup of coffee."

She rolled her eyes, smiling. "Is that all it takes?"

He mulled it over, trying to pinpoint the exact moment he became enthralled with her. "I was watching you at Walt's about a month ago. You were waiting on another trucker. Little guy with red hair. Kind of a jerk."

"Albert?"

Cam didn't know his name. "He reached for something while you were clearing his table and bumped into your arm. His coffee spilled everywhere. I thought he was going to start yelling. You calmly dropped a towel on the table, didn't say a word. You just stared at him. He wiped up the mess and apologized to you."

"It was his fault."

"Yes, it was. But most waitresses would have pretended otherwise."

"They get better tips than me."

"I like you the way you are."

Her lips parted in wonder, as if she was touched by the compliment. He returned his attention to the road, his gut clenched with unease. Yeah, he was in over his head. He needed to pump the brakes on this conversation. He'd just told her how much he *liked* her. That wasn't what you said to a woman you couldn't commit to.

"There's a rough section coming up," he said, avoiding her gaze. "You should get in the back."

She took off her seat belt and climbed into the berth to give him space. It didn't feel like much of a separation. He was still hypersensitive to her presence, aware of her every move. He thought about the unidentified dead body in Willow, frozen in a snowbank. He thought about Jenny, slipping away. The dark discussion he'd been dreading loomed like storm clouds on the horizon. Maybe Tala would clear her name with the police, and he'd move on with his heart intact.

Or maybe he was kidding himself, and it was too late for a clean break.

Chapter 13

December 13
69N
-11 degrees

Tala curled up on the narrow bed in the berth and tried not to panic.

She was getting dangerously attached to Cam. A former cop.

She was falling in love with him, in fact.

This was a total disaster.

She wished she could say she didn't know how it happened, but she did know. He'd rescued her and given her shelter. He'd been a perfect gentleman. He hadn't expected sexual favors. He'd been reluctant to put his arms around her because he knew it would result in his arousal—but he hadn't hesitated to hold her hand. The unselfish choices he'd made had set a series of events into motion, from their chaste embrace at the cabin, to his protective actions in the parking lot, to their sizzling encounter in the weight room.

He'd made her feel valued and respected from the start. He'd seen her as a person, not just a pretty server. He'd noticed something special about her before they even met. He'd admired her as a waitress. How could she resist that?

He was handsome and thrilling and he said nice things. He could control himself. He was capable of being kind and gentle.

But…he'd never love her. He was too hung up on his dead wife. He couldn't erase the woman he'd dedicated his life to and replace her with Tala. He wasn't ready to let go. It would take time for him to open up his heart again.

She didn't have time, unfortunately. She had three madmen chasing after her, threatening to silence her forever.

She closed her eyes and took deep breaths. She wasn't thinking straight. She couldn't trust her emotions right now, with all the stress she was under. Of course she felt attached to Cam, after everything he'd done for her. He was a good man. She was attracted to him. Maybe she'd confused desire and gratitude for deeper feelings.

The fact that she hadn't slept much last night didn't help. She'd convinced herself that Cam was going to leave her behind—or turn her in. He might not be a cop anymore, but he wasn't a typical trucker. He'd come to Alaska to be alone in his grief, not to settle down in a new place. She didn't think he'd make roots here. Maybe he'd go back home and work on the farm. Maybe he'd return to the police force. He wouldn't stay a trucker. He was too physical. He needed to get out and live.

And she needed a backup plan. She couldn't count on Cam to keep her safe, or even stick around. He wasn't ready to make a commitment. He wouldn't want to get tied down to someone like her. She could travel with him for as long as possible, and be ready to run. Or she could hide out in Prudhoe Bay, and be ready to fight.

She'd tossed and turned for hours, weighing her options. In the morning, she hadn't made a decision, but she'd bought herself some insurance. Actually, she'd stolen it. She'd stolen the identification from Lily's wallet.

Tala didn't look like Lily, but they were both dark-haired and the age was close. It would work in a pinch. If employers in Prudhoe Bay were desperate for service staff, they wouldn't question her ID.

She felt guilty about the crime she'd committed, which was another reason to cool it with Cam. He wouldn't approve. She had to stop mooning over him and face reality. They weren't going to ride off into the sunset and live happily ever after. They were going to spend a couple of nights together at the most. Then he'd move on, with or without her.

"This is Avalanche Alley," Cam said over his shoulder.

She sat upright to watch the road as they started a steep climb. There were snow-laden mountains on one side, sheer cliffs on the other. Now that it was full daylight, she could see every terrifying angle. "What do you do if there's an avalanche?"

"Not much you can do if you're in the direct path. Some trucks get swept off the road. Even if you see it coming, it's hard to stop in this area."

"Great," she said, swallowing hard.

"The maintenance crew comes out every week or so to blast the hillside. They create avalanches on purpose. It's the most dangerous job on the Dalton."

She glanced around for a seat belt and didn't find one. Cam continued driving steadily uphill, around hairpin turns. At one point his tires slipped on the icy surface. He cursed under his breath and made some adjustments to the controls to regain traction. After a long, nerve-racking ascent, they reached a flat stretch of road again.

"You can come back up front," he said.

She returned to her seat and secured the belt. "Are we out of the avalanche zone?"

"We're past the worst part. There's an easy section here, then it gets gnarly again after Nightmare Corner."

"Nightmare Corner?"

"Yeah. That's not for another hour."

She noted that the "easy section" was still flanked by steep cliffs, but the elevation remained steady and the road wasn't as narrow. There were places to pull over. After they passed an idling rig, Cam picked up his radio receiver. He had a short conversation with the driver that Tala didn't understand.

"Is he okay?" she asked.

"He's fine. Eating lunch."

"Do you ever pull over to eat?"

"Why, are you hungry?"

She shook her head. The twists and turns made her queasy.

"I don't stop on the Dalton unless I have to, and most other truckers do the same. We're superstitious."

"Of what?"

"There's a story about a trucker from the old days

who pulled over to take a nap. He froze to death. His engine died and he didn't wake up. Since then, everyone who stops between Coldfoot and Deadhorse seems to have some kind of trouble. Gears freeze or whatever. They blame it on Gary's Ghost."

"We had a spirit like that in Yellowknife. My father called him Nahani, the Woodsman. He told me not to wander too far, because Nahani was always in the woods, hunting for souls to take to the spirit world."

He arched a brow. "I don't know if Gary hunts souls, so much as causes delays."

She laughed. "Your spirits aren't as strong as ours."

"Did you believe in the Woodsman?"

"Oh, yes. My dad showed me his tracks one day. There was a set of footprints in the snow that suddenly disappeared. He said the Woodsman could leap to the tops of trees, or turn into a wolf or rabbit. I used to look for him, because I wanted to see how he did it."

He adjusted his gears and switches to accommodate for the level ground. "You weren't afraid of him?"

"I was, but I thought I could run away really fast if I saw him. One day I followed his tracks for several miles before I lost the trail. Then I turned around, and my dad jumped out from behind a tree. I screamed so loud I scared the birds out of the branches."

He smiled at her story. "Was he the Woodsman?"

"Maybe," she said, smiling back at him. "He was the best hunter and tracker in the area."

"Did he hunt alone?"

"He did. When we needed extra money he led hunting expeditions, but he didn't enjoy it. He wasn't into killing animals for sport. And he was a loner, especially after my mother left. He never got over her."

Cam grunted his understanding. He could relate to that problem. Tala wondered if her father would have been happier—and lived longer—if he'd found someone new to love. Her chest tightened with sadness at the thought. Spending time with Cam made her realize how important relationships were. What if she couldn't get over him? She might follow in her father's footsteps and pine away forever.

She fell silent, wishing she'd met Cam under better circumstances. She also wished she could smother her feelings for him.

"Hang on," he said, his brow furrowed. "There's a snowdrift."

She grabbed the handle above the passenger window to brace herself. Seconds later they hit a mound of snow in the middle of the road. It was a nasty surprise of a speedbump. Cam took the jolt in stride, as if these hazards were common. He held the wheel steady as they went over two more in rapid succession.

"Having fun yet?" he asked.

She released a ragged breath, shaking her head.

"Yeah, it's not for everyone."

"But you enjoy the danger."

"I don't mind it."

"Did you enjoy arresting people?"

He gave her a sidelong glance. "I was a highway patrol officer, so I didn't make arrests. I wrote tickets."

She went quiet again. The conversation had veered into uneasy territory, and the road was treacherous enough. Another rig appeared about a mile in the distance, barreling toward them. Her heart dropped as she noticed something in its path. It wasn't a snowdrift, which could be driven over, but a total obstruction.

Cam swore and reached for his radio as the other driver hit the mini-avalanche. Snow exploded over the rig's grill and front window. It was too late for the trucker to slow down, and he couldn't self-correct. Tala let out a terrified scream as the vehicle jackknifed, slid out of control and went plummeting down the cliff.

Cam shouted into the receiver to report the emergency. He pulled to a stop about a hundred feet from the obstruction. He reached for his parka before he climbed out. "Stay here," he ordered.

Tala didn't stay. She tugged on her own jacket before joining him in the bitter cold. The snow must have tumbled across the road seconds or minutes ago. She studied the mountainside on her right, wondering if another, bigger, avalanche might follow. She hurried to catch up with Cam.

He was on the opposite side of the road, standing above a sheer drop. He'd grabbed a heavy length of rope from somewhere. She looked down, her stomach roiling. There was a smoking, busted-up rig below. The windows were smashed, the cab filled with snow. It was half-buried, half-dangling, thirty or forty feet from the edge. It didn't look secure. She could easily imagine the wreck sliding further down the cliff and exploding in flames.

There was no movement but snow flurries. No sound besides the wind.

"I have to get down there," Cam said.

She gaped at him, incredulous. "How? There's nothing to tie a rope to."

He studied the area, his jaw clenched. There were no safety rails or natural features to use as an anchor. His truck was too far away, and there were too many hazards. The snow wasn't stable. Another vehicle could come around the corner any moment. Dropping the rope, he cupped his hands around his mouth and shouted down at the wreckage.

"Hey! Can you hear me? You have to get out! I'll throw you a rope!"

Tala was aware that help might not arrive anytime soon. They were in the middle of nowhere. If the driver was alive, he could very well die before emergency services responded. While she watched, breathless, fingers poked out through the broken window.

"He's alive," Cam and Tala exclaimed at the same time.

The fingers wiggled once, and stilled. They waited for more movement. Cam shouted encouragement until his voice went hoarse. It became clear that there would be no self-rescue. The man couldn't dig himself out of the snow-packed cab. He was going to suffocate.

"I'll go," Tala said, picking up the rope. "I can't hold your weight, but you can hold mine."

"No," Cam said, his eyes wild. "It's too dangerous."

"It's the only way."

He raked a hand through his hair, cursing. "You shouldn't even be out here. I told you to stay in the goddamned truck!"

"He'll die if we do nothing."

After a few seconds of watching her fumble with the rope, he took control and secured one end around her waist. He tied the other end to his own waist. Taking up the slack, he held it in a tight grip. "Whatever you do, don't get the rope caught on the wreckage. If it starts to fall, we'll all go down with it. You have to stay clear."

"I understand," she said. "You've got me?"

"I've got you. Go slow."

She had to brace her boots on the snowy rock face, which made a slippery surface, and lean back into the abyss. Cam gave her a few tips, but mostly he just shut up. His face was taut with worry, his mouth a hard line. Then she couldn't see him anymore. He lowered her with sure hands, steady as a rock. Seconds ticked by and her blood rushed in her ears.

She thought about her father, and how he'd died fighting. She knew he'd been awake after the crash. He'd swum to the surface and tried to punch through the ice. His knuckles had been broken from the effort. He'd needed help, but no one was there.

She couldn't save her father, but she could save this trucker. She could keep fighting.

When she reached the wreck, she fell to her knees on the hood and started scooping out snow with her bare hands. There was a limp arm to guide her. She freed him to the shoulder. His fingers twitched and tears rushed into her eyes. Redoubling her efforts, she tunneled a path toward his head. A weathered face appeared, with a gray mustache and unhealthy pallor. His eyes opened, bloodshot and confused.

"What happened?"

She sobbed with relief. "He's alive," she cried up at Cam. "He's alive!"

The man tried to move, groaning. Tala kept digging. She wept into the snow. After several more minutes, his upper body was exposed and he could breathe easier. He looked more alert, but they weren't out of the woods yet.

"Help me," she panted, tugging on his arms.

He strained forward. Together, they freed him from the snow-packed cab. The truck made an ominous creaking sound.

"Uh-oh," the man said.

Another rope got tossed down to them a moment later. She glanced up the cliff, disoriented. Her arms were tired from digging, her face and hands numb. There was a second figure next to Cam. Nahani, her mind whispered. The Woodsman.

"What's your name, girl?" the trucker asked.

"Tala."

"I'm Phil."

"Anything broken?"

"I don't think so."

She helped Phil loop the rope around his waist. He tied the knot himself. It looked secure. Collapsing on the snow-covered hood, she gave Cam a weak thumbs-up. She started shivering uncontrollably, and she didn't have the energy to climb.

Luckily, she didn't have to do anything. The other men lifted her to the top. Then she was in Cam's arms, warm and safe. He wrapped a blanket around her shoulders and pressed his lips to her forehead.

She didn't want to let go—ever.

But she had to, because their work wasn't done. The figure beside Cam wasn't the woodsman. It was another trucker named Robert. A third man arrived on the scene and offered his assistance. They brought up Phil slowly. He was heavier than Tala, and possibly injured, but leaving him down there wasn't an option.

Phil made it to the top safely. He seemed alert. He had a bump on his head, and some tenderness in his ribs. Tala gave him her blanket. After a short rest, he was able to stand up. He embraced Tala and professed his gratitude.

"You're the prettiest trucker I've ever seen," he said, and everyone laughed.

"I'm not a trucker," she said. "I'm a waitress."

Everyone laughed again, for no particular reason. They were all giddy from the close call and successful rescue. Cam had been right about truck drivers. They weren't antisocial. When someone needed help, they banded together.

"Are you sure you're not my guardian angel?" Phil asked.

"I'm just me."

Phil squeezed her shoulder. "I have a daughter your age," he said, his voice thick. "She wouldn't have a dad right now if it weren't for you. That was a very brave thing you did. I don't know why you did it."

"I told her not to," Cam said, and they all laughed some more.

Tala flushed at the attention, but she felt good about her actions. Phil wasn't exaggerating. He probably would have died if she hadn't dug him out of the snow. "I couldn't have done it without Cam."

Cam nodded an acknowledgment. His quick thinking in grabbing the rope, and his strength in holding her weight, had been essential to the rescue. "It was a group effort," he said, including the others.

Phil thanked everyone with handshakes and claps on the back. The rest of the men grabbed shovels and started clearing the road. They worked with brisk efficiency, part construction crew, part rescue team. Taking a break to help save a guy was no problem, but now they were all business. They had loads to deliver and deadlines to meet.

Tala stood on the sidelines with Phil. She watched Cam shovel until the formal "first responders" appeared. There were two EMTs in a modified ambulance, and a policeman in an SUV. She froze at the sight of the officer's navy blue winter uniform. Her panicked mind supplied the wrong face, morphing him into one of the killers. Then she saw Duane. She blinked to dispel the image, but she couldn't shake the bad feeling. She started shivering again, from a mixture of fear and stress.

There was no escaping an interaction with the authorities. If she tried to avoid them, it would look suspicious.

The EMTs escorted Phil to the ambulance to take care of him. They returned her blanket, which she held with numb hands. The policeman didn't stop to talk to her, which was a relief. She had no idea what to say to him. She'd told Phil her real name. Cam wouldn't lie for her. She was stuck.

While she stood there, trembling, Cam stepped forward to give a statement to the officer. She didn't want to tell a story that might contradict his, so she listened intently. Cam gave the details of the accident without embellishment. Just the facts.

The officer seemed surprised by her part in the rescue. He glanced over the cliff's edge. "She went down there to dig him out?"

Cam nodded.

"Whose idea was that?"

"Hers."

"So you lowered her toward the wreck?"

"Yes."

"How were you planning to get her out?"

"I thought I could pull her up. Then she and I could pull him up."

"That would have been extremely difficult."

Cam didn't argue. Tala hadn't thought that far ahead. They were lucky the two other men had arrived to help.

The officer brandished a pen and notepad. "What's your name, hero?"

"Cameron Hughes."

"And you, miss?"

"Tala Walker," she mumbled, her lips numb.

"Tara?"

"Tala. *T-A-L-A.*" If he returned to his vehicle and entered her name in his computer, he'd get a notification of her outstanding warrants. But maybe he wouldn't bother. As far as he knew, she hadn't done anything wrong.

"You're traveling together?" the officer asked Cam.

"Yes. That's my rig."

"I need to sit down," Tala said. "I feel lightheaded."

The officer shrugged, closing his notebook. "Go ahead."

Cam thanked him and grasped Tala's arm to lead her away. She stumbled forward on unsteady legs. She half expected the policeman to shout at them to stop, but he didn't. She glanced over her shoulder. He wasn't even watching them.

She made it as far as the passenger side of the truck. Then her knees buckled and everything went dark.

Chapter 14

Cam caught Tala before she fell.

He swept her into his arms as her eyelids fluttered closed. She made a moaning sound, resting her head against his shoulder. He lifted her into the cab and deposited her into the passenger seat with a grunt of exertion. It was warm inside, because he'd left the engine running and the heat on. He adjusted the blanket over her body to keep her cozy. By the time he got behind the wheel, she was awake again.

He handed her a bottle of water. She drank half of it and gave it back.

"Are you okay?" he asked.

"I'm fine."

"You fainted."

"I know."

"You also saved a man's life."

"I remember. Can we go now?"

The road was clear, but Cam wasn't in a hurry to leave. He took off his parka and used the restroom while they were stopped. She set aside her blanket and did the same, without help. He grabbed some snacks from the mini-fridge. He had fruit juice and whole wheat crackers. She accepted both.

He didn't think she needed medical attention. Her color looked better. He turned the heat all the way up. Then he put on his seat belt and pulled forward. The other truckers waved goodbye as they left the scene. Cam waved back.

"I guess the secret's out," Tala said.

"Which secret?"

"You're riding with an unapproved passenger."

"They don't know you're not approved."

"This story will get around."

He agreed that it would, and he didn't really care. If he was going to get fired for having a sexy, mysterious companion who rescued strangers, so be it. There were worse ways to go. "What you did was amazing."

"Stop," she said, nibbling on a cracker. "You're embarrassing me."

"I'm sorry I told you not to do it."

"It's okay. I wouldn't have wanted to watch you go down there, either."

He kept his eyes on the road, but his thoughts lingered on her. Her face, her actions, her uncommon bravery. "You were fearless."

"I wasn't fearless. I just fainted."

"That doesn't change anything."

"If you'd fainted, would you feel like a tough guy?"

He laughed at the question, shaking his head. He hadn't felt very tough while she was digging in the snow.

He'd been sick with terror and worry. If the wreckage had slipped, they might have all gone with it. He'd held the rope in a death grip, determined to hang on, no matter what. Letting go wasn't an option.

It still wasn't.

He came to the startling realization that he couldn't walk away from her. He'd been willing to risk his life for her. He wanted more than one night with her. A lot more.

The idea of getting seriously involved with anyone rattled him. He glanced in her direction, frowning. Her actions had been incredibly heroic. She was beautiful and exciting. He enjoyed talking to her, and he wasn't much of a talker. They were having a good time together, despite the circumstances. They'd just executed a daring rescue. Maybe he was high on adrenaline and temporarily enamored.

Yes. That explained it.

Relief washed over him, rinsing away the aftereffects of panic. Danger always heightened the senses. They'd bonded in the hotel room the first night. He felt a strong connection to her, and he still wanted her in his bed, but this infatuation would pass. Eventually.

"I told that cop my real name."

He flinched at her sudden words. "What?"

"I told him my name. Do you think he'll search me in the system?"

"Cops don't have time to run everyone without cause. They do it for a clear violation or suspicion of a crime."

"You said my picture was on TV."

He grunted an acknowledgment. Her photo had probably been distributed to every law enforcement agency in Alaska, not just the local news outlets. "If he recognized you, he would have said so."

She went quiet, huddled beneath the blanket.

Cam didn't tell her that her real name would appear in the police report. As soon as that information was entered in the database, it would trigger an alert about her outstanding warrants. Which might not attract much notice, all by itself. Many districts were understaffed and unable to hunt down every offender. If her name came up as a person of interest in a murder investigation, that was different. Locating her would become a high priority.

Cam felt guilty about the role he'd played in her evasion. Although he hadn't lied to the police officer, he'd kept her secrets and helped her slip away. He'd been reluctant to betray her confidence before he'd heard her side of the story. When they stopped at the hotel in Prudhoe Bay, they'd have a frank discussion. He'd ask her about the dead man in Willow. He didn't think she'd want to warm his bed afterwards. Which was probably for the best, considering his overwrought feelings. Sleeping with her wouldn't help him disconnect.

He noted that she was still shivering. "Are your clothes wet?"

"Just my jeans."

"Take them off. You can wear my sweatpants."

She went to the berth to get changed. He focused on the road, not watching her undress. She returned after a few minutes. He didn't ask her to stay in the back. It was warmer up front, and he could keep an eye on her condition.

Daylight faded quickly. North of Coldfoot, in the dead of winter, they got three or four hours of sun at the most. It messed with everyone's circadian rhythms. Sometimes Cam felt like a vampire, only half-alive. Before he met

Tala, he'd embraced the dark. Now he found himself wanting more light.

He rounded Nightmare Corner without incident and navigated the remaining obstacles. There were drifts and cliffs and narrow passages. Nothing he couldn't handle. While he drove, he thought about how lucky they'd been to witness that accident. If the other truck hadn't been coming toward them, Cam might not have seen the obstruction. It could have just as easily been him crashing into the snow mound and flying off the road.

And Phil would be dead right now, if not for Tala. Cam couldn't have climbed down to the wreckage on his own. Help hadn't arrived for ten minutes or more. Tala's quick thinking had saved the man's life.

There was some chatter on the radio about the accident, but not much. The story would circulate tomorrow. Once the truckers in Coldfoot Camp heard the tale, they'd spread it all over Alaska. Embellishments would be added. By the time Cam returned to Fairbanks, they'd be saying he'd sledded down an avalanche and picked up a guardian angel. The speculation about Tala would run rampant. He groaned, imagining the gossip. They'd assume she was his girlfriend, or his paid companion. Someone might realize she was the missing waitress from Walt's Diner. The trucking company would question him about the incident. If they frowned on his behavior, Cam wouldn't get any more ice-road contracts.

Which was a shame, because working on the Dalton had kept him alive for the past three years. The extreme danger had triggered his survival instincts. He'd needed a challenge as much as he'd needed solitude. But maybe he didn't need either as much as he used to.

The hours ticked by and the temperature dropped.

As he approached Deadfoot, he braced himself for a confrontation with the site supervisor, or even the police. His eyes felt grainy, his neck tight with tension. He pulled into the yard and parked, letting the engine idle. There were several other rigs in the area. Tala had fallen asleep in the passenger seat with her backpack clutched to her chest.

He picked up the radio to check in. "Hughes," he said, and recited the order number. Tala jerked awake with a start. Her backpack tumbled to the ground between them.

"You're clear to continue to Prudhoe Bay."

Cam replied an affirmative and ended the transmission. So far, so good. He hadn't been called into the office. No one had even mentioned the accident. Maybe they were too busy to deal with him right now. Truck yards were notoriously chaotic. Shrugging, he removed his seat belt and reached for his parka.

"What are you doing?" Tala asked. Her voice was husky from sleep.

"Taking off the chains. I'll be right back."

He climbed out, wincing at the cold bite of wind. He put on his gloves and removed the sets of chains. By the time he was finished, his face was numb. He hurried back to the cab to get warm. Tala handed him a cup of instant soup, which she'd heated in the microwave. He accepted it with gratitude.

"You don't need chains for the ice road?" she asked.

"It depends on the temperature and conditions. When it's really cold, tires have good traction, and the weight of the load helps them grip. The main danger isn't slipping so much as breaking through."

Her eyes widened in distress. Too late, he remembered the story of her father's death.

"Sorry," he said gruffly. "The ice gets slushy at the end of the season. Right now, it's rock-solid, and they test it every week."

She put another cup of soup in the microwave, avoiding his gaze.

"This section is the safest part of the route. It's wide and flat, and the speed limit is ten miles per hour. You'll be bored."

"I won't be bored," she said.

He sipped his soup instead of arguing. She went into the bathroom and slid the door shut. The motion caused her backpack to tip on its side. A book fell out, so he picked it up and flipped through the pages. He'd never read a graphic novel before. He'd expected it to be like a comic, with superheroes and action reels.

It had action reels. Just a different kind of action than he'd anticipated. There were several lovingly detailed illustrations of a couple having sex.

The microwave dinged, which startled him into returning the book to her backpack. He noticed an ID card inside. He was already snooping, so he glanced at the card quickly before putting it back. She emerged from the bathroom and retrieved her soup. They finished the meal in silence. His thoughts boomeranged from erotic art and hot memories to stolen IDs and frozen wastelands.

"Are you sure you want to come with me to Prudhoe Bay?" he asked.

Her brow furrowed. "What choice do I have?"

"There's a camp here like the one in Coldfoot. Separate bunks for men and women."

"Is that what you want? Separate bunks?"

"No."

"Then let's keep going."

He tossed his empty cup in the trash, feeling conflicted. A part of him wanted to confront her right now about the ID and everything else. Another part of him, centered below the waist, wanted to take her to the hotel and not talk at all. He drummed his fingertips against the wheel, searching for a good compromise.

"When we get there, we need to have a conversation about what happened in Willow."

She drew in a sharp breath and held it. For a moment he thought she might refuse. She seemed more comfortable with the idea of sharing her body than telling her secrets. Then she gave a terse nod.

He felt a mixture of relief and unease as he pulled forward. He hoped he hadn't negotiated himself out of her bed. Sleeping with her was a bad idea. It would cross a line he couldn't come back from, but he was willing to take that chance. He'd do anything to touch her again. He could sacrifice his ice road contract. He could even give up on staying numb and protecting his frozen heart.

The pages of her graphic novel had captured his imagination. It read like a window into her desires. Her reaction to last night's orgasm had been telling. She wasn't experienced in receiving pleasure. Giving her a taste of what she'd been missing was an irresistible temptation. If she let him, he'd show her how good it could be.

The ice road was as uneventful as he'd promised. At night, the frozen pathway looked like regular asphalt, tracked with snow. Broad daylight turned it into a sparkling mosaic, crystal blue in some places, foggy gray in others. There were clear sections that resembled glass, and you could see the ocean beneath it.

Ice crackled under his truck's weight as they traveled

toward the bay. It was a disconcerting sound, but normal. The ice shifted and moved with the weight of the vehicle, like a reed that would bend rather than break.

"Why do you have to go this slow?" she asked, gripping her armrests.

"Driving over ice causes waves to form under the surface. The faster you go, the more powerful the wave. When two opposing waves crash together, it creates a surge of energy, like an earthquake."

"So if two trucks go toward each other too fast, the ice cracks?"

"Yes. That's why the route is restricted to a few trucks at a time traveling at low speeds. There's no rush hour. No crashing waves."

"No ice-quakes."

"No ice-quakes," he agreed.

The information didn't seem to calm her nerves. She kept her eyes on the surface, as if searching for signs of trouble. Cam wasn't worried about the ice failing. All his fears and anxieties were focused elsewhere.

Time stretched into infinity on the way to Prudhoe Bay. Although the distance was short, the route was slow and arduous. It took over an hour to reach the construction zone, and another hour to unload the trailer. Then they were on the road again.

The best hotel in the bay was located between the sprawling oil fields and a small airport. It offered private, comfortable rooms for executives and engineers who could afford the expense. Truckers tended to choose the cheapest accommodations, so there were no other rigs in the parking lot. Cam paid at the front desk while Tala waited outside. Then they grabbed dinner in the empty café. He was too nervous to eat much. She nibbled on fruit, which drew his attention to her lips. Her braids were softly mussed, her eyes luminous. She wasn't the most beautiful woman he'd ever seen, but she was close. She was breathtaking.

It dawned on him that he couldn't remember every detail of Jenny's face anymore. When he conjured an image of her, it was from a photograph he'd memorized. She'd had a great smile. She'd laughed often, but he didn't hear the sound in his head. He couldn't picture her hand gestures, or the exact shade of her hair. He no longer felt the crushing pain of loss, either. Just a faint ache.

When they were finished, they went down the hall to his room. It wasn't as cozy as Ann's Cabins, or as rustic as Coldfoot Camp. The walls and carpet were a nondescript beige. A large bed with white sheets and a thick comforter took up about half the space. He set his duffel by the flat-screen TV. She placed her backpack in the only chair.

They stared at each other for a couple of seconds. He cleared his throat, trying to think of a conversation opener.

Then she ambushed him.

She rushed forward and collided with his chest. He made a sound of surprise as she wrapped her arms around his neck and pressed her lips to his. He didn't object to her kiss, though he recognized it as an attempt to silence him. The move worked like a charm. She touched her tongue to his and twined her fingers in his hair. Her mouth was hot and sweet and eager. He responded with an enthusiastic groan. He'd accept a frantic groping by a beautiful woman. His body didn't care about the reasons for her urgency. She was clutching his hair and rubbing against him. He responded predictably.

She kept moving forward until he fell back on the bed. He brought her on top of him, forgetting everything he'd meant to say. She straddled his waist, just as she had the previous night. The thought of repeating that sequence without clothes on exploded in his mind. His hands slid under her shirt, seeking warm skin and soft breasts. She was wearing a bra with lacy cups. His thumbs brushed over her taut nipples, making her gasp.

She stared down at him, lips parted. Tulips in spring. He imagined that mouth on his chest, trailing lower. He shuddered in anticipation. She rocked her hips back and forth, dipping her head to kiss him again. He felt deliciously trapped underneath her, and he liked it, but he needed to take control. If he let her set the pace, this would be over in minutes.

He wanted to undress her slowly and learn every inch of her body. He wanted to show her the consideration her husband hadn't.

Her dead husband.

Oof.

He broke the kiss, panting. He'd forgotten their talk, which really needed to happen now. Waiting until after wouldn't be gentlemanly. It would ruin the trust they'd built. He wished he didn't care, but he did. She'd thawed out his heart, and now he couldn't just bang her.

Very carefully, he lifted her off him and set her aside.

"What's wrong?" she murmured.

"We have to talk."

"Now?"

"Yes. Now."

She glanced at his erection, her gaze half-lidded. "I'd rather do something else."

Smothering a groan, he rose from the bed. "So would

I, but I have to say this first. You know that news report I told you about, with your photo?"

"Yes."

"There's been an update. The police found a dead body in Willow."

She swallowed visibly. "Oh?"

"Foul play is suspected. They ran your picture again without the fake name."

Her face paled as she digested this information.

"You're not just a missing waitress any longer, Tala. You're connected to a murder investigation."

Chapter 15

Tala's breaths quickened and her thoughts spun out of control.

She wasn't sure how to interpret this new development, or Cam's insistence on sharing it. Didn't he want to sleep with her? His body was clearly ready, and he'd responded to her kisses, only to push her aside and share this news.

Sure, she'd had an ulterior motive. She'd jumped on him to avoid this very conversation, but it hadn't worked. She wasn't sexy enough to tempt him. Her chest tightened with shame. Cheeks flaming, she stared at the carpet beneath his feet.

"Was it self-defense?" he asked.

Her gaze rose to his face. "What?"

"Did Duane come after you, and you defended yourself?"

She blinked in confusion. It dawned on her that he

thought she'd been an active participant in the murder. He thought the dead body in Willow belonged to Duane. She rose to her feet and crossed her arms over her chest, frowning. "When did you watch the news?"

"This morning, in Coldfoot."

"You saw it this morning, and you didn't tell me?"

He inclined his head.

"Why did you wait?"

"I didn't know how you'd react."

She gaped at him, incredulous.

"I thought you might freak out," he said, raking a hand through his hair. "I decided not to bring it up until we were alone and in a safe place."

"You waited until you had control of the situation, and I couldn't run away."

"That's not fair."

"Isn't it?"

"I could have waited until tomorrow morning," he said pointedly.

She would have preferred that. "Why didn't you?"

"Because I care about you," he growled. "I actually want to help you even more than I want to sleep with you!"

"Maybe you just want to ruin it," she shot back. "You're afraid to sleep with me. You'd rather avoid intimacy and stay true to your dead wife."

His eyes narrowed in warning. "We're not talking about my dead wife right now. We're talking about your dead husband. I'm not trying to ruin my chances to be with you. I'm trying to keep you safe. I'm thinking about the long term."

"The long term? Really?"

"You don't believe me?"

"You're not ready for that, Cam. You have to let go before you can move on."

"I'll work on it, if you meet me halfway. Tell me what happened in Willow."

"I can't."

"Why not?"

"Because you'll call the police. You were a cop. You know them."

"I don't know any cops in Alaska. I won't call them."

She sat down, twisting her hands in her lap.

"I want to protect you, but I can't do it blindly. I need to understand what you did and who we're up against."

"I didn't do anything."

"Come on, Tala. A dead body turned up the day after you went missing. You have to know something."

"You think I killed him?"

"I wouldn't blame you if you did."

He meant it. She could read the sincerity in his stellar brown eyes, along with strength and kindness. He wasn't perfect, but he was a good man. She wouldn't find a better person to share her secrets with. The prospect of reliving those dark details made her break out in a cold sweat. She took a deep breath, wondering if it was possible to explode from anxiety. "The dead man isn't Duane," she said finally. "I'd kill him in a heartbeat, but I didn't."

"Did he hire someone to track you down?"

"He wouldn't do that."

"Why not?"

"Because he's a loner who enjoys the hunt. He'd come alone. This has nothing to do with him."

Cam frowned at this news. "If it's not Duane, who is it?"

"A customer," she said, moistening her lips. She had to tell him the whole story. "He walked in the diner with two other men, first thing in the morning. They ordered breakfast. A cop came in around the same time. He sat at the counter by himself. There was a weird vibe between them, like they knew each other, but they were pretending not to."

"Were they regulars?"

"I hadn't seen any of them before."

"What kind of cop?"

"State police. He had a white squad car and a dark blue uniform."

"Go on."

She swallowed hard. "The three men ate breakfast and left. Two of them didn't finish their plates, which was a little strange. I took out the trash while they were still in the parking lot. When I heard the gunshot, I crouched down and hid. The cop stood watch while they loaded the body into the trunk of a car."

"What kind of car?"

"An old sedan. I don't know."

"Who did the shooting?"

"The blond one, I'm assuming. He had the gun."

"Was this same guy from the Walmart parking lot?"

"Yes."

"Why did you run?"

"Because the cop told them to clean up the mess and pointed to the diner. They went inside to get me. I waited until the cop left. Then I started running."

"Did they see you?"

"I don't think so, but I left the trash gate open. There was nowhere to hide. They must have figured I ran to the truck stop."

"The cop was the leader?"

"I guess."

"Shooting a guy in a public parking lot isn't a smart move."

Tala nodded in agreement. "The cop seemed angry about it. Maybe it wasn't supposed to go down like that."

"Something was supposed to go down. They were too nervous to eat."

"The victim ate."

"He didn't know what was coming," Cam said, pacing the room. "For whatever reason, they killed him on the spot. Then they had to deal with you. When you ran away from the diner, they knew you'd witnessed the crime. They probably saw my truck pull out of the lot and head north. So they dumped the body and came after us."

The succinct summary gave her chills. "And now I'm doomed."

"You're not doomed," Cam said. "We'll figure this out."

Tala took a few deep breaths to calm herself. He sounded optimistic, in addition to sympathetic. He hadn't questioned her story or acted suspicious. His faith in her was reassuring. She supposed the details weren't as shocking as he'd imagined. "Are you glad I'm not a murderer?"

"I'm kind of disappointed your ex is still alive, actually."

She smiled at his dark joke. His opinion mattered to her, because she cared about him. She was glad he hadn't judged her. He hadn't criticized her for running away. He'd believed her. She felt like a weight had been lifted off her shoulders. She didn't feel alone anymore. Maybe they could figure this out—together.

He stopped pacing and studied her. "I understand why you don't want to call the state police."

"I don't want to call any police."

"What if we went to someone I trust in Seattle?"

"How would I get there?"

"I'll take you."

She stood, shaking her head. Talking to him was one thing, but she wasn't ready to make a decision of this magnitude. Going to Seattle with Cam meant stepping out of her comfort zone. It meant working with law enforcement and trusting a justice system that hadn't served her people well, historically. It meant opening herself up to prosecution for her own crimes. It meant that she had to stop running and hiding. That was a lot.

He waited for her to respond, not pressuring her.

"I'll think about it," she murmured.

"That's what you said when I offered to set you up in a cabin in Fairbanks."

Her pulse kicked up a notch at the reminder. They were still circling around the idea of sleeping together. The comment he'd made earlier about giving her lots of orgasms hung in the air between them. She wanted to return the favor—and not because she felt grateful, or obligated. She wanted to be with him for herself.

His gaze lowered to her lips and lingered there. Her seduction attempt hadn't failed; it had been momentarily interrupted. There was no lack of desire on his part. His intentions hadn't changed.

Her cheeks suffused with heat. "I should take a shower."

"Be my guest."

She grabbed her backpack before heading into the bathroom. It had clean white tiles, a small sink and a new-looking bathtub. She hadn't taken a bath in ages, so she filled the tub for a nice soak. She took the time to wash her hair and shave her legs. He was going to see her naked, up close and personal. She didn't know if they could be together "long term." If tonight was all they had, she wanted it to be special.

When she emerged from the bathroom, fresh-scrubbed and wrapped in towels, Cam was standing by the only window. The hotel wasn't fancy, and the oil fields in the distance didn't improve the bleak landscape, but the sky was spectacular. Northern lights trailed across the starry expanse, misty and ethereal.

His gaze wasn't on the view, however. It was on her flushed face, her damp hair and bare shoulders. He examined the length of her legs, taking the scenic route. His expression was taut with desire, his fists clenched. Male attention had often made her self-conscious, even afraid. Cam's gaze made her feel powerful and deliciously sexy. She wasn't afraid he'd hurt her. Anticipation sizzled across her skin.

He seemed eager to get started, but he didn't pounce on her. "Do you want me to shave?" he asked, touching his beard.

"No. I like you the way you are."

With a slow nod, he brushed by her and disappeared in the bathroom. She applied vanilla-scented moisturizer to her arms and legs while he showered. Then she sat down by the heating vent to comb her hair. He finished his shower and came out wearing only the sweatpants she'd borrowed. She'd left them in the bathroom for him. His hair was tousled and wet. He had a towel draped around his neck.

Her eyes traveled from his handsome face to his well-muscled torso. Last night, his sweatpants had molded to his male parts in a vaguely revealing manner. Tonight, she could see he wasn't wearing a stitch underneath them. His waistband rode low on his flat abdomen. He toweled his hair while she finished combing hers.

"Leave it down," he said, watching her.

She set aside the comb and put her toiletries away. Her heart was racing, her stomach fluttering with excitement. She was already aroused and he hadn't even touched her yet.

He moved to the edge of the bed and sat down. Letting her come to him. She went. She kept her towel clutched in a death grip, but she went. She stood before him, trembling. He rested one hand on the outside of her thigh, just above the knee. His palm was warm and strong.

"We don't have to do this," he said.

"I know."

"We could cuddle instead."

She was too nervous to laugh. He didn't want to cuddle, judging by his arousal. His sweatpants strained at the front.

"I have a condom in my pocket. Good?"

"Good."

"Maybe we should establish some signals."

"For what?"

"If you want me to go slower, you can tap my shoulder."

She touched his shoulder with two fingertips. "Slower."

He nodded. "What about stop?"

She placed her palm on his chest, as if preparing to push him back.

"Got it."

She slid her hand to his biceps and squeezed.

"What's that?"

"Keep going."

His lips curved into a smile. She gave his arm another squeeze. He took the hint and stopped talking. She liked his idea, but she didn't think she'd need the first two signals.

She twined her arms around his neck as he lifted his mouth to hers. He kissed her languidly, not rushing. She parted her lips for his tongue. He tasted like mint, clean and hot. Every stroke of his tongue seemed designed to melt her from the inside out. Her nipples pebbled against the damp towel and heat pulsed between her legs. She twisted her fingers in his hair, moaning. His hands moved under her towel, to her hips, and urged her closer. She straddled his waist eagerly. He reclined on his back with a low groan. His erection surged against her.

They kept kissing, and her towel fell away. She didn't feel embarrassed, even when he paused to look at her. She felt desired on a deeper level. He saw more than a sex object, and that made her want to show him everything. She arched her spine, putting her breasts on full display. He moistened his lips at the sight.

"I fantasized about this last night," he said, his breaths ragged. "I imagined you naked on top of me." His big hands skimmed her sides, settling on her rib cage and framing her breasts. "You're so beautiful."

"Touch me."

He cupped her soft flesh, pushing her breasts together to create a deep V between them. She groaned as he stroked his thumbs over her nipples. He replaced his hands with his mouth, sucking the taut nubs. She squeezed his arm, because it was so good. Her hips moved back and forth, seeking the same friction they'd generated last night.

"Do you ever touch yourself?" he asked.

"Yes," she breathed, shuddering.

"Show me."

He rested his weight on his elbows, giving her space. She moved her hands to her breasts. She used a softer touch than he did, circling her wet nipples with her fingertips. Then she pinched them lightly.

His erection throbbed against her, and his jaw clenched with arousal. He lifted her off his lap abruptly, tossing her on her back. His gaze settled between her legs. Her first instinct was to close them, but he didn't let her. He braced his hands on her inner thighs, spreading her wider. "More."

She blinked at the command. He wanted her to continue the show. Maybe she did need those first two signals. They flashed in her mind like a safety net, available if she chose to use them. There was comfort in knowing she could stop him anytime she wished. But she didn't want to stop. His eyes blazed with spectacular intensity. She longed to please him, and herself. She slid her hands down her belly. Her fingertips skimmed her sensitive flesh. Shivering, she slipped one finger inside.

"That's it," he said.

She added another finger, pumping in and out. She was very slippery and warm. He watched her movements as if mesmerized. When she removed her fingers from her body, he grasped her wrist and brought them to his mouth. He sucked one, then the other. Her stomach quivered at the erotic sight.

He didn't tell her to keep going, but she did. He didn't have to hold her legs open, either. She circled her clitoris, thighs parted wide.

"That's pretty," he said, his throat working. "That's so pretty. I'm going to come, just looking at you."

She moaned, stroking faster.

"Can I taste you?"

He already had, and she hadn't objected. She nodded her permission. A few minutes ago, she might have been too shy to ask for this, or even allow it. Now she was panting for it. When he settled his mouth between her legs, she clutched his hair and held him there. He smiled at her boldness, murmuring his approval. Then he touched his tongue to her. He sucked and licked her clitoris as tenderly as he'd kissed her mouth. He savored her as if she were a delicious treat. She'd never felt anything so heavenly. Pleasure rushed over her in endless waves. They rippled beneath the surface, gaining speed. She watched his tongue, warm and wet and precisely placed. He eased off the pressure, letting her teeter on the edge of orgasm.

She needed another signal, for Finish Me, please!

Animal sounds emerged from her throat and her head thrashed against the blankets. She fisted his hair desperately. He sucked her harder, and that was all it took. The wave broke in a brilliant surge of energy, crashing through her. She sobbed and shuddered and bucked against his mouth in helpless ecstasy. The immense power of it overwhelmed her. She'd never come like that on her own.

When she opened her eyes, he was watching her. She

released his hair, murmuring a vague apology. Languid satisfaction drizzled through her bones. She couldn't move. He seemed amused by her stupefied state. He wiped his smug mouth with one hand and rolled off the bed, heading to the bathroom. He filled a cup at the sink and drank. Then he brought the water to her. She sipped it.

He rejoined her on the bed. Instead of climbing on top of her, he stretched out on his back, tucking his hands behind his head. His erection jutted against the front of his sweatpants, proof of his desire. And yet, he waited patiently for her to recover.

He'd given her the best orgasm of her life, and he wasn't in a hurry to get his. The level of caring and generosity overwhelmed her.

Tears sprang to her eyes and her throat closed up. "I've never..."

He grasped her hand and held it. "I know."

He brought her knuckles toward his lips for a kiss. Tender emotions swelled inside her. She wanted to tell him she loved him, but she was afraid to ruin the moment. She didn't think he was ready for that level of emotion. So she showed how she felt instead.

She climbed on top of him and pressed her lips to his. His tongue penetrated her mouth in bold strokes, hinting at pleasures to come. She moaned at the thought. His erection felt huge and hot against her stomach. With another man, she might have been wary of his size. With Cam, she was excited. She needed him inside her, filling her to the hilt.

She broke the kiss and trailed her mouth down his chest. She touched her lips to his collarbone, his sternum, and lower. He threaded his fingers through her hair, caressing the long strands. She kissed his taut belly. He'd wanted this last night, and he wanted it tonight. His eyes blazed with hunger. But when she tugged at his waistband to release his erection, he groaned and stopped her.

"Next time," he said. "I won't last a second in your mouth."

"I don't care if you last."

"I do."

She reclined on the bed, acquiescent. He removed the condom from his pocket and took off his sweatpants. His arousal bobbed straight up against his belly. She moistened her lips in anticipation. He was long and thick, swollen with veins. It looked painful, and she longed to soothe that taut skin with her tongue.

He rolled the condom over his shaft. She parted her thighs in invitation. His nostrils flared at the sight. He stretched out on top of her, taking her mouth again. She slipped her arms around his neck and kissed him back. His latex-covered length slid along her swollen cleft, sending sparks of sensation all through her body.

He didn't rush to enter her. He feasted on her neck and breasts, flicking his tongue over her stiff nipples. She slid her hand between them and gripped his shaft. He inhaled a sharp breath, his gaze locked on hers. She guided him to her opening. With a low groan, he gave her what she wanted.

Although she was slippery from her orgasm, and eager to accept him, it had been months since she'd accommodated a penis. Never one this large. He pushed inside carefully, inch by inch. His arm muscles trembled from the effort of holding himself in check. When he was about halfway in, he had to thrust forward. She gasped at the intrusion, bracing her palms on his chest. He withdrew immediately.

It took her a moment to realize that she'd given the stop signal. He was breathing heavily, his stomach quivering.

Tears sprang into her eyes again and she kissed him, laughing a little. If she hadn't been sure of her feelings before, she was sure now. She loved him. She squeezed his arm and wrapped her legs around his waist. He seemed hesitant, so she whispered in his ear.

"I want you inside me."

He reentered her slowly, but he didn't need to. The twinge of discomfort she'd felt after his initial penetration was gone. She used her heels to urge him forward. He drove into her slick heat, making them both groan with satisfaction. She kissed him with an open mouth, squeezing his arms and neck and everything she could reach.

He buried himself in her, again and again. They kissed and touched and thrust together, limbs entangled. His mouth had been amazing, but this was even better.

This was pure ecstasy.

He reached between them to stroke her clitoris at regular intervals. His caresses seemed designed to keep her in a pre-orgasmic state. Tension built to an unbearable point inside her. She begged for release, sobbing his name. He licked his fingertips and made her come. She fisted her hands in his hair, screaming and shuddering.

He soothed her with a thorough kiss, still moving on top of her. Seconds later, he reached his own climax. His hips jerked forward in heavy thrusts. He let out a hoarse cry and drove deep inside her.

They collapsed together, totally spent. He didn't withdraw. She didn't want him to. She stroked his damp back for several moments. Finally, he pulled out, holding the condom in place, and went to dispose of it in the bathroom. When he returned, they crawled under the blankets. She cuddled up against him, drowsily satiated. She felt happy and safe and well-loved. Even if it was just physical for him, it wasn't for her.

She fell asleep and dreamed of a better future.

Chapter 16

December 14
70N
-17 degrees

The sun didn't rise until midmorning.

For the first time in years, Cam slept late. He'd stayed up half the night with Tala, reaching for her over and over again. Every time he touched her, she responded with enthusiasm. So he kept doing it. He'd probably *over*-done it, but he hadn't heard any complaints from her side of the bed. Her soft cries of pleasure had urged him on.

He finally got up, spurred by hunger and a niggling feeling of unease. He had no idea what to expect from Tala. They'd discussed the danger she was in and considered their options. He'd offered to take her to Seattle, but she hadn't accepted. He didn't know if they'd get stopped on the way. She was right to be concerned about state police.

He studied her nude form as he pulled on his sweatpants. She was curled up on one side, facing away from him. Her dark hair spilled across the white pillows, black as ink. Her vibrant skin made a pretty contrast with the pale bedding. Every inch of her was smooth and supple. The sheets were tangled low on her hips, exposing her elegant back and the upper half of her buttocks. His blood heated with arousal, despite the marathon of sex they'd engaged in. He entertained the idea of climbing back into bed with her. Kissing his way up her spine, taking her from behind.

A notification from his phone interrupted that fantasy. He retrieved it from his duffel with a frown. He hadn't realized there was cell service in this frigid wasteland.

Deadfoot was a dead zone, unsurprisingly. Prudhoe Bay was more of an industrial hub, so it made sense that they had cell towers. He'd never spent the night here, and he wasn't big on staying connected, anyway.

He rubbed his sleepy eyes and glanced at the screen. Mason. Of course.

Tension gripped him. Feeling guilty on several different levels, he ducked into the bathroom to check his messages. Mason had sent him a series of cryptic texts. When Cam tried to return his call, Mason didn't pick up. Cam silenced his phone and set it aside. He'd try again later. He realized that he hadn't told Tala about his brother or the background check last night. He winced at the thought of having that conversation this morning.

He studied his reflection in the mirror, contemplative. He looked tired but satisfied. Every moment with her was worth it.

Cam used the toilet and washed his hands quickly. Then he opened the door. Tala was still in bed, in the same position he'd left her. Her eyes were closed, her face serene. The heating unit next to her rattled and hummed with constant white noise. His movements hadn't woken her. Relieved, he tucked his phone away and climbed back into bed with her. He'd tell her about Mason…later. She made a sleepy sound when he touched his lips to her bare shoulder. When he slid his hands beneath the blankets to capture her hips, she murmured a faint protest.

"It's getting late," he said.

"You didn't let me sleep last night."

He pushed her hair aside and kissed the nape of her neck. "Mmm."

"Are you trying to keep me in bed or wake me up?"

"Lady's choice."

She groaned and pulled away from him, declining his offer. Which was probably for the best, since they were out of condoms, and he needed to get on the road as soon as possible. He also needed to call Mason.

She rose from the bed, stark naked. His breath caught in his throat at the sight of her. He hadn't seen her in the daylight before. White rays filtered in between the layers of curtains, illuminating her lovely curves. She was all dark hair and soft skin. Angelic, otherworldly…and achingly beautiful.

"Jesus," he said in a hushed voice.

She covered herself with her hands, self-conscious.

His gaze rose to her face. "I can't get enough of you."

She moistened her lips. Her eyes were troubled, as if she had something important to say. But she ducked into the bathroom before he could ask. His stomach growled, reminding him that they'd skipped dinner last night. He rose from the bed and pulled on his clothes. He didn't want to leave the hotel yet. He wanted to stay in this room, with her, forever.

She emerged from the bathroom in a towel, with her hair caught up in a messy bun. He watched her rifle through her backpack, his chest aching. She started getting dressed. Her brow furrowed with discomfort as she tugged on her leggings.

"Are you okay?" Cam asked.

She seemed startled by the question. "I'm fine."

"If I hurt you, I want to know."

"You didn't hurt me."

"You're sore?"

"A little."

Guilt flooded him. He shouldn't have reached for her so many times. "I'm sorry."

"Don't be."

"I went overboard."

"And I loved it."

He groaned, wrapping his arms around her from behind. He pressed his lips to her head. "When you're ready, I'll kiss it better."

She squeezed his forearm. "You're insatiable."

"Only with you," he said, and meant it. He'd shared some special nights with Jenny, but they hadn't been like this. He'd been so young and green. He'd learned how to be a good lover with her, not before her.

Looking back, he hadn't been a perfect husband. He hadn't focused on her needs as much as he should have. He hadn't spoiled her with thoughtful gifts. He hadn't known their time together would be so short.

With Tala, he knew. He wasn't the same person he'd

been before. In some ways, he was less giving. Less accessible. He was colder and harder to reach. But he was also more aware of the casual cruelty of life, and better able to appreciate its shining moments.

Losing Jenny had torn him apart. Being with Tala made him feel whole again.

He was faced with another dilemma about what to tell her, and when. Yesterday he'd been reluctant to bring up contentious topics. Today the stakes were even higher. Last night hadn't been a one-off for him. It had felt like a new beginning.

His stomach growled again. "Are you hungry?" he asked, releasing her.

"Starving."

"We can eat breakfast before we leave."

She nodded her agreement. He put on his boots while she finished getting ready. They brushed their teeth side by side at the bathroom sink. It was quietly domestic, and he relished every second. She'd borrowed one of his flannel shirts to wear with her leggings. She had to roll up the sleeves. The hem reached her upper thighs. The outfit reminded him of the day they'd gone shopping together in Fairbanks. It seemed like weeks ago. They'd spent more consecutive hours together than some couples who'd been dating for months.

"I like you in my shirt," he said gruffly.

"It doesn't fit."

"That's why it's sexy."

She laughed at the claim, as if she didn't believe it. He felt the urge to scoop her up and carry her off to bed again. Instead, he let her slip away. He didn't want to scare her by coming on too strong. She'd escaped an abusive relationship less than a year ago. She'd witnessed a murder and been attacked by strangers. He understood why she'd be wary of entering a new relationship. He was willing to take things slow, but he was also ready to fight for her. She was in danger, and he would protect her by any means necessary.

That was one of the benefits of becoming a rough, tough Alaskan trucker. He could get uncivilized quick. He'd tear apart anyone who hurt her. He'd fall on them like a grizzly ripping into a salmon. Teeth bared, roaring.

But he couldn't let his caveman instincts take over with Tala. She needed space, not domination. She needed the freedom to make her own decisions. He'd been an animal last night. Today he would soften his approach. Instead of tossing her over his shoulder and declaring her his woman, he had to win her gently.

The hotel café was empty except for two other customers, single men at separate tables. One was reading blueprints. The other was focused on his plate, facing the opposite direction. Despite the late hour, there were some buffet-style breakfast items available. Cam piled a plate with turkey sausage and scrambled eggs. Tala had oatmeal and fruit. They both went for seconds. They'd worked up quite an appetite.

"What's the plan for today?" she asked.

He took a sip of coffee. "First the ice road, then the Dalton. I always try to drive straight through on the way back."

"We won't stop in Coldfoot?"

"Not if we don't have to. The return trip is mostly downhill, so it goes faster. When the weather's good, I can get to Fairbanks in fourteen hours or less."

She went quiet, glancing around the café. The airport runway was visible through a single window. He vaguely remembered hearing a few planes take off and land during the night. There was a mounted television in the corner displaying weather updates, but no news. It was a cold, clear day. Perfect for the ice road.

"Have you decided on coming with me to Seattle?" he asked.

She arched a brow. "Is that what you wanted me to focus on last night?"

"No," he admitted, raking a hand through his hair.

"I didn't think at all."

He couldn't prevent the rush of male satisfaction her words inspired in him. He'd given her hours of mindless pleasure. He couldn't wait to do it again.

"I was hoping my performance had convinced you."

She swallowed hard and looked away. He didn't press her for answers. She wasn't ready for a long-term commitment. Maybe he wasn't, either. The physical component was more comfortable for both of them than exposing themselves emotionally.

Wiping his mouth with a napkin, he cleared their empty plates from the table. They returned to the room to gather their belongings. His bag was already packed. She still had some toiletries in the bathroom.

"I'll warm up my rig," he said. "Meet me in ten minutes?"

She nodded, picking up her hairbrush.

He left the hotel and crossed the parking lot in purposeful strides. Despite the brilliant sunshine, the chill in the air stole his breath away. He doubted the high would rise above zero. In the dark afternoon and early night, temps would plummet further. He'd driven in cold shots of –30 and –40 before, so he wasn't worried about freezing. Even if he broke down on the road, he had survival gear. He could handle the weather.

Tala was another story. She might be the death of him.

His phone rang, interrupting his thoughts. It was Mason.

"Hello?" Cam answered.

"Where the hell have you been?"

"On the road. You know I don't get service out here."

"Then how are we talking?"

"I'm in Prudhoe Bay. It's more developed."

"I've been trying to call you all morning."

"I had a late night."

Mason made a huffing sound. "I'll bet."

"Did you mention Tala's name to the local police?"

"Not yet, but the sheriff from Willow keeps leaving me messages. He wants to know why I was so interested in the missing waitress case. I have to return his call."

Cam dragged a hand down his face. "Can you blow him off?"

"No, Cam, I can't. It's regarding a homicide. I can't blow him off just so you can get blown by some hitchhiker."

"She's not a hitchhiker."

"Stowaway. Whatever."

"You've got the wrong idea about her."

"So you weren't drilling her all night?"

"That's none of your business."

"I've seen pictures of her, Cam. I understand the attraction."

"Maybe I just want to help her."

"If that's true, you have more issues than I thought."

"You know who has issues?" Cam shot back. "You have issues. You're so messed up over your divorce that you can't imagine spending time with a woman for any reason but sex. Angry revenge sex."

"Some women like angry revenge sex."

"Yeah? Do they come back for more?"

"They would if I let them."

Cam grunted his skepticism.

"I can't believe you're lecturing me about women. You've been avoiding them for years. You probably don't remember how to get one off."

"I remember."

Mason laughed in approval. "Good for you. Next time find a partner who isn't under investigation."

Cam headed back into the hotel lobby, which was deserted. "Did you call to heckle me or share information?"

"Both," Mason said. There was a sound of rifling papers, as if he'd made notes. "They found a dead guy in Willow with a receipt for Walt's Diner in his pocket. He was a hardcore criminal with an extensive record."

"Local?"

"From Anchorage."

"What else?"

"I talked to a detective in Whitehorse, where your girl was arrested. He had a vivid recollection of her. Everyone who saw her thought she was innocent."

"Why?"

"Pretty young women don't assault police officers very often. Her blood alcohol level was zero. The arresting officer said she seemed more afraid than defiant. She refused to give a statement, other than an apology. When her husband came to bail her out, he was a real asshole. They immediately suspected him."

"Why not drop the charges?"

"They were hoping she'd roll on him."

"Did they follow up?"

"They sent a unit to question the husband after she failed to appear. He claimed he didn't know where she was and declined to file a missing-person report."

"He doesn't want her found."

"Not by them, no."

Cam nodded in agreement. "This matches everything she's told me."

"Did she say he sent some thugs to kidnap her? Because that doesn't add up. Laramie's a scumbag, but he's a low-level scumbag. He doesn't have the money or power to hire professionals."

"She said he wasn't involved."

"Who is?"

Cam didn't answer. "Have you seen the case file?"

"No, I don't have access. But now this sheriff is breathing down my neck because I reached out first. I have to tell him something."

"I need more time," Cam said.

"More time to do what? Screw the truth out of her?"

"I'm trying to convince her to come to Seattle and sit down with you. She doesn't trust the cops here. She's afraid they won't believe her."

"What if I don't believe her?"

"You will."

"Cam, you're my brother, and I love you, but I can't do this. I can't stall for three days while you drive halfway across the country. You're asking me to ignore a direct request from a colleague while you continue to harbor a fugitive. And get laid."

Cam turned to stare out the lobby windows, searching for the words to convince Mason. His brother was a diehard skeptic on a good day. On a bad day, he was an unfeeling bastard. Cam had been numb for years, so he could relate. Accessing his emotions wasn't easy. Communicating them to Mason was damned near impossible. "I don't care about getting laid. I care about her."

"You hardly know her."

"You don't understand how I feel."

"I understand everything," Mason replied. "You couldn't save Jenny, and it broke you. That's why you went to Alaska, to be broken and alone and miserable. Now you have the chance to save someone else, and you're obsessed with playing the hero. It's not about her. It's about you, and your rescue fantasy."

Cam couldn't dispute any of Mason's observations. "Do you ever get tired of being the most cynical person on earth?"

"You brought me into this. You called me first, remember?"

"I wanted your support," Cam growled. "Not your judgment."

"I withheld judgment about your stupid ice-road job."

"No, you didn't."

"What do you expect me to say? I think you're making a huge mistake. You're putting your life in danger for a piece of ass."

"I already told you—"

"I know what you told me, so save it. I'm required to share information with other law enforcement officials unless I have cause to suspect corruption or negligence. I have to give them her name and let them investigate."

Cam cursed under his breath. He returned to the breakfast area and sat down at a quiet table. After a short hesitation, he told Tala's story. It was a betrayal of her trust, but he didn't have a choice. If he didn't share the details, Mason would cooperate with the investigation and they'd never make it to Seattle. He'd get pulled over in Fairbanks, or even sooner.

"You're saying that a statie is part of this crew?" Mason asked.

"Yes."

"Jesus, Cam. You need to file a report."

"With who? The state police are the only agency out here. There's nothing else for hundreds of miles."

"What about tribal police?"

"They don't have jurisdiction on the Dalton."

"You can call the FBI."

"I can, but I doubt Tala will talk to them, and what help could they offer at this point? A field agent wouldn't get here for days. They'll tell us to come to them. Until we get back to Fairbanks, we're on our own."

Mason didn't dispute him.

"If you give Tala's name to the sheriff, there's a chance he'll notify state police to be on the lookout."

"So what? They don't know she's with you."

"Yes, they do." He summarized the incident on Avalanche Alley.

Mason made an incredulous sound. "This girl is even crazier than you are."

"She saved a man's life."

"Is she an adrenaline junkie?"

"I don't think so. She fainted from stress afterward, and she doesn't like the Dalton."

"No one with common sense would like the Dalton."

"Thanks," Cam said, sarcastic.

Mason fell silent for a moment. "I have a bad feeling about this."

"You have feelings?"

"Maybe I can get on a late flight to Fairbanks."

"You don't have to do that."

"Yeah, I do. I'm your brother."

"Okay, but promise me one thing."

"What?"

"Don't tell Mom."

Mason let out a short bark of laughter and hung up. Cam stared at the screen of his phone for several seconds, smiling to himself. He couldn't dismiss Mason's concerns, but the remoteness of Prudhoe Bay added a measure of security. The police presence here was tiny. They'd already met a state trooper on the road, and they'd left a good impression on him. The danger of getting apprehended in this area was very low.

Once they returned to Fairbanks, he'd have to proceed with caution. Cam assumed the killers were still there, waiting for another opportunity to strike. His smile faded at the thought of a second attack on Tala. He couldn't let anything happen to her.

Here in Prudhoe Bay, the main challenge wasn't avoiding the bad guys. It was surviving the elements, and navigating the tricky space he'd entered with Tala. He hadn't convinced her to stay with him.

Tucking his phone away, he left the breakfast area. Tala still hadn't come down, so he went back outside and warmed up his truck. He'd get diesel in Deadhorse. He didn't need chains. His gauges looked good. When Tala didn't arrive to meet him, he started to worry. She didn't take that long to get ready.

He got out of his rig and glanced around. Miles of vast oil fields stretched toward the ocean in the west. On the east side of the hotel, a plane took off from the airport and accelerated with a low roar. The airport was within walking distance.

His blood went cold at the sight. While he'd been on the phone with Mason, he'd kept his back to the lobby. Had she quietly approached, without him realizing? Had she overheard his conversation?

"Son of a bitch," he said, turning off his engine. He rushed toward the front entrance of the hotel and ran down the hallway. He still had the key card, so he opened the door. The room was empty. He searched every inch of the space, frantic. He even looked in the shower stall. She wasn't there.

He couldn't believe it. She was gone.

Chapter 17

Tala found a laundry room with an alternative exit.

She snuck out the door, her heart racing. It opened to the opposite side of the building. Frigid air sucked into her lungs as she started running across the hard-packed snow. The airport was less than a block away, and she moved fast, but the distance seemed endless. She was completely exposed. Her light gray parka and dark leggings made a stark contrast to the blinding white tundra.

The cold soaked through her thin leggings and stung her cheeks. She didn't dare moisten her lips. Her breath huffed out in telltale clouds, like a flag waving over her head. She clutched her fur-lined hood with one hand and kept running.

Running was what she knew. It was her fallback.

What else could she do? She'd seen Cam on the phone in the breakfast room. He'd looked like he was trying to have a private conversation, which triggered her suspicions. Instead of making her presence known, she'd stood hidden in the doorway to listen. She couldn't hear every word, but she'd heard enough. He'd called someone, probably his police officer buddy in Seattle, and told her story.

She hadn't agreed to that. She hadn't even agreed to *go* to Seattle.

He'd betrayed her. She couldn't believe he'd shared her secrets. He'd argued about giving her name to the state police. She didn't trust the person he'd spoken with at all. She didn't know if she trusted Cam anymore.

Which was a real shame. Because she was in love with him.

Her chest seized at the realization, adding to her anguish. Less than twelve hours after she'd bared her soul to him—and her body—he'd broken her heart.

Tears froze on her face as she stumbled forward. She felt conflicted about leaving, despite his shady behavior. He'd given her the best night of her life. He'd been sweet and caring in the morning. His desire for her wasn't in question, and his feelings seemed sincere. Even so, he hadn't said a word about calling his contact. He hadn't consulted her.

He'd also searched through her belongings.

While she was packing up, she'd noticed some rearranged items in her backpack. Her book was in the inside pocket with the stolen ID. She was already upset about that invasion of privacy when she'd caught him on the phone.

She didn't look back as she raced toward the airport. She half expected him to stop her, or to call out her name. He must not have noticed her escape, because he didn't come after her. There was a twisted sort of irony in her actions. She was fleeing the hotel the same way she'd fled the diner. One hosted a love scene; the other, a murder scene.

She arrived, breathless, in the terminal. She didn't have any money for airfare. Even if she did, she was afraid to use the ID. She'd headed this direction on impulse. Instead of approaching a kiosk for ticket information, she sat down in an empty seat and bent forward with her head in her hands.

She had to think. Think.

She didn't feel safe in Prudhoe Bay. Cam had been right about the extreme isolation of the place. If she hadn't given the police her real name for the accident report, she might have been able to lay low here. That was no longer an option.

She glanced around the airport terminal warily. She could hide in the bathroom if Cam showed up. Her stomach clenched at the thought. She'd run away from the only person who wanted to help her.

Damn it.

She wished she wasn't in love with him. She wished he hadn't been so good to her. It was incredibly difficult to accept this turn of events. How could he spend the night in her arms, making her die with pleasure, and then go behind her back in the morning?

Maybe he'd been shady all along. Maybe he wasn't who he seemed. All she knew for sure was that he'd hurt her. When a man hurt her, she ran.

It occurred to her that he might not come looking for her. She'd mentioned staying in Prudhoe Bay to work. She'd left without saying goodbye. That was a big deal to him. Frowning, she rifled through the zippered pocket of her backpack. She had several quarters, and a business card with Cam's phone number on it.

She stood abruptly, taking a deep breath. There was a pay phone in the corner. She walked toward it and dialed a number. Not Cam's. Her mother's. After she inserted the required amount of change, the call went through.

"Hello?"

"Hi, Mom. It's me."

"Tala?"

"Yes."

"You haven't called in so long! I was getting worried."

Tala swallowed back a surge of guilt. Her mother sounded surprised and excited, not disapproving. She held the receiver in a tight grip, unsure what to say.

"How are you?"

"I'm okay," she hedged.

"How's Duane?"

"Uh… I don't know. I left him six months ago."

Her mother gasped. "Why?"

"He hit me."

"Oh, no," she said, as if it pained her to imagine. She repeated the phrase several times. Then, with resolve: "I'm going to send Clark."

"No, Mom."

"I'll send Clark *and* Bear."

Tears sprang into Tala's eyes at her mother's protective attitude. Tala didn't want anyone to beat up Duane on her behalf, but she appreciated the offer. "That's not a good idea."

"We'll all come. Where are you?"

"I'm in Alaska. Prudhoe Bay."

"What are you doing in Alaska?"

"It's a long story."

"Do you need anything? How can I help, *nitânis*?"

The term of endearment brought tears from her eyes. "I just wanted to hear your voice."

"It's nice to hear yours."

"I was wondering…did Dad ever mistreat you?"

"He never laid a hand on me. We just argued a lot."

"About what?"

"Oh, many things. We were so young when we got married. I thought it would be romantic to live in the wilderness with him. Instead I was cold and lonely and bored. I didn't have any friends. The other women hated me."

"Why?"

"Because they all wanted your father! He was the best-looking man in Yellowknife, and I was an outsider. A silly city girl."

"You weren't ever happy?"

"I was happy after you were born. I loved you so much, but I didn't love him. I couldn't forgive him for keeping you."

"What do you mean?"

"It was against tribal law for me to take you away from Yellowknife without his permission, and he wouldn't give it. I couldn't get full custody. Equal custody would have interrupted your schooling. You wanted to stay with him, so I had to let you go."

"I didn't know."

"You were little."

She wondered why her mother hadn't told her this before. Maybe, as a rebellious teenager, she wouldn't have listened. "I'm sorry."

"Don't be. It was better for you to spend those years with him. He was taken too soon. Now he's gone, but I am here. You can come to Billings. There will always be a place in my home for you."

Tala's throat closed up with emotion. "Okay."

"You'll come?"

She blinked the tears from her eyes. It felt good to know her mother wanted her around. If Tala needed to go to Montana, she could. This knowledge helped soothe her overwrought feelings about Cam.

"Right now, I'm waiting for a ride to Fairbanks. I'll call you after I get there. We can plan a visit."

"Be careful, *nitânis*."

She promised she would and said goodbye. She hadn't expected her mother to be so sympathetic. She'd anticipated doubt and criticism. Living with Duane had brainwashed her into assuming the worst of people.

Which brought her back to Cam. She had to give him a chance to explain. He was her only way out of this place, and she needed to face her emotions. She wiped the tears from her cheeks, noticing a broad-shouldered figure at the entrance. He opened the door and located her in seconds. He looked relieved, and more than a little bewildered. She waited, heart pounding, as he strode toward her.

She crossed her arms over her chest. Her hands were shaking. She didn't like confrontations, but they needed to hash this out. She deserved some answers, and he deserved an explanation.

"Why did you run?" he asked.

"I heard you on the phone."

He didn't make any excuses, or offer any denials. "You could've asked me about it instead of taking off. What were you going to do, stow away on a plane?"

Her cheeks heated at his sarcasm. "I called my mother."

"What did she say?"

"She said I could come to Montana."

"Is that what you want?"

She gave a stiff shrug.

"I can't believe you left without saying goodbye."

"I can't believe you talked to the police without my consent!"

"I was talking to my brother."

"Your brother?"

"He's a detective in Seattle."

She sat on the bench again, her knees weak.

He took the space next to her. "I should have told you about him. I was wrong."

She gaped at him, stunned by the admission. He'd actually said he was wrong.

"I called him after you were attacked in Fairbanks. You begged me not to call the police, so I called him." He raked a hand through his hair, seeming chagrined. "I asked him to run a background check on you."

The breath sucked out of her lungs. "You didn't."

"I was worried about you."

Tala struggled out of her parka, flushing. She remembered his pointed questions in the weight room. He'd interrogated her just like a cop. "You knew about my record and warrants. You knew before I told you."

He inclined his head.

"What else do you know?"

"I know the dead guy they found in Willow had a receipt for Walt's Diner in his pocket. He was a career criminal."

"Do they think I killed him?"

"I'm pretty sure you're not a suspect. You left your

purse at the scene. That indicates a terrified witness, not a cold-blooded killer."

She fell silent, trying to process the disturbing news.

"Look, I asked Mason not to give your name to the police. He needed a reason. That's why I had to tell him everything this morning." His steady gaze met hers. "It started off innocent, and sort of snowballed."

She hugged her parka to her chest. He'd lied to her, or at least misrepresented the truth. He'd promised not to call the police, but he'd called his brother, a detective. If she'd been thinking clearly, she would have anticipated this. Cam was a former cop, after all. She should have left him in Coldfoot after he'd admitted to his law enforcement background. She could have hitched a ride back to Fairbanks with that tour group. Instead, she'd stayed with him and let her hormones take over.

"I'm sorry," he said quietly.

"You took my choices away, just like Duane used to. You decided what was best for me, and now I'm trapped."

His jaw clenched with anger. "That's not fair."

"Isn't it?"

"No, it isn't. I'm not Duane. I'll *never* be like Duane."

"Did you search through my things?"

He flinched at the accusation. "Not really."

"Not really?"

"I saw the ID you stole, if that's what you mean."

"You invaded my privacy."

"You robbed someone at my place of work!"

She flushed with guilt. She shouldn't have done that, but two wrongs didn't make a right. She still felt betrayed by him.

"I'm not holding you against your will," Cam said,

lowering his voice. "You don't have to run away from me like you ran away from Duane. You want to go to Montana, go to Montana. Maybe you'll be safe there."

She heard the warning in his "maybe." He was trying to suggest the opposite, that she wouldn't be safe in Montana. She might be putting her family at risk by hiding there. It was a chilling realization. "You think I'll be safe if I talk to the police, but they won't protect me. They'll send me back to Canada and I'll go to prison."

"You won't go to prison. That's for longer sentences. If anything, you'll go to jail."

She leapt to her feet. "You're not helping, Cam."

He rose with her, grasping her arm. "All you have to do is tell the truth about what happened at the rally. They'll probably dismiss the charges against you and arrest Duane. Then he'll go to jail, where he belongs."

She pulled away from him in frustration. He didn't understand how difficult it would be for her to point the finger at Duane. The last time she saw her husband, he'd beaten her unconscious. It wasn't fair to ask her to make a statement that would infuriate him. Or one that would put her in the crosshairs of hardcore criminals, for that matter. She didn't have any faith in the system. When there were men like Duane in uniform, it was hard to believe in justice.

"You make it sound so easy," she said. "All I have to do is be honest and everything will work out."

"It's better than running forever."

"When are *you* going to stop running?"

His eyes darkened. "What do you mean?"

She gestured at the bleak landscape, visible through the terminal windows. "You don't belong here. You're not an Alaskan recluse, or a trucker. You came to escape, just like I did." She paused, studying him. "Or maybe you came to die."

"That's ridiculous. I don't want to die."

"Then why did you choose this job, above all others? Why this road?"

"It's not that dangerous."

She laughed harshly. "You're in denial. You should be saving lives at accident scenes or whatever you used to do. Instead you're courting death in hopes of getting reunited with your precious Jenny."

"I don't want to reunite with Jenny," he growled, closing the distance between them. "I want to be with you."

"For how long?"

His eyes darkened at the question. He fell silent, unable to answer.

She wasn't surprised by his reluctance to make promises. He was as gun-shy about relationships as she was. "Even if I clear my name and the police catch the killers, I'm still married. I'll have to go back to Canada and take care of my legal issues."

"Can we focus on the next few days?" he asked. "Let's make it to Seattle first."

She turned away from him, her heart aching. She couldn't imagine a happy ending for them. He was a former-cop-turned-extreme-driver. He liked her right now because they were on an adventure. He liked to chase danger, even if he didn't admit it. When the ice melted and the excitement died down, he'd lose interest.

"At the very least, come with me to Fairbanks," Cam said. "You can't stay here."

She couldn't argue with him anymore, so she stared out the terminal window. The oil refineries in the distance puffed out chutes of smoke, and snow flurries danced through the air like poisoned ashes. Polluted before they even hit the ground.

Cam wrapped his arms around her and pressed his lips to her hair. His embrace felt warm and reassuring. He was hard and strong and unyielding. She wanted to trust him. She wanted to forget her troubles, and escape into a fantasy in which love conquered all.

"I'll keep you safe," he said against her ear. "I promise."

She leaned into his chest, eyes closed.

"If you stop running, I'll stop with you. I'll fight for you, if you let me."

"Okay," she murmured, giving in. She couldn't resist him. She'd play along, for now. She'd hope for the best but prepare for the worst. She'd stay alert.

And if she had to run again—she'd run.

Chapter 18

They were back on the road by noon.

Storm clouds gathered across the sky, intersected with clear spots of blue. Brilliant sunshine shone through the patches, illuminating the slabs of ice beneath the spinning wheels. The road appeared to have been made from shards of crystals, crosshatched into a giant puzzle on top of a gently sloshing ocean. Later in the season the top layer would turn to slush.

Tala didn't speak while they were on the ice. She stared out the window, her face pale. Cam couldn't blame her. It was an unsettling experience.

He filled his gas tank in Deadhorse before they moved on. He didn't check in with the office for fear of being stopped and questioned about yesterday's accident. The possibility of getting pulled over by a supervisor truck or patrol vehicle loomed. There was nothing he could do to prevent it, so he focused on other things. His rig, the road, the weather, the woman beside him.

The woman he wanted, who didn't trust him.

He knew he'd screwed up this morning. He should have told her he'd been talking to Mason. He'd taken a gamble and lost. He'd apologized for the mistake, and she'd seemed willing to forgive him, but he wasn't convinced she would cooperate with the police. She might run away at the first opportunity.

He considered some solutions to her legal problems. He believed she'd be exonerated if she told the truth about Duane and the murder in Willow. She didn't have to stay in Canada. He had an apartment in Anchorage. She could live with him.

Cam stayed quiet about this option. It was too much, too soon. She'd rushed into a bad situation with Duane. She wouldn't be eager to tie herself down again, and they hadn't known each other long enough to take that plunge. Even so, the idea of sleeping next to her every night appealed to him. He wanted to spend as much time with her as possible. He wasn't going to change his mind.

For the rest of the day, they avoided contentious topics. He didn't press her about going to Seattle, or talking to his brother. He considered telling her that Mason was coming to meet him in Fairbanks, but decided not to worry her. They'd cross that bridge when they came to it. He was afraid of setting her off again.

Most of the hours passed in silence. She curled up in the berth and went to sleep. He drank coffee to stay awake. Twilight faded into endless night. He drove on and on, into the snow-laced dark. They passed Nightmare Corner and Avalanche Alley. Before he knew it, they were in Coldfoot. He'd made excellent time, and he didn't want to stop to rest. The other truckers would grill him about the rescue, and Tala. He decided to blow through camp and continue to Fairbanks.

"Wait," Tala said, before he passed by. "I have to return the ID."

"To who?"

"The front office. I can say I found it in the parking lot."

Cam had a better idea. "I'll put it in the mailbox."

She shrugged, so he went ahead and took care of it for her. They didn't stay in Coldfoot long. After a light dinner of soup and crackers, they were on the road again. When they were about two hours from Fairbanks, he remembered something important.

"My gun," he said.

"What gun?"

"It's in a locked box under the bed." He found the key and handed it to her. "We should keep it close."

"You think we'll need it?"

"I doubt it. I just want to have it within reach before we get to Fairbanks." He couldn't protect her without a weapon. The killers were armed. They might still be in the area, waiting for his truck to cruise down the main drag.

"Is it loaded?"

"No."

She retrieved the metal box and brought it up front. After fitting the key into the lock, she opened the lid. His 9 mm handgun was inside, under a pile of photos he hadn't looked at in years. The first was of Jenny frolicking at the beach in California. She was dripping wet and smiling in a skimpy striped bikini.

"Sorry," he said gruffly. "I forgot those photos were in there."

"Did you stare at these and stroke your gun?"

"Pretty much."

Her face revealed a mixture of sympathy and horror. Cam realized she'd been using "gun" in the literal sense.

"I mean, no," he said, flushing. "The gun is for protection only. I thought you were talking about…something else."

"Why are the pictures in here?"

"I locked them up so I wouldn't look at them anymore. I was spending too much time wallowing in grief."

She removed the gun and the clip, leaving the photos in the box without browsing through them. He was relieved. They weren't all sexy pics, but there were a couple of nudes mixed in with holiday photos and vacation shots. An embarrassing assortment. She studied the gun carefully before loading it.

"You know how to use that?" he asked.

"I've handled a 9 mm before. Where should I put it?"

"Here," he said, indicating the pocket next to his seat.

"I'll leave the safety on."

He grunted his approval. She tucked the gun away, where they could both access it easily. Making preparations for a shootout didn't brighten the mood in the cab. Or maybe it was the photos that caused tension. Either way, Tala stayed quiet, her face pensive. Cam didn't turn on the radio to break the silence. He let it echo between them. He wished he was better at making conversation. He wanted to know more about Tala. He wanted to hear her childhood stories. To share her hopes and dreams.

"What would you do for a living, if you could do anything?" he asked finally.

"Anything?"

"Anything," he repeated.

"I'd like to finish school first. I need at least another year to graduate."

"You're getting a degree in life science?"

"Earth science."

"Then what?"

"I'm not sure. Something outdoors. Maybe a wildlife biologist, or park warden."

"What's a park warden?"

"I believe you call them 'park rangers' in the US."

He arched a brow. "Are you aware that park rangers are law enforcement officers?"

"Yes," she said ruefully.

He didn't point out that she couldn't apply for that kind of job with a criminal record. She probably already knew.

"Don't judge me, Cam. You're a trucker with a sociology degree."

"Have you thought about search and rescue?"

"No."

"You'd be great at it."

"Why don't *you* do search and rescue?"

"We could do it together."

"Is that your fantasy?"

He mulled it over. "My fantasy is you and me in a cozy cabin with a fireplace. I'll chop some wood. You can braid your hair."

She smiled, a little sadly. "Sounds nice."

"What's your fantasy?"

"Freedom."

He couldn't argue with a fantasy. He wanted to give her whatever she needed, including freedom. Maybe she'd come back to him if he let her go. The idea disturbed him too much to contemplate, so he focused on the road. She took out her book, flipping sleek pages. He wondered how many of the images were sexual.

"I didn't realize graphic novels were so graphic," he commented.

Her lips parted in surprise. "You looked at it."

"I got a few ideas from the illustrations."

"You did not," she said, rolling her eyes.

He conceded her point. He hadn't needed any extra inspiration to give her pleasure. "Well, I enjoyed the art."

She closed the book abruptly. Her cheeks were flushed, as if she was picturing a similar scene from last night. He'd spent some quality time with his mouth between her legs—and he'd relished every second. If she left him, he hoped she'd think of that memory often. He could live with being the best she'd ever had. But he'd rather live with *her*.

"Why did you search my bag?"

"I didn't mean to."

"That's hard to believe."

"The book fell out. I glanced at a few pages and put it back inside."

"Then you saw the ID."

"Then I saw the ID," he confirmed. He didn't feel the need to apologize, because it had been an accident. But he tried to consider her perspective and respect her feelings. "Did Duane snoop through your things?"

"Yes. He always hid my purse so I couldn't leave."

"I wouldn't do that."

Her gaze searched his, as if gauging his sincerity.

"I wanted to look at the book, just to see what you were reading. I didn't mean to invade your privacy."

She nodded her acceptance. "I shouldn't have stolen the ID."

"Nobody's perfect."

"Most people aren't criminals."

"I like you the way you are."

Tears filled her eyes at the comment. "You said that before."

"It's still true."

"I like you the way you are, too," she said softly. "I'll never forget you, Cam."

His throat tightened with emotion. He couldn't deny his feelings any longer. He was in love with her. Head over heels in love with her.

And she was going to run away again, because she didn't believe they could be together. Because she was a petty criminal, and he was a former cop. Because the world was a terrible place sometimes. Because happy endings didn't happen every day.

He considered pulling over to talk, but they were on a downhill curve, and there was a bridge coming up. After he crossed it, he could find a quiet spot to park. He'd tell her he loved her and convince her to stay. If she wouldn't listen to his words, he'd show her with his hands. He would kiss her and touch her until she believed him. He had it all planned out.

Unfortunately, his plans were thwarted.

As he rounded the corner, shifting into a lower gear, he spotted a major problem. Someone had parked a white Chevy Suburban at an angle near the end of the bridge. It was obstructing both lanes, headlights beaming across the railing.

There was no room to maneuver. He couldn't get around the vehicle. He'd have to slow to a stop in the middle of the bridge. He engaged his jakes, cursing under his breath. That was when he noticed another vehicle parked on the side of the road beyond the bridge, barely visible in the grainy dark. It was a black SUV, lying in wait.

Fear spiked through him.

"This is an ambush," Tala said, her eyes wide. She was savvy enough to recognize the danger.

"If I stop, they'll shoot us."

She reached for the gun.

"Not yet," he said, easing off the jakes. "Get your head down and brace for impact."

With a muffled shriek, she bent forward and covered her head. He wasn't eager to get in a shootout against two or three armed men. They were already posted up. They could have a cadre of weapons, including long-range rifles. His 9 mm was no match for that kind of firepower, but his rig could do plenty of damage. The killers probably weren't expecting him to play demolition derby. They'd underestimated his survival instincts.

Instead of slowing down, he increased his speed, barreling toward the Suburban. Seconds from impact, a man jumped out of the vehicle and ran for cover. Cam wished he hadn't escaped, but the minor detail didn't change his trajectory. He smashed head-on into the side of the truck. The Ice Storm crushed the Suburban with brutal force. It was a jarring crash.

Tala screamed, cowering lower.

Cam anticipated some steering failures and other complications. He'd worried about losing control and jackknifing over the side of the bridge, but that didn't happen. His rig took the hit like a champ. There were no flames obscuring his view. The Suburban was stuck to his grill, bent and twisted and smoking.

He pressed on the gas and kept going. He hadn't done anything to even up the odds yet, except refuse to be a sitting duck. He needed to wreak some more havoc, or the ambush would succeed and they would die. As soon as he cleared the bridge, he veered to the right, where the other SUV was parked.

"Stay down," he said to Tala.

There were two men inside the second vehicle, and they didn't jump to safety like their quick-thinking friend. Maybe they didn't realize he was coming for them next. Maybe they wanted to stand their ground and shoot. Whatever. Bring it on.

He bore down on them like a freight train, unwavering. Bullets peppered the windshield, making Tala shriek again. Pain exploded in his left shoulder, so he knew he'd been hit.

Gritting his teeth, he wrenched the wheel toward the SUV and ducked his head. The Suburban stuck to his grill smashed into the SUV.

This time, there was fire. Not just bullets, but an exploding gas tank. The Suburban went up in flames, and his rig didn't fare much better. It jackknifed and rolled into a ditch, scraping across the frozen earth. He got slammed around inside the cab, despite his safety belt. Metal screeched and buckled. His shoulder burned and his leg twisted underneath him. Tala was still screaming, or maybe it was him.

His head cracked into the side window, and then there was nothing. No sound, no pain, no fire, no light.

Chapter 19

Tala couldn't believe what was happening.

She'd been worried about an ambush in Fairbanks, which was still a hundred miles away. It hadn't occurred to her that the killers would attack them on the Dalton. Cam had insisted that the road was too dangerous for regular vehicles, and she'd seen the evidence with her own eyes. She hadn't expected an early strike.

The killers had executed their plan with military precision and chilling foresight. They'd known when the Ice Storm was coming. They couldn't have set up on the bridge otherwise. She realized that as she braced for impact.

The first crash had been blindly terrifying. She wanted to lift her head to look, but Cam had shouted at her to stay down. Bullets peppered the front of the rig, and chaos erupted. They'd hit a second target. A gas tank exploded. That stupid metal box flew across the cab, slamming into Tala's elbow. Pictures of Cam's beautiful dead wife spilled out everywhere. For a surreal moment, they were suspended in the air. Frozen in time.

Then the action kicked into fast-forward. Flames and snow blurred together. She was jostled this way and that. Glass shattered inward, along with a cold blast of air. The world pitched sideways and came to a shuddering stop. Her seat belt jerked and held.

She glanced around woozily, trying to orient herself. The smell of smoke and gasoline burned her nostrils. An engine idled high, like a racecar before takeoff.

It was a bad wreck, and they were trapped inside it. The semi had rolled over onto the driver's side. Her seat belt held her in place, sort of dangling above Cam. He was slumped behind the wheel, motionless.

"Cam," she cried, grasping his shoulder. "Cam!"

He moaned in response. He was alive!

She reached out to turn off the engine. Panic gripped her in an icy fist. The front windshield was broken. Snow and cold seeped in, but her main concern was fire. They were dangerously close to two burning vehicles. And what about the inhabitants? She had no idea where the killers were. They could be inside the flaming wreckage, or roaming free. She couldn't see through the smoke. She couldn't breathe, couldn't think.

"Radio," Cam mumbled.

She grabbed the CB and pressed the button. "There's been an accident," she said in a shaky voice. "It's serious. We're on the Dalton Highway, near the bridge. I need an ambulance and police. Please hurry!"

She didn't listen for a response. She hung up the receiver and released her seat belt, promptly falling against Cam. He grunted in pain as she jostled him.

"Sorry," she said. "I have to get you out."

He didn't argue. She took off his seat belt and considered her options. He was a big, heavy man. She couldn't drag him far. The driver's-side door was blocked. The most expedient route was through the front window.

Decision made, she attempted to pull him toward her. He sucked in a sharp breath when she gripped his right arm. His shirt was torn and damp. She could smell the blood on him. Her stomach dropped.

"You're shot."

He seemed half-conscious, and not fully aware. His eyes drifted shut.

"Stay with me, Cam. Are you injured anywhere else?"

"Head...ankle."

"Maybe I shouldn't move you."

He wrenched his eyes open. "You have to."

She didn't want to cause him pain. She also didn't want them to burn to death, or get shot like fish in a barrel. She nodded her agreement. "This will hurt."

He gritted his teeth in preparation.

She put her arms around his waist and heaved. He helped her as much as he could. When she freed him from the cramped space behind the wheel, it was easier to maneuver. She crawled through the safety glass and over the hood, pulling him along. He used his good leg to push off. Then they were both clear, tumbling into the bitter cold.

She dragged him a few feet away from the wreckage. He collapsed there, his breaths ragged from exertion. She didn't think he could walk. The concussion was probably more of a factor than his busted ankle. The blood on his shoulder appeared minimal. She didn't see any other wounds, but he could have internal injuries.

Heart racing, she inspected their surroundings. It was a nightmarish scene. There were two bodies inside the black SUV. The Suburban looked empty. Maybe there was another corpse inside, buried under smoke and twisted metal.

"One got away," Cam rasped.

Tala swallowed hard. There was a killer on the loose, lurking in the shadows. She glanced around warily, unable to locate the threat. She felt the urge to flee, as always, but she couldn't take Cam with her.

"Go," he told her. "Run."

She ignored the order. She wasn't going anywhere. Her instinct to run couldn't compete with her love for him. She wouldn't leave him to die. He might die anyway, because of the cold. It was below zero, and he was injured, lying in the snow. They weren't even wearing jackets. They had no protection from the elements, and the flames from the wreck didn't warm them. Hypothermia would set in quickly—if the killers didn't finish them off first.

Cam didn't say anything else. Maybe he'd passed out again.

Running wasn't an option. She had to stand her ground and fight, for both of them.

She needed Cam's gun. In the chaos, she'd forgotten to grab it. Getting out of the truck had been her only focus. She studied the wreckage, noting that the fire had died down. Flames were no longer licking at the front of the rig. She didn't think it would explode if she went back inside. Either way, she had to risk it. She needed the gun and their jackets, too. She'd get both, save Cam and shoot whatever moved in the burning dark.

She didn't tell him about her plan. He wasn't in any position to object. She crawled across the hood with caution. Safety glass clung to her clothes and bit into her palms as she climbed into the cab. The gun was still in the pocket beside the driver's seat. She emptied her backpack and shoved it inside.

Her parka was easy to locate. She tossed it out the front window and searched for his. It was wedged against the driver's side door, caught on a piece of twisted metal. She yanked it free, panting, and threw it on the hood. Then she grabbed the sleeping bag from the berth.

When she returned to the front of the cab, the firelight shifted. Someone was standing outside, blocking the glow of the flames. He was a dark shadow, faceless and menacing. Her panicked mind supplied a picture of Duane. It was a nasty illusion, but reality was worse. The man tilted his head to the side to reveal his true features. It was the blond man from the diner. The rude roughneck with the gun.

"Look who we have here," he said, peering inside the cab. "It's that pretty little waitress from Willow."

Tala stared at him in horror. She clutched the sleeping bag to her chest. The heavy material would protect her from the elements, but it wouldn't stop a bullet. The gun she needed was in her backpack, out of reach.

He gestured to the burning vehicles behind him. "You did me a favor with those two. Now come on out and do me another."

She didn't move.

"If you cooperate, I'll make it quick. No suffering."

"Lay a hand on me and you'll be the one suffering."

He drew a pistol from his coat pocket. Metal glinted in the firelight, reflecting the menace in his eyes. She was about to lunge for her backpack when a flash of motion startled them both. Someone tackled the killer in a clumsy rush.

It was Cam.

She screamed in protest as Cam took the other man to the ground. He was too weak to win this fight. She couldn't believe he'd gotten up on his own. He was going to get shot again! He was going to die for her. She couldn't let that happen. She grabbed the gun from the backpack, her heart pounding with adrenaline.

Cam had risked his life for her, despite his injuries. He might not be able to move beyond the first strike—but that was all she needed. He'd given her an opening to save them both. She scrambled across the hood. Cam and his opponent were grappling in the snow. She disengaged the safety with shaking hands. The killer shoved Cam backward and raised his weapon.

Cam sprawled there, motionless.

A gun went off, but it wasn't the killer's. It was the one in Tala's hand. She squeezed the trigger twice in rapid succession. Two bullets struck her target in the chest. He slumped forward, dropping his weapon in the snow. Blood bubbled from his lips. He drew in a last breath and went completely still.

Tala inched forward, ready to fire again if he so much as twitched. He didn't. He wasn't breathing. She picked up the loose weapon and secured it in her backpack. Then she knelt by Cam's prone form. Flickering light illuminated his face. She hoped they weren't in danger from another explosion. Most of the flames had dissipated, and she didn't smell gasoline anymore.

"Did you get him?" he asked, eyes closed.

"I got him."

He grunted his approval. She retrieved both parkas, her throat tight. He was already shivering, his brow furrowed with pain. She couldn't imagine how he'd managed to stand, let alone launch an attack. Blinking the tears away, she inspected his shoulder. It appeared to have been grazed by a bullet. A small amount of blood seeped from the wound.

"Can you sit up? I need to put on your jacket."

With her help, he struggled into a sitting position. She eased him into his parka carefully, zipping up the front, before he reclined again. He had a bump on his temple. She scooped up a bit of snow and applied it to the tender spot.

"I had something to tell you," he said, wincing. "Before the crash."

"Shh," she said. "Rest now."

"It was important."

"We're alive. That's the most important thing."

He closed his eyes, his breaths labored. "I thought… he was going to kill you."

She donned her own parka, shivering. She was lucky Cam had intervened. If he hadn't, she wouldn't be here. Instead of dwelling on the close call, she grabbed the sleeping bag and covered them both. It was incredibly macabre to cuddle next to a dead man, with two other corpses burning in the background. She considered moving, but jostling Cam might exacerbate his head injury. Another trucker would come along soon.

"Why didn't you run?" Cam asked.

She reached out to hold his hand. "I couldn't leave you."

Two truckers arrived a few minutes later. Then the police came, followed by a fire truck and an ambulance. They didn't let her ride to Fairbanks with Cam. She watched as the EMTs loaded him into an ambulance. She'd barely stepped away before she was relegated to the backseat of squad car. Although she wasn't cuffed, she felt like a criminal. She wasn't given any updates about Cam's condition on the way. As soon as they arrived at the station, she was taken to an interview room, where she recounted the pertinent events in vivid detail.

Her statements were honest; there was no benefit in lying now. She'd been caught at the scene of the crime. If she didn't talk, she'd look guilty.

Guilti*er.*

She told the truth about Duane, because her story didn't make sense otherwise. He was the reason she'd come to Alaska to hide. He was the reason for her arrest in Canada, and for her failure to appear in court.

She also told the truth about the two IDs she'd stolen, in the interest of full disclosure. She found out that she wouldn't be extradited to Canada because the charges against her weren't serious enough. Also, they confirmed she wasn't technically a foreign national. Full-blooded First Nations members were allowed entry from Canada to the US and vice versa. It was similar to dual citizenship. She had the protection of both countries. She was supposed to return to Canada of her own volition to take care of her warrants, but no one would be tracking her down with a dragnet.

Several hours passed in the interrogation room. Two detectives asked her a thousand questions, many of which were repetitive. She wasn't sure if they were trying to trip her up, or just being thorough. Either way, it was exhausting.

She received medical treatment for her minor cuts and scrapes. She was photographed, fingerprinted and given a hot meal. She was left alone to eat. She wanted to see Cam. They wouldn't even tell her where he was or how he was doing. He might be in surgery, or in pain. Her eyes welled with tears of anxiety.

She pushed aside the tray and buried her head in her arms. Moments later, a third detective appeared. He was younger and better-looking than the others. He had an athletic build and dark, close-cropped hair. His rumpled suit fit him well.

"Can I make a phone call?" she asked.

"I'd like to ask you a few questions first."

She wiped the tears from her cheeks, nodding her permission.

He took the seat across from her. His gaze moved over her in a measured sweep. She couldn't tell if he was assessing her feminine attributes or judging her mental state. He had a pretty good poker face. A good face in general, with strong features. There was something familiar about them.

"You're Cam's brother," she said.

"And you're his damsel in distress."

She didn't argue with the description, though it rankled. "Is he okay?"

Cam's brother passed her a card with his name on it. Mason Hughes, Seattle PD. "He has a concussion and a broken foot. The bullet wound isn't serious."

"He's conscious?"

Mason nodded. "He says you saved his life."

"He saved mine. More than once."

"He's a regular Boy Scout, isn't he?"

Tala didn't know how to respond to that. Mason's flat expression made her nervous. "When can I see him?"

"They gave him some pain meds. He'll be out for hours."

"I want to be there when he wakes up."

Mason studied her with interest. "My brother is infatuated with you. I'm sure he feels even closer to you now that you've braved death together, but I'm concerned about his judgment. Since he met you, he's been behaving erratically."

She bristled at the accusation. "Since he met me, or since he lost his wife?"

"He's had a hard time dealing with his grief," Mason acknowledged. "I'm glad you came along, because he needed a diversion."

First she was a damsel, now she was a diversion. She narrowed her eyes at his wording. Mason Hughes was trying to insult her without being too obvious about it. He was one of those psychological cops, trained to mess with people's minds.

"The problem is, he doesn't know you're a diversion. You're a beautiful woman, and he's been living like a recluse. He's not equipped to discern between psychical attraction and something deeper."

Tala just stared at him. She had her own poker face, and she could use it. He was an intimidating figure, tall and stern-looking. Before she met Cam, she'd gone out of her way to avoid men like this. Now she didn't feel so helpless. She'd regained a sense of her former strength. She didn't have to run from everything that scared her.

Mason leaned forward. "Do you follow what I'm saying?"

"You're saying that Cam is too broken to know his own heart."

"Exactly," Mason said, pleased with her comprehension.

"What do you want from me?"

"I want you to let him recover in peace."

"You think I'm disturbing his peace?"

"I think you have outstanding warrants and a crazy ex-husband." Mason drummed his fingertips against the table the same way Cam drummed his on the steering wheel. "Cam doesn't need that kind of stress right now."

She swallowed hard. "Cam can make his own decisions."

"I'll buy you a bus ticket," Mason said, undeterred. He removed several hundred dollars from his wallet and placed it in front of her.

Tala couldn't believe he had the nerve to bribe her in the middle of a police station. Shady deals like this were the reason she didn't trust law enforcement officers. The arrogance of his attempt galled her. "I don't want your money."

"Don't do it for the money," Mason said. "Do it for Cam. Don't drag him off to Canada to fight your battles."

She picked up the cash and threw it in his face. "Cam was right. You're an asshole."

Mason retrieved the loose bills from the ground, his brow furrowed. "Is that what he said?"

"He said you were bitter about your divorce."

"Well, he told me you're a firecracker in bed."

She drew in a sharp breath. "He did not."

Mason gave her an assessing look. "Okay, he didn't. But I bet you are."

"He's going to be furious when he hears about this."

Cam's brother returned the cash to his wallet. "If you don't tell him, I'll take you with me to the hospital. They won't let you see him without me. You're not family."

She nodded, curling her hands into fists. "Fine."

"Think about my proposal while we're there."

"I don't have to think about it. I wouldn't ask him to come to Canada, and I'd never pit him against Duane."

Mason shrugged, as if her intentions weren't important. He didn't seem bothered by her refusal to accept his bribe. Maybe he'd done it to test her loyalty to Cam—or to plant seeds of doubt in her mind.

Mission accomplished.

Was she foolish to believe that Cam wanted a long-term relationship, like he'd claimed? That he might, someday, love her with the same intensity he'd loved Jenny? She didn't know if she should stay and hope. She didn't want him to get hurt again.

Mason Hughes didn't think she was a good choice for Cam, and maybe she wasn't. Maybe she should leave him alone. He was injured. He'd suffered from a concussion. He didn't need any more grief or trauma in his life.

She followed Mason down the hall, her thoughts in turmoil. Mason was wrong about one thing; Cam wasn't broken. He was strong. He could decide for himself. She had to give him a chance to make up his own mind. She wouldn't give up without a fight.

And she wouldn't, under any circumstances, leave without saying goodbye.

Chapter 20

December 15
65N
5 degrees

Cam drifted in and out of consciousness for several hours.

Tala was there, holding his hand. She kissed his knuckles periodically.

Mason was there, too. He didn't do anything but lurk in the background and pace around. Cam appreciated his brother's presence, though he was hardly a calming influence. He wanted to tell Mason to relax, but he couldn't keep his eyes open.

When the drugs wore off, he woke to a bright room, a full bladder and throbbing pain. Mason was there, staring at him.

"Where's Tala?"

"She went to the cafeteria."

Cam studied his surroundings blearily. He was in a hospital bed, his busted-up foot propped on pillows. In addition to a gunshot wound, he had a sprained ankle and something called a "proximal fracture" in the bone on the side of his foot. Apparently those two injuries went together like peanut butter and jelly. They'd immobilized it with bandages and a medical boot. He wasn't supposed to put weight on it—or drive—for several weeks. He took the pain pill by his bedside with water. Then he gestured for Mason to help him. "Bring me those crutches."

"Why are you getting up?"

"I have to take a piss."

Mason gave him the crutches with reluctance. Cam managed to make it to the bathroom and back without falling down. His sutured arm didn't hurt as much as his foot, but it didn't feel good. Neither did his head, for that matter.

"I called Mom," Mason said.

Cam muttered a string of curse words.

"I had to. You're in the hospital, and you almost died."

"I didn't almost die. I have a broken toe."

"Metatarsal. It's attached to your toe."

"Whatever."

"Also, you were shot."

"You didn't tell her that, did you? It's a graze. It's nothing."

"She wants to book a flight. You have to call her and talk her down."

Cam changed the subject. "How's Tala?"

"She's fine," Mason said. "She answered all of the

questions they threw at her. The detectives found her very credible, and your story corroborates hers."

"They don't think she was involved?"

"No. They're more concerned about who the cop was working for. The guy they executed at the diner was a police informant. The cop might have been there to identify him for his buddies. Whatever they were up to, they're all dead now. You and your girlfriend don't have to worry about retaliation."

"Are we supposed to stay in town while they wrap up the investigation?"

"Nah. This is open-and-shut."

"What about her warrants?"

"She's supposed to take care of it on her own. They won't be detaining her. She's not exactly a menace to society. The guys at the station were falling all over themselves to get her a cup of coffee."

Cam was relieved by the update. He'd been interviewed in the ER early this morning, while he was waiting to get X-rays. He hadn't known for sure if Tala would talk to the police. This was a big step for her. She'd set aside her fears and told her story to strangers.

She'd also shot a man and killed him, to save Cam. It was surreal.

"I'm in love with her," Cam said.

"You're on drugs," Mason said. "Literally."

"I was in love with her before the accident."

"You were high on adrenaline then."

A nurse entered the room breezily to check his vital signs. Cam was glad for the interruption, even though she scolded him for getting up on his own. "You need to keep that foot elevated as much as possible. Don't make any major decisions today, because you're recovering from a head injury. The medication will make you sleepy. You can do as much activity as you feel comfortable with tomorrow."

"When will I be released?"

"Late afternoon or early evening."

She took his lunch order and left, smiling at Mason on her way out. Cam's phone was among the effects brought to him from the accident scene. He called his mother, who was "worried sick," and wanted to fly to Fairbanks immediately.

"Don't waste your money," Cam said. "By the time you get here, I'll be out of the hospital."

"Where will you go?"

"There's a hotel across the street."

"Why don't you come home with your brother?"

"I can't fly," he said. "I'm supposed to keep my foot elevated."

"For how long?"

"I don't know, Mom. I just woke up."

"Someone needs to take care of you, and Mason can't do it. You know he's a workaholic."

Mason, who could hear their conversation, rolled his eyes.

"I'll be fine. I can take care of myself." And if he couldn't, he'd ask Tala to help him. He couldn't wait to see her again.

"Are you sure?"

"Positive."

"When will I see you next?"

"I'll come home for Christmas."

She inhaled a delighted breath. "You will?"

"Sure," he said. He'd already promised Mason he would, and the holidays didn't seem like a big deal anymore. Maybe he could convince Tala to come with him. Then his family could interrogate her instead of him.

"Call me later and let me know how you're doing. I mean it."

"I've got to go, Mom. Love you."

"I love you, too, sweetheart."

He hung up on that positive note. Tala entered the room with two coffee cups. She handed one to Mason, who nodded his thanks. Then she approached Cam's bedside. Her hair was in loose waves, freed from the braids. He wanted to bury his hands in that hair and kiss her until they both lost their breath.

"Can you give us some privacy?" Cam asked Mason.

Mason took a sip of coffee and almost choked on it. He didn't refuse to leave, though he seemed annoyed by the request. "Remember your patient instructions," he said, glancing at Tala. "No major decisions."

"You're turning into our mother," Cam said.

Tala ducked her head to hide a smile. Mason gave them both a dark look and continued out the door.

"Has he been rude to you?" Cam asked.

She touched her lips to his, making a noncommittal sound.

"I'll tell him to cut it out."

"He's just being overprotective. He thinks I'm going to throw you in front of Duane."

"I wouldn't mind mixing it up with Duane."

"I'd mind," she said, holding his gaze.

He threaded his fingers through the rumpled silk of her hair. He wanted to immerse himself in it, and disappear in her. "You're a sight for sore eyes."

"How do you feel?"

"Better, now that you're here."

"What instructions was he talking about it?"

"I'm supposed to take it easy. No heavy lifting."

"Or heavy thinking?"

"Something like that."

"You called your mother?"

"Yes. I said I'd bring you home for Christmas."

Her mouth fell open. "You didn't."

"You're right. I didn't. But I'd like to."

She pulled away from him, her brow furrowed.

"You don't want to meet my family?"

"That's not it," she said, crossing her arms over her chest. "I just have to go back to Canada for a while. I have to get my life in order."

"Alone?"

She nibbled on her lower lip. "Maybe that would be best."

"Best for who?"

"You're injured, Cam. You can't even drive."

"I can sit next to you."

"You need to rest."

"Exactly. This is the perfect time for a vacation. My truck is totaled, and I can't work. We'll stay here in Fairbanks for a day or two. Then we can rent a vehicle and take a road trip. You can drive, can't you?"

"I can drive a sled, a snowplow and just about anything else."

"Then what's the problem?"

"I don't want you to feel obligated to come with me."

"I don't feel obligated," he said, grasping her hand. "I love you."

Her eyes filled with tears. "What?"

"I'm in love with you."

"You are?" she asked in a hushed voice.

He nodded, his throat tight. "I thought you were going to die last night. I know what that kind of loss feels like, and I can't survive it again. That's why I can't let you go. I want to spend the rest of my life with you, Tala."

She blinked the tears away. "I don't know what to say."

"You don't have to say anything. Just stay."

"Okay."

He smiled at her easy acceptance.

"You're not supposed to be making any major decisions," she reminded him.

"We can talk about it again tomorrow. I won't change my mind."

She pressed a kiss to his temple. The swelling had gone down, but it was still tender. "You should be resting."

"I am tired," he admitted.

"I'll let you sleep."

"Can you book a hotel room? They're releasing me this afternoon."

"Which hotel?"

"The one across the street. Take my wallet." He glanced around drowsily and located a large plastic bag in the corner. "Our stuff is in that bag. They brought it from the accident scene. If you need clothes or anything, it's in there."

She sorted through the bag, selecting a few items. She kissed him goodbye once more before she left.

He was asleep before her footsteps faded down the hall.

Chapter 21

Tala zipped up her parka as she exited the hospital.

It was a brisk winter day, cold and bright. She went snowblind for a few seconds before her eyes adjusted. Then she continued toward the hotel, which was less than a block away. It was nice to stretch her legs and get some air.

She paid for a room with one of Cam's credit cards. The first thing she did was strip for a shower. Her clothes smelled like smoke and gasoline. Maybe even burnt flesh. When she closed her eyes, she saw melting corpses. She imagined bits of gore in her hair, even though she'd made a clean kill.

Shuddering, she soaped and scrubbed until her skin was raw. She climbed out of the stall, feeling better. She found a hairdryer and used it on high heat. Then she got dressed in her wrinkled sweater and jeans. At least she had fresh underwear, and her body was clean. She scanned a laminated list of hotel services, noting that there was a laundry room on the first floor. She could wash their clothes tonight.

She didn't want to be away from Cam for too long, so she grabbed her backpack and headed out again. She felt restless and uneasy. She was still in shock from the series of traumatic events. Nothing seemed real to her. Had Cam's words of love been a sweet fantasy, or a lovely dream? She couldn't believe he'd offered to come to Canada with her.

His brother wouldn't be pleased. Mason clearly disapproved of their whirlwind relationship. Tala couldn't really blame him. They'd known each other less than a week. Her love for Cam defied explanation.

Amazingly, he'd said he loved her, too. She'd been so stunned that she hadn't even told him she returned his feelings! A little part of her, the part that she'd been trying to overcome since she'd escaped Duane, didn't believe he meant those words. Some things were too good to be true.

She zipped up her parka, shivering. She couldn't shake a vague stirring of doom. Her grandmother's voice echoed in her ears like an omen. She'd often spoken of ill winds and the calm *before* the storm.

What if they weren't out of the woods yet?

The sun had already dipped low in the sky, and the temperature had dropped to below freezing. She pinpointed several common-sense reasons for her anxiety. She'd spent the night in an interrogation room, after a harrowing near-death experience and several days of stress. She'd witnessed a murder. She'd shot a man, point-blank. No one would feel lighthearted and hopeful after what she'd been through.

Cam's brother didn't inspire any warm fuzzies, either. She hoped he wouldn't make any more trouble for her. She understood his concerns for Cam. They both needed time to recover. She'd nurse him back to health, and heal herself.

Deep breaths.

She put on her hood as she crossed the parking lot. The hairs at the nape of her neck stood on end. She hurried toward the front entrance of the hospital, her heart pounding. As she approached the double doors, they opened unexpectedly.

Duane was on the other side.

She froze in her tracks, stunned. This time, he wasn't a figment of her imagination. He was really there.

He strode forward, like a hunter with his prey in sights. Instead of calmly walking past him, into a public waiting room, she panicked and stayed outside. Gasping cold air, she retreated. Her first instinct was to cut and run.

She moved backward slowly, keeping her eyes on him. That was how she ended up in a deserted parking lot with her abusive husband.

He looked the same, for the most part. Handsome features belied his ugly nature. He was tall and lean, with disheveled blond hair and a short goatee. He wore his favorite hunting jacket, swamp-grass print with a sheepskin lining.

Something was different about him. Or maybe *she* was different.

She could see the physical qualities that had attracted her to him, along with the strength he'd used against her, but he didn't appear as intimidating as he used to. He looked pale and reedy. Cam was the bigger man in more ways than one, and he exuded confidence. Duane didn't. He had a scared-rabbit glint in his eyes.

She realized, with shock, that Duane was afraid of *her.* He was afraid of getting hurt. The knowledge didn't make her feel powerful or safe. Cornered animals were the most dangerous. He could still do terrible damage to her.

Even so, she stopped retreating. It was too late to flee. She could try to escape into the lobby, but he might grab her. She didn't want to trigger his predator instincts, and she was done running from him. Also, they had important matters to discuss. She might as well stand her ground and get on with it.

"How did you find me?" she asked, lifting her chin.

"I saw your picture on the TV. Missing waitress from Willow."

"This isn't Willow."

"You were on the news again this morning. Deadly accident near Fairbanks."

She crossed her arms over her chest to hide her trembling hands.

"I drove all night to get here. I thought you were hurt."

"I was hurt the last time you saw me. Remember what you did to my face?"

His mouth thinned with displeasure. He didn't like being reminded of his abusive ways. "It won't happen again."

"I know. I won't let it."

"You made your point, Tala. I was wrong to do what I did. You ran off to make me sorry. Well, I'm sorry. Are you happy now? Can we go home?"

She shook her head, incredulous.

"You got a new man? Is that it?"

"It's none of your business."

"I knew it," he said, spitting in the snow. "I knew you couldn't keep your legs shut."

"I'm filing for divorce."

"You won't get a penny."

She stifled the urge to laugh. Even if he had money—which he didn't—she wasn't interested in it. "I'll tell you what I want. Listen carefully."

"Why should I?"

"Because I'm pressing charges if you don't."

He made a scoffing sound. "You can't do that. You've got no evidence." He gestured to her unmarred face.

"Sure I do," she said. "I took pictures."

His eyes narrowed with suspicion.

"I'll show them to the police, and I'll tell them everything. I'll tell them what happened at the rally, too."

"They won't believe you."

"Yes, they will. It's the truth."

He glanced around the parking lot warily. "What do you want?"

"I want you to clear my name. Go to Whitehorse and confess to the assault."

"I'll go to jail," he sputtered.

"That's your problem," she said. "Hire a lawyer and submit a plea bargain, or do whatever you have to. When they drop the charges against me, I'll file for divorce and walk away. You won't have to worry about everyone knowing you're a wife-beater. But you really should get some help with that, Duane. You need it."

He stared at her for a long moment, his nostrils flared. "You goddamned bitch," he said through clenched teeth. "I loved you."

She recoiled in fear when he stepped forward. She'd

seen that look before. She'd seen his neck turn red with fury just before he struck. Duane's switch had flipped. He was beyond caring about making a scene now, beyond listening to reason. The urge to run gripped her again, but she didn't get the chance. She stumbled over a concrete divider and fell on her behind. Before she could scramble to her feet, Duane advanced. He loomed over her with a raised fist.

Then a man flew out of nowhere and knocked *him* on his ass.

It was Mason Hughes.

Her unexpected defender hit Duane with a right cross so well placed he spun around in a full circle before he went down. Duane stayed down, seeming stunned by the blow, but Mason wasn't finished with him yet. He straddled Duane's waist, lifted him by the collar and punched him again.

Duane's head rocked back against the snow-covered asphalt.

Mason drew back his fist a third time.

"Stop," Tala said, grasping his elbow.

"You want to take a shot?" Mason asked. "I'll hold him for you."

"No, I don't want to take a shot. I need him conscious."

Mason let go of Duane's collar, with reluctance. Duane gazed up at them blearily. Blood dribbled from his nose and continued down his chin.

"Remember what I said about confessing?" she asked.

"I remember."

"If you don't do it, I'll see you in court."

"And I'll see you in a dark alley," Mason said.

Duane grimaced, his teeth stained red. "I hear you. Now get your dog off me."

When Tala nodded her permission, Mason allowed Duane to his feet. Duane wiped his nose and spat blood in the snow. Then he started walking across the parking lot in angry strides. He didn't appear to enjoy being on the receiving end of violence.

"One more thing," she called after him.

"What?"

"Do you have my purse?"

He kept walking toward his truck. It was parked at the far edge of the lot, among a cluster of similar trucks and half-covered in new-fallen snow. She figured he'd brought her purse along. They couldn't cross the border without her ID. Sure enough, he tossed her purse out the window and took off in a squeal of tires.

She rushed forward to retrieve her purse from the ground. Her wallet was there, with her drivers' license and tribal card.

Victory.

She studied Mason with new eyes. He'd really grown on her in the past few minutes. "Why did you do that?"

He massaged his knuckles. "Do what? I didn't do anything."

"Thank you, all the same."

"It was my pleasure."

"I thought you wanted to get rid of me."

"Not that way," he said, watching Duane's truck until it disappeared. "Does he usually have a gun on him?"

"He keeps one in his truck."

Mason moved his gaze to Tala. Although he didn't say anything, his expression revealed his concern for Cam's welfare. This basic human emotion was much more effective than the bribe he'd attempted earlier. He'd asked her not to put Cam in the line of fire. She didn't think Duane would shoot anyone, but she couldn't be sure. He was a man scorned, and he wasn't known for handling rejection well.

Duane might confess to the assault at the rally. Not because it was the right thing to do, but to avoid the scandal of domestic violence charges. He might sign the divorce papers and let her go without a fight.

Or he might make her life hell, just because. She removed Cam's wallet from her pocket and handed it to Mason, feeling glum. Mason accepted the item in silence. They stood side by side in the snowy parking lot.

"I misjudged you," Mason said finally.

She was startled by the admission. Mason seemed even less likely to admit to a mistake than Cam. They were cut from the same stubborn cloth. She had her own stubborn streak, so she could sympathize.

"Cam says he's in love with you. I don't want him to get hurt again."

Her knees felt weak, so she sank to a sitting position on the curb.

"Are you all right?"

"I'm fine. I just need a minute."

He stayed right there with her, his arms crossed over his chest. She could tell he was cold. His jacket would suffice in Seattle, but it didn't have enough insulation for an Alaska winter. Now the adrenaline was wearing off, and he could feel the chill.

She took pity on him. "I'd rather be alone, if you don't mind."

He nodded curtly and walked away. Anxiety welled

up inside her once more. She wanted to be with Cam, but she also needed some time to herself. She needed time to think. Mason had helped her stand up to Duane. He'd asked her to leave Cam alone, and she felt obligated to consider his request.

So she did. She considered it very carefully.

It wouldn't be the end of the world to go to Canada without him. She could give him some space while he recovered from his injuries. She didn't have to leave forever. Just until the conflict with Duane passed. As much as she appreciated Cam's support, she could manage without him. She'd been doing it for months. She was an independent woman, capable of handling her own business. If Duane followed her suggestions and cleared her name, she'd come back to Alaska. If he didn't...perhaps it was best to stay away. Cam had been through enough heartache and struggle. He'd almost died trying to protect her.

Mason's concerns weren't unwarranted.

She rose to her feet, pulse racing. She understood Mason's perspective, but she had to consider Cam's needs, also. He said he loved her. He planned to introduce her to his family. He'd asked her to stay. She'd already told him she would.

Ultimately, this was her decision. If she wanted to go, she could go. If she wanted to stay, she could stay.

She studied the looming structure of the hospital, with its glinting windows and geometric shapes. She could walk inside and be with Cam right now, but the prospect of sitting in a quiet room with Mason Hughes didn't appeal to her. She couldn't take any more tension or stillness. She wanted space to move around. Physical activity would clear her head. She needed to run for a little while.

She turned away from the hospital and headed toward freedom.

Chapter 22

Cam slept most of the afternoon.

When he woke up again, it was dark outside. His head felt better. His foot still hurt and his arm was sore, but he could endure the discomfort. He declined a second pain pill in favor of over-the-counter stuff. He wanted to stay awake.

Mason brought him some flannel pajamas to lounge around in. Cam decided to take a shower before he changed clothes. He smelled like blood and diesel and sweat. It would be easier to bathe here than in a hotel room, so he rose from his hospital bed. There was a safety chair in the shower stall, ready to go. The nurse gave him a plastic baggie to cover his foot. Sitting down to shower felt strange, but it was better than falling on his ass. He washed off, toweled dry and got dressed on his own.

He couldn't wait to get discharged. He was looking

forward to a night of snuggling with Tala. Maybe more, if he was lucky. When he emerged from the bathroom, Mason was sitting in the corner, reading a newspaper. He didn't look up.

"Where's Tala?" Cam asked.

Mason rattled his paper. "I don't know."

"Did she come back from the hotel?"

"She did. Then she left again."

Cam figured Tala didn't want to spend time with his surly brother. Cam didn't blame her. He pictured her reading one of her graphic novels in the lobby, or grabbing a cup of coffee. The nurse arrived with discharge forms, which he scanned quickly. She told him the doctor would come in to go over patient instructions.

"Do you want some ice for that hand?" she asked Mason.

Cam glanced at his brother in surprise. His knuckles were raw and swollen. "I'm good," he said, closing the newspaper.

The nurse said goodbye and exited the room.

Cam's gut clenched with unease. "What happened to you?"

"I ran into Duane Laramie."

"Where?"

"Right here, in front of the hospital. He was arguing with Tala."

"How did he find her?"

"I don't know," Mason said. "I didn't get the chance to interrogate him. I saw her fall down, so I intervened."

Cold fury enveloped Cam. "He hit her?"

"No. I got there first."

"Did you straighten him out?"

"I punched him a few times. I couldn't knock him

out because she wanted to talk to him. She threatened to take him to court if he didn't confess to assaulting that police officer."

Cam rubbed a hand over his mouth, contemplative. It was a better deal than Duane deserved. If he cleared Tala's name, she wouldn't press domestic violence charges against him. "Did he agree?"

"He'd be a fool not to, but he didn't say yes or no. After I let him up, he threw her purse out of his truck and drove away."

"Jesus, Mason. Why didn't you tell me?"

"You were asleep."

Cam grabbed for his crutches. One of them clattered to the floor. "She almost gets attacked by her ex, and you don't wake me up? You left her alone in the lobby? What the hell is wrong with you?"

Mason picked up the crutch for Cam. "I don't think she's in the lobby."

"Where is she?"

His brother shrugged, avoiding his gaze.

Cam's vision went red. He didn't know what Mason was up to, but he couldn't stay in the hospital another minute. He was leaving right now to find Tala.

"Where is she?" he repeated, his voice low.

"I don't know," Mason said. "She never came in from the parking lot."

"Did Duane take her?"

"I'm pretty sure she walked away on her own."

"Why would she do that?"

"I might have said something that upset her."

"You *might* have?"

"Okay, I did. I suggested that you'd already been shot once because of her—"

"I didn't get shot," Cam growled. "It's a *graze*."

"—and maybe she should leave you alone until things blow over."

"You son of a bitch. How dare you?"

Mason flinched at Cam's vehemence. "I'm your brother. I was worried about you."

"So you chase off my girlfriend? That's your way of helping me?"

"You've been racing toward death since you got here," Mason said, raising his voice. Now they were both shouting. "I thought you hooked up with her to accelerate the trip!"

Cam wanted to tackle Mason. He pictured them wrestling on the floor, knocking over trays of medical supplies. If he didn't have a broken foot, he'd have launched himself at his brother, fists flying.

"I wasn't racing toward death," he said curtly. "I was already dead inside. She makes me want to live again."

Mason fell silent for a moment. "I'm sorry."

"She's the opposite of whatever you're thinking. She's the best thing that's ever happened to me. She shot a man to protect me, for Christ's sake. You had no right to blame her for my injuries."

"I was looking out for you."

"I didn't need you to look out for me," Cam said. "I needed you to look out for *her*. She's a victim of domestic violence, and her abuser's in town."

Mason raked a hand through his hair. "Do you want to go after her, or yell at me?"

"Go after her," Cam said.

They didn't wait around to listen to the doctor's orders. Mason gathered Cam's belongings and headed out the door. Cam followed him down the hall, clumsy on his crutches. His foot throbbed and his arm burned as he loped along. He wanted to pick another fight with Mason in the elevator, but he saved his breath. They'd already spent too much time arguing. He had to focus on finding Tala.

They looked in the lobby, the gift shop and the cafeteria. She wasn't there.

"Maybe she went back to the hotel," Mason said.

"Let's check it out."

Mason brought his rental car to the front entrance of the hospital so Cam didn't have to maneuver across the parking lot. Crutches didn't mix well with snow and ice. Cam didn't thank him for the courtesy. He was too angry to speak.

"She returned your wallet," Mason said. "It's in the glove compartment."

Cam glanced in his wallet and found a key card with the room number. Mason drove the short distance to the hotel and pulled into a parking space. He hopped out to help Cam with his crutches.

"Be careful. It's slippery."

Cam offered a curt two-word response as he exited the vehicle. He wasn't in the mood for Mason's brotherly advice. They entered the hotel lobby and walked down the hall. Tala had booked him a room on the ground floor. She wasn't inside, but he noted the evidence of her presence. The scent of shampoo lingered in the bathroom, and a damp towel hung on the rack. There were no clues to her current whereabouts. She'd taken her backpack and clothes with her. The graphic novel she'd been reading was sitting in the middle of the bed.

He wasn't sure if she'd meant to leave it behind. Maybe it was a subtle hint that their erotic encounters hadn't been important to her. They were fleeting pleasures, easily forgotten. Abandoned at the first opportunity.

He picked up the book and threw it against the wall, very close to his brother's head. Mason ducked to avoid the object, which wouldn't have hit him anyway. Pain stabbed down Cam's arm from the sudden motion, and one of his crutches fell to the carpet. He struggled to maintain his balance.

Mason hurried to help him sit on the edge of the bed. "Settle down, Cam! You're going to end up right back in the hospital."

"I should put *you* in the hospital," Cam said.

Mason shoved him until he sat down. "Dream on, little brother. You can't even take me when you're healthy."

Cam considered punching his lights out. "I could take you right now."

Mason leaned forward and pointed at his chin in offering. "Make my day. You think I won't hit you back just because you're injured?"

Cam didn't really want to fight. Not in his current condition. His entire body ached and his brain felt scrambled. Hurting Mason wouldn't bring Tala back. So he took a deep breath, trying to refocus. His crutches were in a heap on the floor. He had a busted-up foot and a bandaged arm. And his brother was still getting in his face, taunting him.

Cam had to laugh at Mason's pugnacious expression. "You're ridiculous."

Mason straightened abruptly. "You started it."

"Give me my crutches."

"Don't be stupid."

"We have to keep looking for her."

"You're in no condition to be out on foot in this kind of weather. You weren't even officially discharged."

"I'm fine," Cam said, his irritation rising again. "We're driving around, not climbing Denali."

"One of us should stay here in case she comes back. That's you."

It wasn't a bad plan, but Cam didn't trust his brother to find Tala. Mason was the one who'd scared her off. "She won't talk to you."

"She doesn't have to. I'll just make sure she's safe."

"Okay," Cam said, because he didn't really have a choice. They were wasting time arguing about it. "You'll want to check the airport."

"What about the bus station?"

"There's no bus service in the winter. This isn't Seattle."

"Where else?"

Cam raked a hand through his hair. "I don't know. She might go to a diner or a bookstore. She likes books."

"I see that."

"If all else fails, I can get on a CB and ask the truckers to be on the lookout. Do you know what her husband drives?"

Mason's eyes narrowed. "Yeah, I do."

Cam swallowed hard. He couldn't finish that thought, but he didn't have to. Mason knew the statistics for domestic homicides better than Cam did. If she'd been harmed, Cam would tear Duane apart with his bare hands.

"Stop mad-dogging me," Mason said. "She'll turn up."

"She'd better, or I'll kill you."

They stared at each other for a tense moment. Mason looked a little choked up. Cam glanced away, clearing his throat. His brother meant well, and he seemed sorry. It was difficult to hold a grudge against Mason. He had emotional issues, and not just because of his divorce. In his line of work, he dealt with unspeakable atrocities.

"Go on," Cam said. "I'll keep my phone handy."

Mason nodded and left the room, his gaze sharp with determination.

Chapter 23

Tala ran until her muscles ached and her lungs burned.

When she got off the treadmill, she was breathing hard, her skin damp with sweat. Her head was clear, and she felt better.

Much better.

She preferred running outdoors, but that wasn't an option in this nasty weather. The hotel gym was nice enough. She'd changed into her leggings before she left the hotel room. She ran barefoot on the treadmill, her muscles flexing. She ran off her tension, and her troubles. She ran without running away.

Then she started a load of laundry and waited for Cam. He'd said he'd get discharged sometime today. After she put the clothes in the dryer, she wandered down the hall and found an empty office area. There were a couple of desks for guests to work quietly. There was a cozy-looking chair and a phone.

On impulse, she settled in to call her mother. The hotel clerk charged the long-distance fee to Cam's room. Tala waited for her mom to pick up. Once again, she sounded happy to hear from her.

"When are you coming to visit?" her mother asked.

"I'm not sure."

"What about Christmas? Bear will be here."

"Oh, *now* you want me to hang out with Bear?"

Her mother laughed. "You don't have to."

Tala switched the phone to her other ear. "I met someone here in Alaska, but I don't know if it's going to work out."

"Why not?"

She struggled to find words for her feelings. "Maybe I'm supposed to be alone."

"Of course you're not. Why would you say that?"

"Dad didn't have anyone."

"He had you."

"That's not what I mean. He didn't have girlfriends. After you, he gave up on love."

"He didn't give up on love. He had a girlfriend."

"Who?"

"Helen Barclay."

"Mrs. Barclay? The music teacher?"

"That's her."

"She was married."

"Yes. That's why he kept it a secret."

"Where did you hear that?"

"There was gossip around town. They started seeing each other when you were eleven or twelve. It went on for years, until her husband caught them. He moved the family to Edmonton. Helen wanted to stay in Yellowknife, but your father told her not to. They had two little girls, and he didn't want to break up their family."

"She came to the funeral."

"Yes. She loved him."

"I never knew," Tala said, her voice breaking. "That's so sad."

"I didn't tell you to upset you, *nitânis*. I just wanted you to know your father had love in his life, even after me. He worked hard and he never gave up on anything. I think he learned not to be so selfish after what we went through in our divorce. He became a better man."

Tala was glad her mother had told her about the ill-fated affair. She wasn't sure if it brightened her outlook, but it did color her perspective. She said a quick goodbye to her mother, rising from the chair.

She'd always thought of romantic love as something beautiful and fleeting. It was the rainbow after the storm. It didn't last. Maybe she'd been wrong. Maybe love was the storm, too. Maybe it was the wind and the rain and the thunder. It wasn't a settled feeling, static and unchanging, but it didn't have to fade away. It could be calm one day and tumultuous the next.

Her mother said love was hard work. Tala had never been afraid of hard work. She loved Cam, and she was willing to fight for him.

She couldn't run away from love anymore.

She had to tell him how she felt, right now. She left the office and hurried down the hall, her heart racing. She had to get back to the hospital and confess her feelings to Cam. He'd said he loved her, and she'd left him hanging. She'd been afraid to say the words back to him. Afraid to put herself out there. Afraid to get hurt again. She was still afraid, but she couldn't let fear stop her from getting what she wanted. Maybe this time everything would work out. Maybe it wouldn't. Either way, she had to try.

She was her father's daughter. Unlucky in love, perhaps, but not a quitter.

Feeling giddy, she ducked into the laundry room to retrieve their clean clothes. Then she headed down the hall with her arms full. When she opened the door to the room, someone was inside, waiting for her.

She let out a startled shriek and dropped everything on the floor.

It was Cam.

Her heart couldn't take another shock, even a good one. She clutched the center of her chest and tried not to hyperventilate.

He stood, with some difficultly. He seemed as surprised to see her as she was to see him. He was wearing flannel pajamas, and he had crutches under his arms. His left foot was encased in a heavy black medical boot. He looked injured, but still strong. Still ruggedly handsome. Her chest swelled with love for him. She wanted to throw her arms around him and kiss him senseless, but she was afraid to knock him off balance.

"You came back," he said.

She closed the door and locked it behind her. They stared at each other for a taut moment. Emotions welled up inside her, spilling over. She rushed into the comfort of his embrace. He managed to hug her back without falling. He smelled like snow and heat and man. She closed her eyes, relishing his warmth. "I love you."

His body went tense. "You do?"

She pressed her lips to his neck. "I should have told you earlier."

"I thought I'd lost you," Cam said, hugging her closer.

"I've been here all afternoon."

He released her abruptly, his expression incredulous. "You've been here at the hotel? This whole time?"

"Where did you think I was?"

"I thought you ran away!"

"I didn't run away. I came here and ran on the treadmill. Then I called my mother and did some laundry."

He stared at her as if he couldn't fathom these ordinary things. "My brother said Duane attacked you in the parking lot."

"He did, but he's gone now."

Cam lowered himself to the edge of the bed. "How did he find you?"

She took his crutches and placed them nearby. Then she sat down next to him and told him the whole story. "I think your brother broke his nose."

"I guess he did one thing right," Cam muttered.

"It almost makes up for the attempted bribe."

Cam narrowed his eyes. "He offered you money to leave me alone?"

"Yes."

He dragged a hand down his face. "I'm sorry."

"Don't be. It's not your fault."

"He's out looking for you right now."

She laughed merrily at that turn of events. "Are you sure he wants to find me?"

"I told him I'd kill him if he didn't."

Her amusement died at this dark claim. "Cam, I don't want to cause trouble between you and your brother."

"You're not causing trouble. It's him."

"He doesn't want you to get hurt."

"I'm not going to get hurt," Cam said, stretching out his injured leg.

"You're already hurt."

He ignored this observation and took his phone out of his pocket. "Should I tell him I found you, or let him sweat a little longer?"

"Tell him."

She waited while he had a short conversation with his brother. They spoke to each other in grunts and monosyllables.

"He wants to apologize," Cam said.

Tala shook her head, grimacing.

"She's busy," Cam lied. He listened to Mason for a minute. Then he said goodbye and hung up. "Mason talked to the state police. They spotted Duane's truck in Delta Junction. It's halfway to the Canadian border."

"He's going home."

"Looks like it."

She was relieved by the news. She hadn't figured Duane would stick around to cause trouble with a busted nose. She'd stood up to him, and he'd run off with his tail between his legs. Good riddance.

Cam set his phone on the nightstand and stretched out on his back. She put a pillow under his ankle to prop up his broken foot. She retrieved the clean laundry from the floor and folded it. Then she cuddled next to Cam, enjoying his warmth. He had a great physique for snuggling. He was lean and solid. Steady as a rock.

"Do you want kids?" he asked.

"Right now?"

"Now, later, whenever."

"Why do you ask?"

"It's good to be on the same page about some things."

She considered the question carefully. "I'd like to be a mother."

"When?"

"Before I'm thirty, I guess."

He seemed to find this timeline acceptable.

"What about you?"

"I'm past thirty already."

"I know."

"Before I'm forty is good. I don't want to be too old."

"There are a few things we should discuss before we plan the next five years, Cam."

"Okay."

"I'm planning to finish college. You already know that. I'd like to go to school in Billings, where my mother lives. I want a chance to repair our relationship. We've spent too many years apart."

Cam pointed out the obvious. "I can't be an ice-road trucker in Montana."

"You could be a regular trucker."

He made a noncommittal sound. Maybe after the ice road, highway hauling didn't hold the same appeal. "What if I returned to law enforcement?"

"Would you consider it?"

He arched a brow. "I thought you hated police officers."

"That was before I fell in love with one."

Cam smiled at her answer. "I can look for work in Montana. I'll live wherever you want to live. When you're ready to get married and have babies, we'll do that. You want me to come home to you every night, I'm there. How does that sound?"

She smiled back. "Too good to be true."

"Maybe we've earned it."

"My grandmother used to say, 'After the storm comes the rainbow.'"

"Do you believe it?"

"I'm trying to."

He shifted into a more comfortable position. "We'll make it work."

"How do you know?"

"Because you're a warrior, and I'm your soldier. I'll do anything for you. Together, we can't lose."

She studied his handsome face, contemplative. Maybe he was right. Last night he'd dragged himself upright, half-conscious and bleeding, to tackle the gunman. "You're unstoppable."

He propped a finger under her chin. "So are you."

Tears filled her eyes. "I love you, Cam."

He touched his lips to hers. "I love you, too."

She kissed him until they were both breathless. His hands roved over her body, squeezing her waist and the curves of her bottom. She could feel his arousal swell against her hip. She gentled the kiss, reluctant to encourage him. He grasped her thigh and tugged, as if urging her to climb on top of him.

"We can't," she said.

He stared at her mouth intently. "Why not?"

"You need to rest."

"I need you more."

She kissed him again, biting his lower lip. "I don't want to hurt you."

"If you do, I'll give the stop signal."

She laughed at his eagerness. "No, Cam. Not tonight."

"Tomorrow?"

"Tomorrow," she promised.

She snuggled against his chest. He grasped her hand.

They fell asleep like that, fingers entwined and limbs entangled. Just the two of them against the world, united by love, unbroken and unstoppable.

Chapter 24

Big Sky, MT
45N
21 degrees

Three weeks later.

Cam's recovery went well.

He wasn't great at resting, but he tried to relax as much as possible. They lounged around the hotel for almost a week. Tala took care of his every need and then some. She even indulged him with exercise. He spent many quality hours underneath her. He thought he'd get bored with reclining positions, but he didn't. She had a knack for being on top, and he loved watching her. He loved every inch of her sweet body, sliding all over him.

While they were in Fairbanks, they did a few other

things besides making love. Cam submitted his resignation to Northern Lights Trucking Company, on their request. They weren't pleased about his unapproved passenger or the melee on the Dalton. They launched an insurance investigation, with predictable results. Cam had broken the rules of his contract, so he was liable for all the damages.

Cam could pay for his own hospital bills, but his rig was unrepairable. He had to sell it for parts. His ice-road trucker days were over. A month ago, he'd have been devastated by this turn of events. In his current state of sexual bliss, it was hardly a blip. He'd already decided to move on with Tala.

They'd hired a lawyer to help Tala with her legal issues. Although Duane hadn't caused any more trouble in Fairbanks, he hadn't taken the initiative to confess to the assault at the rally. Tala's attorney had to send him a letter of encouragement, along with the divorce papers. Duane responded by hiring his own defense. In the end, he'd cooperated with investigators. He pleaded guilty to disorderly conduct.

This outcome frustrated Cam, because it felt like another travesty of justice. Duane was a menace to society, a coward and an abuser of women. But instead of a stiff punishment, he'd gotten a slap on the wrist. Cam had to let it go, however. In addition to clearing her name, Duane had signed the divorce papers.

Tala was a free woman.

When Cam was cleared to travel, he rented an SUV and headed south. Driving was still uncomfortable for him, so Tala took the wheel. They visited Denali National Park. He was an expert on his crutches after the first week. After Denali, they passed through Willow.

She visited Walt at the diner. He'd managed to sleep through the excitement and remain unscathed.

For Christmas, they flew to Tacoma and spent several days on the farm. She didn't really warm up to Mason, but she hit it off with his parents. Tala enjoyed cooking and was genuinely interested in the land. They loved her.

Before they left, his mother pulled him aside and said, "Marry her."

"I'm working on it," Cam replied.

Their next stop was Billings, Montana. Although Tala hadn't seen her family in years, and her younger brothers hardly knew her, they accepted her with open arms. Her older stepbrother, the one she'd had a crush on, was now a sheriff's deputy in Great Falls. When Tala mentioned Cam's previous profession, Bear gave him a curious look.

Later, Bear approached Cam for a private talk. Cam thought he was going to get grilled about his intentions toward Tala. Instead, Bear told him about an employment opportunity in Big Sky. They'd offered Bear the position, but he didn't want to relocate to a sleepy mountain town. The sheriff there needed a deputy, and not some wet-eared rookie. He was looking for someone with enough experience and education to train for the sheriff's position. The current sheriff planned to retire in another year.

"I didn't mention it in front of Tala because I don't know how serious you are about her," Bear said.

Cam smiled at the brotherly comment. "I want to marry her."

"What does she want?"

"To finish school and be near her family."

"So you're staying in Montana?"

Cam nodded. "I told her I'd look for work here."

Bear seemed satisfied by his answers. "If you're interested in the deputy job, I'll put in a good word."

Cam thanked him with a handshake. He was interested—very interested. A sleepy mountain town sounded perfect after what he'd been through. He'd had enough excitement to last a lifetime. Now he wanted to settle down in a peaceful place.

He mailed in an application, listing his credentials with the Seattle PD and adding Bear Klamath as a reference. He didn't tell Tala about the opportunity. Big Sky was more than a hundred miles from Billings and he wasn't sure how she'd feel about living there. If he got an offer, he'd ask her to come with him.

They spent the next few days touring Yellowstone National Park, which was nearby. Cam had never been there, and Tala hadn't visited in winter. It was a snow-covered wonderland. He didn't need his crutches anymore, but he still had to wear the medical boot. He couldn't wait to take it off.

While they were at the Yellowstone Lodge, Cam received a message from Sheriff Dugan in Big Sky. It was a request for a FaceTime interview. Cam waited until Tala was in the shower to step outside and return the call.

Sheriff Dugan was a no-nonsense lawman in his late sixties. He explained that the job was physical, the weather was challenging and the terrain was rugged. He needed someone with patience, fortitude and stamina.

Cam liked the sound of the job. He told Dugan about his nine years on highway patrol and his recent stint as an ice-road trucker.

"Ice roads, huh? You must have nerves of steel."

Cam didn't agree or disagree.

"You're not afraid of extreme conditions."

"No, sir."

"How do you know Bear?"

"He's my girlfriend's stepbrother."

"Well, you look healthy enough to do the work and you have the right background. A degree in sociology is better suited to this position than criminal justice. You'll be keeping the peace more than investigating."

Cam wanted to pump his fist in triumph. "Yes, sir."

"We get tourists all year round. Summertime's the busiest. Lost hikers and vehicular accidents are common. It's mostly quiet, though."

"I like quiet."

"Good," Dugan said. "There's a cabin by the old sawmill that comes with the job. Drive out there and take a look before you decide. Bring your girlfriend."

"I'll do that."

Cam jotted down the address for the cabin. Dugan needed an answer within a few days. It was a great opportunity, but he had to discuss the details with Tala. He checked the directions to Big Sky on his phone. It was only an hour away from the lodge.

When Tala was ready to go, her hair blow-dried and bags packed, he drove them north. Big Sky was off the beaten path a little, about ten miles from a major highway. He suggested they have lunch there. Tala shrugged her agreement, nose in a book. He continued through the rustic little town, with its snow-covered roofs and chimneys chugging. There was a busy café with a Help Wanted sign in the window.

Tala perked up when she saw it. "We could eat there."

"We'll come back to it," he said, continuing past the

café. A few minutes later he found the cabin on Sawmill Road.

"Are we lost?" Tala asked.

"No," Cam said. "I wanted to surprise you."

He got out and opened the passenger door for her. She followed him toward the cabin. The key was under the mat, as promised. He unlocked the door and stepped inside.

It was a well-built cabin. The fireplace in the living room promised cozy nights. There was a small kitchen with modern appliances, a full bath and a single bedroom. Good lighting and sturdy hardwood floors. With some furniture and rugs and stuff, it could be transformed from an empty space into a quaint little home.

He glanced at Tala. "What do you think?"

"Is it for rent?"

"I got a job offer here in Big Sky. This place comes with it."

"A job offer? To do what?"

"Sheriff's deputy. I'd train to take over as sheriff."

She blinked at him in surprise. "I didn't know you'd applied for any jobs."

"Your stepbrother told me about the opening. It seemed too good to pass up."

"It is," she said, twirling around in a slow circle. Her attorney had arranged for her belongings to be packed and shipped from Duane's house to her mother's. Tala had told him about her grandmother's furs and other cherished items. She could keep them here. She could decorate however she liked.

"I don't have to take the offer," he said. "I came to Montana to be with you. If you don't want to live here, we won't."

She inspected the bathroom. "How far away is Bozeman?"

"Thirty miles."

"Montana State University is in Bozeman. I could go there."

"You would do that?"

She returned to his side and twined her arms around his neck. "As long as we're together, I'll be happy."

Relief and love overwhelmed him. "So will I."

"This is a beautiful town."

"It's two hours away from Billings. Ten hours from Tacoma."

"Some distance from family is good. Especially from your brother."

He laughed, hugging her closer.

"Maybe I'll apply to that café."

"You don't have to."

"I want to."

He lowered his head to kiss her. She kissed him back sweetly, threading her fingers through his hair. He couldn't believe his luck. A month ago, he'd been completely numb. Tala had thawed him from the inside out.

"Will this be exciting enough for you?" she asked.

"You're all I need for excitement."

"You said your fantasy was a cozy cabin."

"And yours was freedom."

"We got both."

"We did, didn't we?"

On impulse, he lifted her into his arms and carried her over the threshold into the bedroom. She laughed at his romantic gesture, which was no easy task with a healing foot. He set her down by the window. There were no furnishings, and it wasn't warm enough to get intimate, but he kissed her until they were both breathless.

"I love you," he said, his heart full.

"I love you, too."

"Always?"

"Always," she agreed, and kissed him again.

* * * * *

Read on for an exclusive sneak peek at Fatal Invasion, *the next sizzling book in the Fatal series from* New York Times *bestselling author Marie Force...*

ONE

"THIS IS A classic case of be careful what you wish for." Nick placed a stack of folded dress shirts in a suitcase that already held socks, underwear, workout clothes and several pairs of jeans. Only Nick would start packing seven days before his scheduled departure for Europe next Sunday, the day after Freddie and Elin's wedding. "That's the lesson learned here."

"Only anal-retentive freakazoids pack a week before a trip." Sam sat at the foot of the bed and watched him pack with a growing sense of dread. "*Three freaking weeks.* The last time you were gone that long, I nearly lost my mind, and I don't have much of a mind left to lose."

"Come with me," he said for the hundredth time since the president asked him to make the diplomatic trip, representing the administration on a visit with some of the country's closest allies. Since President Nelson was still recovering—in more ways than one—from his son's criminal activities, several of the allies had requested he send his popular vice president in his stead.

Sam flopped on the bed. "I *can't.* I have work and Scotty, and Freddie is going on his honeymoon for *two* weeks and… I can't." No Nick at home to entertain her. No Freddie at work to entertain her. The next few weeks were going to totally suck monkey balls.

"Actually, you *can.*" Nick hovered above her, propped

on arms ripped with muscles, his splendid chest on full display. "You have more vacation time saved up than you can use in a lifetime, *and* you have the right to actually use it. Scotty will be fine with Shelby, your dad and Celia, your sisters, and the Secret Service here to entertain him. We could even ask Mrs. Littlefield to come up for the weekends."

Their son's former guardian would love the chance to spend time with him, but Sam didn't feel right about leaving him for so long. However, the thought of being without Nick for three endless weeks made her sick. His trip to Iran earlier in the year had been pure torture, especially since it kept getting extended.

"Why'd you have to tell Nelson you wanted to be more than a figurehead vice president?" She play-punched his chest. "Everything was fine when he was ignoring you."

He kissed her lips and then her neck. "You're so, *so* cute when you pout."

"Badass cops do *not* pout."

"Mine does when she doesn't get her own way, and it's truly adorable."

She scowled at him. "Badass cops are not adorable."

"Mine is." Leaving a trail of hot kisses on her neck, he said, "Come with me, Samantha. London, Paris, Rome, the Vatican, Amsterdam, Brussels, The Hague. Come see the world with me."

Sam had never been to Europe and had always wanted to go, so she was sorely tempted to say to hell with her responsibilities.

"Come on." He rolled her earlobe between his teeth and pressed against her suggestively. "Three whole *weeks* together away from the madness of DC. You know you want to go. Gonzo could cover for you at work, and things have been slow anyway."

There hadn't been a homicide in more than a week, which meant they were due, and that was another reason to stay home. "Don't say that and put a jinx on us."

"Come away with me. Scotty will be fine. We'll FaceTime with him every day and bring him presents. He'll be well cared for by everyone else who loves him." He kissed her neck as he unbuttoned her shirt and pushed it aside. "You'd get to meet the Queen of England."

Sam moaned. She *loved* the queen—speaking of a badass female.

"And the Pope. Plus, you'll need some clothes—and shoes. *Lots* of shoes."

"Stop it." She turned her face to avoid his kiss. "You're fighting dirty."

"Because I want my wife to come with me on the trip of a lifetime? I *need* you, Samantha."

As he well knew, she could deny him nothing when he said he needed her. "Fine, I'll go! But only if it's okay with Scotty and if I can swing it at work."

"*Yes*," her husband said on a long exhale. "We'll have so much fun."

"Will we actually get to see anything?"

He pushed himself up to continue packing. "I'll make sure of it."

"Um, excuse me."

"What's up?"

"My temperature after your attempts at persuasion."

A slow, lazy smile spread across his face, making him the sexiest man in this universe—and the next. "Is my baby feeling a little needy?"

She pulled her shirt off and released the front clasp on her bra. "More than a little."

"We can't have that." Stepping to the foot of the bed, he grasped the legs of her yoga pants and yanked them off.

"Lock the door."

"Scotty's asleep."

"*Lock the door*, or this isn't happening." With Secret Service agents all over their house, Sam couldn't relax if the door wasn't locked.

"This is definitely happening, but if it'll make you happy, I'll lock the door."

"It'll make me happy, which will, in turn, make *you* happy." She splayed her legs wide open to give him a show as he returned from locking the door, and was rewarded with gorgeous hazel eyes that heated with desire when he saw her waiting for him.

"You little vixen," he muttered.

"I don't know *what* you're talking about."

"Sure, you don't," he said, laughing as he came down on top of her and set out to give her a preview of what three weeks away together might be like.

THEY BROKE THE news to Scotty the next morning at breakfast. "So," Nick said tentatively, "what would you think if Mom came with me to Europe?"

Thirteen-year-old Scotty, never at his best first thing in the morning, shrugged. "It's fine."

"Really?" Sam said. "You wouldn't mind? Shelby, Tracy and Angela would be around to hang with you, and Gramps and Celia too. We thought maybe Mrs. Littlefield could come up for a weekend or two if she's free."

"Sure, that sounds good."

Sam glanced at Nick, who seemed equally perplexed by his lack of reaction. They'd expected him to ask to come with them, at the very least.

"Is everything okay?" Sam asked her son.

"Uh-huh." He finished his cereal and got up to put the bowl in the sink. "I'm going to finish getting ready for school."

"Okay, bud," Nick said.

"Something's up," Sam said as soon as Scotty left the room.

"I agree. He didn't even ask if he could miss school to come with us."

"I thought the same thing."

"We'll have to see if we can get him to talk to us before we go—and not in the morning," Nick said.

"I'll ask Shelby to make spaghetti for dinner. That always puts him in a good mood." Sam's phone rang, and when she saw the number for Dispatch, she groaned. "Damn it. You jinxed me!" So much for getting out of Dodge without having to worry about work. She took the call. "Holland."

"Lieutenant, there was a fire overnight in Chevy Chase." The dispatcher referred to the exclusive northwest neighborhood that was home to a former US president, ambassadors and other wealthy residents. "We have two DOA at the scene," the dispatcher said, reciting the address. "The fire marshal has requested homicide detectives."

"Did he say why?"

"No, ma'am."

"Okay, I'm on my way." Thankfully, she'd showered and gotten dressed before she woke Scotty. "Please call

Sergeant Gonzales and Detective Cruz and ask them to meet me there."

"Yes, ma'am."

Sam flipped her phone closed with a satisfying smack. That smacking sound was one of many reasons she'd never upgrade to a smartphone.

"You'll still be able to come with me, right?" Nick asked, looking adorably uncertain.

Sam went over to where he sat at the table and kissed him. "I'll talk to Malone today and see if I can make it happen."

"Keep me posted."

A RINGING PHONE woke Christina Billings from a sound sleep. Two-year-old Alex had been up during the night with a fever and cold that was making him miserable and her sleep deprived. Her fiancé, Tommy, had slept through that and apparently couldn't hear his phone ringing either. He was due at work in an hour and was usually up by now.

"Tommy." She nudged him, but he didn't stir. "*Tommy.* Your phone."

He came to slowly, blinking rapidly.

"The phone, Tommy. Answer it before it wakes Alex." He needed more sleep and so did she, or this was going to be a very long day.

Tommy grabbed the phone from the bedside table.

Christina saw the word *Dispatch* on the screen.

"Gonzales."

She couldn't hear the dispatcher's side of the conversation, but she heard Tommy's grunt of acknowledgment before he ended the call, closing his eyes even as he continued to clutch the phone.

Christina wondered if he was going back to sleep after being called into work. She was about to say something when he got out of bed and headed for the shower.

Nine months ago today, his partner, A. J. Arnold, had been gunned down right in front of Tommy as they approached a suspect. After a long downward spiral following Arnold's murder, Tommy had seemed to rebound somewhat during the summer. But the rebound hadn't lasted into the fall.

In the last month, since his new partner, Cameron Green, had joined the squad, Christina had watched him regress into his grief. He'd said and done all the right things when it came to welcoming Cameron, but he was obviously spiraling again, and she had no idea what to do to help him or how to reach him. Even when lying next to her in bed, he seemed so far away from her.

Sometimes, when she had a rare moment alone, she allowed her thoughts to wander to life without Tommy and Alex at the center of it. She loved them both—desperately—but she wasn't sure how much more she could take of the distant, closed-off version of the man she loved. They were supposed to have been married by now. Like everything else, that plan had been shoved aside to make room for Tommy's overwhelming grief. It'd been months since they'd discussed getting married. In the meantime, she took care of Alex and everything else, while Tommy worked and came home to sleep before starting the cycle all over again.

They didn't talk about anything other than Alex. They never went anywhere together or as a family. They hadn't had sex in so long she'd forgotten when it had last happened. She was as unhappy as she'd ever been. Something had to give—and soon, or she would be forced to decide whether their relationship was still healthy for her. She did *not* want to have to make that decision.

Only the thought of leaving Tommy at his lowest moment, not to mention leaving Alex, had kept her from making a move before now. She loved that little boy with her whole heart and soul. She'd stepped away from her own career as Nick's chief of staff to stay home with him and had hoped to add to their family by now. When she thought about the early days of her relationship with Tommy, when they'd been so madly in love, she couldn't have imagined feeling as insignificant to him as a piece of furniture that was always there when he finally decided to come home.

Christina hadn't told anyone about the trouble brewing between them. In her heart of hearts, she hoped they could still work it out somehow, and the last thing she needed was her friends and family holding a grudge against him forever—and they would if they had any idea just how bad things had gotten. Her parents had questioned the wisdom of her giving up a high-profile job to stay home to care for her boyfriend's child, especially when she'd made more money than him. But she'd been ready for a break from the political rat race when Alex came along, and she had no regrets about her decision. Or she hadn't until Tommy checked out of their relationship.

This weekend they'd be expected to celebrate at Freddie and Elin's wedding, and she'd have to pretend that everything was fine in her relationship when it was anything but. She wasn't sure how she would pull off another convincing performance for their friends. Tommy was one of Freddie's groomsmen, so she'd get to spend most of that day on her own while he attended to his friend.

Dangling at the end of her rope in this situation, more than once she'd thought about taking Alex and leaving, even though she had no legal right to take him. Another thing they'd never gotten around to—her adoption of him after his mother was killed. What would Tommy do if she left with his son? Call the police on her? That made her laugh bitterly. She'd be surprised if he noticed they were gone.

Tommy came out of the bathroom and went to the closet where he had clean clothes to choose from thanks to her. Did he ever wonder how that happened? He put on jeans and a black T-shirt and then went to unlock the bedside drawer where he kept his badge, weapon and cuffs.

She watched him slide the weapon into the holster he wore on his hip and jam the cuffs and badge into the back pockets of his jeans, the same way he did every day. Holding her breath, she waited to see if he would say anything to her or come around the bed to kiss her goodbye the way he used to before disaster struck, but like he did so often these days, he simply turned and left the room.

A minute later, she heard the front door close behind him.

For a long time after he left, she lay in bed staring up at the ceiling with tears running down her cheeks. She couldn't take much more of this.

TWO

SAM WAS THE first of her team to arrive on the scene of the smoldering fire that had demolished half a mansion in one of the District's most exclusive neighborhoods.

"What've we got?" Sam asked the fire marshal when he met her at the tape line.

"Two bodies found on the first floor of the house, both bound with zip ties at the hands and feet."

And that, right there, made their deaths her problem. "Do we know who they are?"

He consulted his notes. "The ME will need to make positive IDs, but the house is owned by Jameson and Cleo Beauclair. I haven't had time to dig any deeper on who they are."

"Are we certain they were the only people in the house?" Sam asked.

"Not yet. When we arrived just after four a.m., the west side of the house, where the bodies were found, was fully engulfed. That was our immediate focus. We've got firefighters searching the rest of what was once a ten-thousand-square-foot home."

"Any sign of accelerants?"

"Nothing so far, but we're an hour into the investigation stage. Early days."

"Has the ME been here?"

"Not yet."

"Could I take a look inside?"

"It's still hot in there, but I can show you the highlights—or the lowlights, such as they are."

Sam followed him up the sidewalk to what had once been the front door. Inside the smoldering ruins of the house, she could make out the basic structure from the burned-out husk that remained. The putrid scents of smoke and death hung heavily in the air.

"That's them there," the fire marshal said, pointing to a space on the floor by a blackened stone fireplace where two charred bodies lay next to one another.

Sam swallowed the bile that surged to her throat. Nothing was worse, at least not in her line of work, than fire victims. Though it was the last thing she wanted to do, she moved in for a closer look, took photos of the bodies and the scene around them, then turned to face the fire marshal. "Anything else you think I ought to see?"

"Not yet."

"Keep me posted."

"Will do."

He walked away to continue his investigation while Sam went outside, carrying the horrifying images with her as she took greedy breaths of fresh air. As she reached the curb, the medical examiner's truck arrived. She waited for a word with Dr. Lindsey McNamara.

The tall, pretty medical examiner gathered her long red hair into a ponytail as she walked over to Sam.

"Fire victims," Sam said, shuddering.

"Good morning to you too."

"Hands and feet bound with zip ties."

"Here we go again," Lindsey said with a sigh. "Looks like it was quite a house."

"Ten thousand square feet, according to the fire marshal."

"I'll get you an ID and report as soon as I can."

"Appreciate it." Sam opened her phone and placed a call to Malone. "I'm at the scene of the fire in Chevy Chase."

"What've you got?"

"Two DOA, bound at the hands and feet, leading me to believe this was a home invasion gone bad. I need Crime Scene here ASAP."

"I'll call Haggerty and get them over there."

"I want them to comb through anything and everything that wasn't touched by the fire, and they need to do it soon before the scene is further compromised. We've got firefighters all over the place."

"Got it. What's your plan?"

"I'm going to talk to the neighbors and find out what I can about the people who lived here while I wait for Lindsey to confirm their identities."

"Keep me posted."

Sam slapped the phone closed and headed for her car to begin the task of figuring out who Jameson and Cleo Beauclair had been and who might've bound them before setting their house on fire. If the bodies were even those of the Beauclairs. Cases like this were often confounding from the start, but they would operate on the info they had available and go from there.

Her partner, Detective Freddie Cruz, arrived as Sam reached her car, which she had parked a block from the scene.

"I guess it was too much to hope our homicide-free streak would last until after the wedding," he said.

"Too much indeed. We've got two deceased on the

first floor of the west side of the home, hands and feet bound."

"Do we know who they are?"

"We know who owns the house, but we're not a hundred percent sure the owners are our victims," she said, passing along the names the fire marshal had given her. "Let's knock on some doors and then go back to HQ to see what Lindsey can tell us."

"I'm with you, LT."

"Any word from Gonzo?"

"Not that I've heard yet."

"He can catch up."

Don't miss Fatal Invasion *by Marie Force, available now from HQN Books.*

COMING NEXT MONTH FROM

HARLEQUIN®

ROMANTIC suspense

Available December 31, 2018

#2023 COLTON COWBOY STANDOFF

The Coltons of Roaring Springs

by Marie Ferrarella

After walking out on Wyatt Colton six years ago, Bailey Norton is back—and asking him to father her child. But a crime spree puts Bailey, their child and Wyatt's ranch in danger. They suddenly have bigger problems than mending their past relationship.

#2024 SNOWBOUND WITH THE SECRET AGENT

Silver Valley P.D. • by Geri Krotow

Instant chemistry between undercover agent Kyle King and local librarian Portia DiNapoli spells instant trouble. Kyle is now torn between completing his mission and getting out of Silver Valley, and protecting the woman with whom he shares the most intense attraction of his life.

#2025 A SOLDIER'S HONOR

The Riley Code • by Regan Black

A security breach has exposed Major Matt Riley and the secrets he's kept for fourteen years, putting the woman he's never stopped loving and their son in grave danger.

#2026 PROTECTING THE BOSS

Wingman Security • by Beverly Long

Designer Megan North has four new boutiques to open over the course of a twelve-day road trip. But someone is targeting her and her business. When the dangers turn deadly, can security specialist Seth Pike save her?

A security breach has exposed Major Matt Riley and the secrets he's kept for fourteen years, putting the woman he's never stopped loving and their son in grave danger.

Read on for a sneak preview of the first book in USA TODAY *bestselling author Regan Black's brand-new Riley Code miniseries,* A Soldier's Honor.

She wasn't accustomed to sharing a bed with anyone.

"And what about us?"

"Us as in you and me?" His gaze locked on her, hot and interested. "Is that an invitation?"

She backpedaled. "I meant us as in what are Caleb and I supposed to do while you're fixing the problem?"

He watched her steadily as he took a long pull from the beer bottle. Setting the bottle aside, he took a step toward her. "Which part concerns you most? Sticking with me for safety, or maybe just the idea of sticking with me?"

The last one, a small voice in her head cried out. But she wasn't that overwhelmed nineteen-year-old anymore. She was a grown woman, a mother with a son and an established career. No matter the circumstance, Caleb's safety was her top priority.

She planted her hand in the center of his hard chest. His heart kicked, his chest swelled as he sucked in a breath. He leaned into her touch, as though his heart was drowning and she was the lifeline. Good grief, her imagination needed a dose of reality.

"Bethany," he murmured.

The blood rushing through her ears was so loud, she saw him speak her name more than she heard it. The blatant need in his brown eyes triggered an answering need in her. Any reply she might have given went up in flames when he lowered his firm lips to her mouth. He kissed her lightly at first, but she recognized the spark and heat just under the surface, waiting for an opening to break free and singe them both. Her hands curled into his shirt, pulled him closer. Oh, how she'd missed this. She'd thought time had exaggerated her memories and found the opposite was true when his tongue swept over hers, as he alternately sipped and plundered and called up all her long-ignored needs to the surface.

Our second first kiss, she thought. As full of promise as the first first kiss had been when they were kids.

"Oh. Ah. Sorry. Never mind." Caleb's voice, choked with embarrassment, doused the moment as effectively as a bucket of ice water.

She muttered an oath.

HRSEXP1218